DAUGHTERS

ALSO BY CORINNE DEMAS

The Same River Twice

Daffodils or the Death of Love

What We Save for Last

If Ever I Return Again

The Writing Circle

Everything I Was

Returning to Shore

Eleven Stories High: Growing Up in Stuyvesant Town, 1948–1968

The Road Towards Home

DAUGHTERS

A NOVEL

CORINNE DEMAS

Little a

This is a work of fiction. Names, characters, organizations, places, events, and incidents are either products of the author's imagination or are used fictitiously. Otherwise, any resemblance to actual persons, living or dead, is purely coincidental.

Published by Little A, New York
www.apub.com

EU product safety contact:
Amazon Media EU S. à r.l.
38, avenue John F. Kennedy, L-1855 Luxembourg
amazonpublishing-gpsr@amazon.com

ISBN-13: 9781662536977 (hardcover)
ISBN-13: 9781662530845 (paperback)
ISBN-13: 9781662530852 (digital)

Cover design by Emily Mahar
Cover image: © Cherry Tree, (oil on canvas) by Katharina Valeeva © Katharina Valeeva; © jessicahyde / Shutterstock

Printed in the United States of America

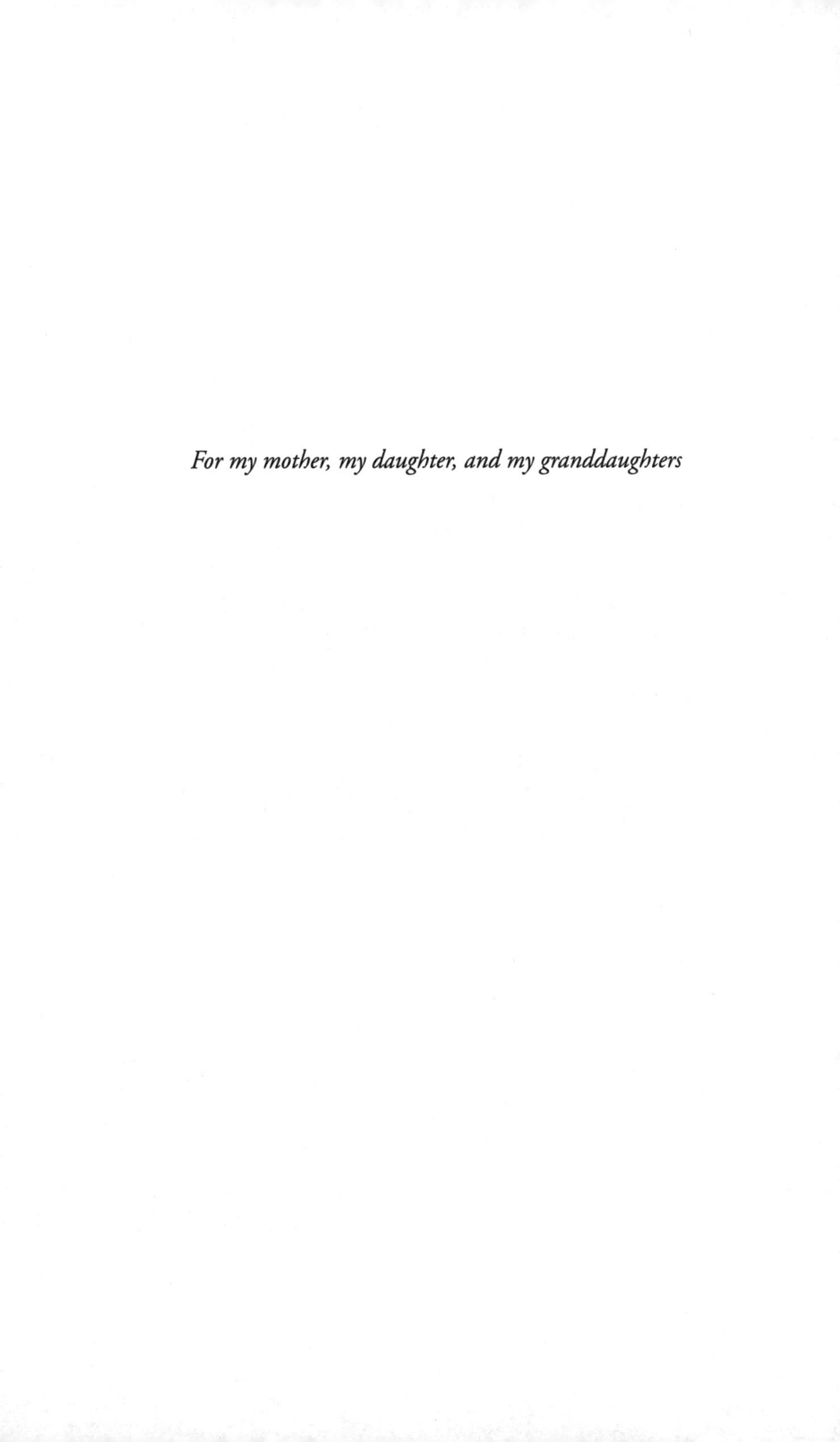

For my mother, my daughter, and my granddaughters

1

Somewhere in the darkness, a phone was ringing. Delia, summoned from sleep, groped for it on her bedside table, but that was overly optimistic; her fingers encountered nothing except a box of tissues and a tube of hand lotion that had lost its cap. Any call in the middle of the night was an emergency, if it wasn't a telemarketer on the other side of the globe. Delia pulled herself up, planted her feet on the cold floor, and surveyed the room. She'd gotten a bright-pink case for the phone to make it easier to spot, but it was hidden now. When she was a kid and her father misplaced his car keys, he'd stand still, look around, and say, "Now if I were a bunch of keys, where would I hide?" But there wasn't time to try that strategy now. She raced across the room towards the ringing, dug frantically through the clothing piled on the chair by the window, and unearthed her phone from the pocket of her jeans. She answered it just in time.

"Hello!" she cried, and in reward heard her daughter's voice. "Where are you, Mom?"

The interrogative nature of Merry's response was reassuring. It didn't sound like an emergency. "Home," said Delia. She would have said "Where else would I be at this hour?" but Merry might find that confrontational.

"I thought you'd never answer." Merry's tone was querulous.

"I had to find my phone." Had it been her older daughter, Kat, Delia would not have admitted this. Kat insisted that Delia keep her phone within grabbing distance so she could call for help in the unlikely event she'd topple to the ground out of earshot of anyone. But this was Merry, who regularly misplaced things, including, on one occasion, her daughter Eloise, when she was a baby in a stroller.

"We're on our way," said Merry.

On their way? Delia might not remember where she'd left her cell phone, but she was certain she'd remember if Merry had mentioned anything about coming to visit. She wasn't sure which question to ask first, and opted for one that seemed neutral.

"Where are you, dear?"

"We're at the airport," said Merry. "Our flight is leaving in like three minutes. We'll be there tomorrow, but we have a layover in Chicago, so who knows when. But don't worry, we'll figure out a way to get home, so you don't need to pick us up at the airport. Unless of course you want to."

Delia ventured a question. "Who is the 'we'? Is Josh getting time off?"

"Josh is not coming," said Merry. "For God's sake, Mom. Use your head."

And before Delia could ask anything more, Merry said, "Gotta go—" her standard line for terminating calls, and hung up.

Delia stood by the window for a moment, looking out over the darkness. She thought about Merry's use of the word "home." Was that promising? The last time Merry had visited she'd objected when Delia had used the term to describe the place where Merry had once lived.

There was no light on in the barn, and the surrounding fields were as invisible as the hill beyond. In the barn the horse and donkeys were all asleep. Reassuringly so. Their lives were uncomplicated, Delia knew, and at times she envied them for this. As for their dreams, she had no idea. The only creatures she'd witnessed dreaming were the dogs, who occasionally yipped in their sleep as if they were chasing squirrels.

No one in their right mind would have bought the old farm in the first place. Even Delia had acknowledged this at the time. Both house and barn were too old, too big, too run down, and there were too many acres to keep track of, but even so, she'd surrendered to its charms. Though implausible and unrealistic, the farm had seemed perversely necessary, like the various men she had fallen in love with in her life. Her husband Bob, still asleep now, had, in the end, given in about the place, and Merry, who was thirteen, the age when she objected to just about everything her mother proposed, had been uncharacteristically enthusiastic. In the two decades since, the house hadn't gotten any younger, smaller, or less run down, nor had the property gotten more manageable, but Delia was determined not to abandon the farm, in spite of the clamor from Kat to move into something more "age appropriate."

It was getting cold by the window, and Delia crawled back into bed. She wished Bob was awake so she could talk to him, but he was breathing heavily, his mouth partly open with his lower lip drooping, unappealingly, on one side. She snuggled down against him, warmed her feet between his legs, and tried to go back to sleep. But it was useless. Merry often did this to her—left her distressed after informing her of one crisis or another. Delia didn't anguish over her two other children as she did with Merry. Was it because Kat and Evan were older and steadier? Or—and this was a possibility she rarely allowed herself to contemplate—was it because (as Kat had once accused her) she loved Merry more?

She nudged Bob's side with her chin, but he stirred only briefly. It was unlikely that he would wake with the sort of delicate prodding she could call accidental. She sat up in bed. "Bob," she said, and she gave him a shake. "Bob, I need to talk to you."

Bob dragged himself from sleep. He seemed more weary than alarmed. He was not a man who was easily alarmed.

"What?" he asked.

"Merry just called."

Bob leaned over and pressed the button on the alarm clock to illuminate the time. He turned back to Delia.

"What's up, Lili?" he asked.

"She's on her way here. She's apparently taking a flight to Chicago now, and will be flying here tomorrow."

"Just Merry?"

"I don't think so. I imagine Eloise is with her. But not Josh."

"Oh for Christ's sake," said Bob. He was fully awake now.

"You'll drive me to the airport to meet them, won't you?"

"Do I have a choice?"

"You always have a choice."

"Right," said Bob. He punched his pillow into a compact ball, stuffed it against his neck, but before he lay down he asked, "How long is she coming for?"

"She didn't say."

"This does not bode well."

"It couldn't be too long," said Delia. "Eloise has school."

"If I recall, Merry was cavalier about Eloise's school attendance when they last visited."

"Eloise was younger then."

"I just hope you're right," said Bob, and he lay down in bed, back to her, pulling the covers up over his shoulder.

Kat and Evan were older when Delia had married Bob, but Merry was only in middle school, and Bob had impatiently endured those years until she departed for college. He was not a man who enjoyed the company of teens or children and felt they should be kept at what he called "a respectable distance." He put up with Eloise when required. He steered clear of the Suzuki pupils who invaded the music room. In fact, thought Delia, it wasn't just children; Bob didn't like people in general, and had chosen to be a radiologist since it involved only minimal interaction with living patients. She'd thought she'd get used to this about him, but she hadn't. Not really. There were a few things she hadn't gotten used to, if getting used to required not just weary acceptance but a touch of forgiveness. Loving someone was an entirely different matter.

Once again she tried to reenter the territory of sleep, but she kept picturing her daughter dragging a disheveled Eloise through the airport while searching for her boarding pass. Merry hadn't offered a clue about how long she might be visiting. Nor had she given any hint of what had happened with Josh. With Merry, anything was possible. Delia looked over at the heap of duvet that was Bob. Even the most taciturn of men had their breaking points. As for herself, well—she would not consider her own breaking point. Mothers were not supposed to have them. She got out of bed and put on a sweatshirt she retrieved from the floor of her closet. It was something she should have relegated to the rag bin, but it had a comforting, shapeless familiarity. That was one of the perks of being married to Bob. He was relatively indifferent to clothing. Early in their relationship, she'd bought and modeled a somewhat itchy black lace negligee, and had been relieved when Bob didn't find it sexy.

The dogs, Juno and Ralph, were curled up on the rug by the woodstove in the living room. They had their own dog beds in the bedroom, but sometimes preferred this spot. Dogs were like that. The fire had gone out just before Delia had headed up to bed, but she could see the glowing embers through the smoky glass doors. Unlike flames that were constantly in motion, embers were soothingly still. Delia sank onto the floor beside the dogs and laid her head against Juno, the mostly-sheepdog's, soft side. "Things will work out, won't they?" she whispered. "They usually do." She stroked Juno's long, tangled fur, fur that smelled of barn and animals and earth. Juno pulled her paws up against her chest—her "aren't I cute!" pose—lifted her head, and reached around to lick Delia. Delia closed her eyes and tried to focus on the feel of Juno's wet tongue against her bare wrist, and not think about what might be going on with Merry.

2

It was late in the morning when Meredith woke up and discovered she was alone in bed. Earlier, before it could legitimately be called morning, Eloise had crawled into bed with her and fallen asleep, leaving Meredith wide awake. Eloise was only fifty pounds, but she was a sprawler. She started off cuddled close to her mother, her face buried in Meredith's side, her stuffed moose wedged between them, but once asleep she stretched out and recklessly flung her arms and legs far apart, claiming acres of bed. But Eloise must have woken up and gone downstairs after Meredith had finally fallen asleep again, and now Meredith was here alone in this bedroom that she'd once called hers. It hadn't been altered since she'd abandoned it years ago, when she'd left for college, so in a sense it was hers still. The print of Escher's *Drawing Hands* on the wall, the batik throw on the butterfly chair, the "earring tree" on the dresser, which she'd made from branches, were just as she'd left them. Even the stuffed penguin was still there, slumped against the pillows on the window seat. It was reassuring and depressing, both. In this room, as in this house, she reverted to being Merry, her totally unsuitable nickname. She reverted to a lot of undesirable things when she was here. Not by choice. It was inevitable. She wouldn't have come here if she'd had better options. Or would she have? She wasn't sure. She wasn't sure about a lot of things these days, though whenever she was with her mother she presented—as best as she could—a façade of certainty. Aggrieved certainty, perhaps, but certainty nevertheless.

Meredith had been too tired the night before to bother to dislodge pj's from her suitcase, and her leggings and top had that mottled look of clothing that had been on duty for nearly two days. She confronted herself in the bathroom mirror—mild, unmemorable features, except for her surprisingly dark eyes. If she made herself up, she might have been striking, but she'd never taken much interest in her appearance, and certainly didn't care about it now.

Her limp hair was slowly growing out from an unfortunate asymmetrical cut—shoulder length on one side and short on the other. She expected her mother would comment on it. No—her mother would restrain herself from commenting, but her raised eyebrows would say it all. And her mother would probably say something about Meredith looking too thin. She always did.

What Meredith wanted was a good, hot shower, but she knew the shower—a jerry-rigged affair in an old clawfoot tub—would be an unpredictable trickle, lukewarm at best. She risked it anyway. Her mother had replaced the moldy shower curtain with a new one, clear, with a dizzying assortment of butterflies. It had a vinyl smell and clung to her thighs and butt in a lascivious way. The towel had bits of lavender stuck to it.

She dug some clean clothes out of her suitcase and kicked the dirty ones under the bed. She expected that Eloise was eating breakfast, and although she was hungry she put off going down too. They'd gotten in late last night, so she'd been spared her mother's inevitable interrogation, but the reprieve wouldn't last. She expected her mother might hold off until Eloise was out of earshot. Not that her mother would question her directly. No, her mother's technique was more subtle. She'd appear patient and receptive, hide her inquisitiveness and let the small talk circle, slowly ensnare Meredith, and ferret out the truth. It was always like this. Her mother managed to draw out Meredith's confessions, and though Meredith regretted it later, she never was able to protect herself. But this time she would hold out. She had to.

Finally hunger won, and Meredith went downstairs. The kitchen's antique charm was intact, but—thank goodness!—the appliances were relatively new. The cloudy white marble counters had softened, somehow, and the cabinets were a pleasing dark wood. Not cherry, something less common: chestnut.

Eloise was in the kitchen, standing on a chair, so she was almost too high for the counter. She was wearing a grown-up-sized apron with the apron strings tied double around her waist.

"We're making waffles," she announced.

"Waffles?"

"Good morning, Darling," said Delia, "I thought you deserved something special for breakfast after all that traveling."

There were a lot of things Meredith felt she deserved. Waffles hadn't been one of them. The bowl was full of batter, and the counter was decorated with batter too. "Aren't you hungry, Honey?" she asked Eloise.

"I already had breakfast. I had oatmeal," said Eloise. "This is second breakfast."

"Would you like some orange juice?" asked Delia.

"Nobody likes orange juice," said Bob. He was sitting at the far side of the table, and Meredith hadn't noticed he was there. "Give the girl a cup of coffee, Lili."

"I've given up coffee," said Meredith.

"Why would you do that?" asked Bob.

"It's not really good for you."

"Jennifer drinks coffee," said Eloise. Nobody said anything. "She does!" shouted Eloise. She jumped off the chair and ran out of the kitchen. Meredith started after her and took her arm, but Eloise shook herself free, gave her mother a fierce look, and fled up the stairs. Meredith stood at the foot of the stairs for a while, then she returned to the kitchen.

"Jennifer?" asked Delia, when Meredith came in.

"Her teacher."

"Should I go to her?"

"I think it's better not," said Meredith, and she did her best to ignore her mother's reproachful look. She took the plate her mother handed her with a waffle in the middle. It looked fleshy and undercooked.

"The maple syrup is on the table," said Delia. "Bob, clear off the papers."

Bob made a show of gathering the pages of *The New York Times.* A scene familiar to Meredith from the past. He always spread out the morning newspaper so it took over an unreasonable area of table, and her mother always tidied it up for him. She never said anything. Even when she didn't say anything, she had a way of shuffling the papers that clearly expressed her exasperation. This morning she was busy at the waffle iron. Bob, long suffering, had developed a neutral, noncombative expression.

"Your sister is looking forward to seeing you," said Delia. "Shall I ask them for dinner tomorrow?"

"How'd she know I'm here?"

"Your mother told her when Kat called this morning," said Bob.

"She called?"

"She calls every morning to check in on us and make sure we haven't died in our sleep."

"Bob!" cried Delia.

"Every morning?" asked Meredith.

"Just a quick call," said Delia.

"At night they gab for an hour."

"Every night?" asked Meredith. She kept herself from adding "Doesn't she have anything better to do?"

"You might want to eat your waffle while it's still warm," said Bob. "It's not very palatable, cold."

"I'll make lasagna," said Delia. "I'll make it with mushrooms. You're still a vegetarian, aren't you?"

"That does not deserve an answer," said Meredith. She poured too much syrup over the waffle and took a few bites. If you put enough maple syrup on anything, it was good.

Her mother was standing there, looking hurt, so Meredith said, "I'll have some orange juice." A peace offering. Delia set a glass for her on the table, and Meredith took a sip. It was fresh-squeezed juice, part of the plot to soften her up. She was afraid her mother would seize this Eloise-free moment to have a serious discussion with her, and sure enough Delia came and sat beside her and placed her hand on Meredith's arm just as she started to get up.

"Eloise has certainly grown!" Delia began.

"Big surprise. I decided to feed her now and then."

"If I'd known ahead you'd be here, Sweetheart, I would have gotten some of the foods you and Eloise specially like, but I can go shopping later. We'll make a list."

"You don't need to get anything special for me. Or Eloise."

"Of course she does," said Bob.

"I'll go as soon as I'm done teaching. I'm sorry, Merry, but I have some students coming this morning. If I'd known you were coming, I would have canceled them."

"I thought you were retiring," said Merry.

"Just a few students," said Delia, but Bob interrupted her.

"Your mother is incapable of retiring. She keeps trying, but the Suzuki parents are a determined bunch. And she won't stand up to them."

"It's just a few students—"

"And their little sisters. And their cousins. And their best friends. I thought when I retired we'd be able to do things together—travel, take a cruise. Instead I'm stuck here, tortured by 'Twinkle' on pint-sized violins."

"You don't like cruises, Bob. You get seasick."

"It was a metaphor," said Bob.

"What about the critters?" Meredith asked him.

"We could get someone to look after them. Or better yet, we could find them new residences. And that brings us to my next point. Your sister thinks it's time we thought about moving on.

Kat has a lot of opinions that make me grind my teeth, but this is one that may have some merit. We're getting a bit old to be hefting bales of hay and shoveling equine excrement. I don't know how Old MacDonald managed. Kat's been trying to get your mother to unload this venerable house and farm and get a nice, undemanding condo, instead."

"I know, she tried to convince me to join her campaign."

"She did?" asked Delia.

"Yup. She actually called me."

"And were you convinced?" asked Bob.

"Of course you weren't, were you, dear?" asked Delia.

Meredith held up her hands. "No comment."

"You love this place, don't you?"

Meredith looked back and forth between Bob and her mother. She had plenty she wanted to say about this subject, but she knew it would inevitably lead to questions about why she was here, and she wasn't ready to face that yet. "I'm going upstairs to check on Eloise," she said. She pushed back her chair and started standing up, but she wasn't fast enough. Her mother pounced.

"What's going on, Merry?" Delia asked. She tilted her head in that way she had to express concern.

"What do you mean what's going on?"

"How come Josh didn't come with you?"

"What, is there some problem with me coming here on my own with Eloise? I need Josh to accompany me?"

"No, of course not! You're always welcome, just as you are, but this seemed like such a last-minute thing, as if—"

"How much advance notice do you need, Mom?"

"I don't need any, dear—it's just that when you called, the way you sounded, made me wonder if—"

"If what?"

"If, well, maybe something had happened."

"Maybe I don't want to talk about it."

"But, Sweetheart, I want to know what I can do to help you—"

"What you can do is just lay off, OK? If you don't want me and Eloise to be here, we'll pack right up and leave—" She heard her old resentful voice assert itself. How had she ended up in this wrangle?

"Oh no, Merry! I want you to stay—of course I do!"

"Then stop the inquisition, all right?"

"But, Sweetheart, I'm only trying to—"

Bob gave his newspaper a brutal shake and laid it on the table. "Delia, what are the chances for a temporary moratorium so I can finish my breakfast in relative peace?"

"You're in luck, Bob," said Meredith. "I'm leaving right now to go see how my daughter's doing."

Just as she got to the doorway Delia called out, "Tell Eloise I'm saving the best waffle for her."

Upstairs, Meredith found Eloise curled up on the window seat, Moosie on her lap, thumb in her mouth. She had Meredith's dark-brown eyes and brown hair, but her face was rounder, and she had a child's small nose. It was hard to tell whether she would still be pretty when she grew up. She was too old to be sucking her thumb, and she pulled her hand away as soon as she saw Meredith. But Meredith had no intention of saying anything, especially now. She had her secret vices too. On the trip here she'd bitten one fingernail down so far it bled.

Eloise pointed to the stuffed penguin on the window seat beside her. Its fabric was stained, and stuffing fluffed out from a hole in its beak. "What happened here?" she asked.

"Looks like the mice chewed it."

"Why?"

Meredith sat down cautiously next to Eloise and tried to gauge her mood. "I think a mommy mouse needed some stuffing to make a nest for her babies." Eloise was a sucker for baby animals. Meredith was relieved when Eloise sank against her, and she put her arm around Eloise's small body, pulling her close.

"Grandma said I could feed the animals," said Eloise. "And she's going to teach me how to clean out the stable—it's called mucking out—and she's going to let me ride Falstaff. He's old, and he's blind in one eye."

"I know."

Eloise sat up and turned to her mother. "You do?"

"Falstaff used to be my horse. Didn't you remember that from the last time you were here?"

"That was a long time ago."

"Not that long ago."

Eloise shook her head. "You're lucky," she said. "You had a horse. I wish I had a horse."

"Horses don't do well in cities. Falstaff can be your horse, too, while we're here, OK?"

Eloise brightened up. "How long are we going to be here?"

Meredith shrugged. "Not sure."

"What do you think?"

Meredith shrugged again. "Don't know."

"I think you know, but you aren't saying."

Did she know? Meredith knew what she was hoping for, but there were things she had to work out first—and things that could go wrong. She gave a little laugh. "Sweetheart, you are wise beyond your years!"

"My ears?"

"Beyond your *years*!"

"What does that mean?"

"It means you're wise as someone who's a lot older than you."

"Like maybe middle school?"

Meredith smiled. "Sure." She kissed the top of Eloise's head.

"What about school?"

"What about it?"

"If we stay here next week, I'll miss school, won't I?"

"It's school vacation week."

"And after that?"

"You don't need to worry about school."

"But what about my tidal pool?"

"Tidal pool?"

"My diorama. For the seashore project. I told you about it. Don't you remember?"

"I don't know, Honey."

"You don't remember anything!"

Zing! But the problem, Meredith thought, wasn't that she didn't remember anything. The problem was that she remembered too much. Her brain was overwhelmed.

Eloise got up from the window seat and put Moosie on the bed. "I'm going downstairs for second breakfast," she said. Meredith pulled herself to her feet to follow Eloise. She didn't want to be near her mother right now, but she didn't want to be left alone here in this bedroom.

"I've kept some waffles warm for you," Delia said when they came into the kitchen. She handed Eloise a plate from the oven. Eloise carried it over to the table and, before Meredith could stop her, took the seat next to Bob. He folded back the newspaper to make room for her.

"Merry?" asked Delia, holding up another plate.

Meredith shook her head. "No. I'm good." She sat down on the other side of Eloise.

Eloise smiled up at Bob. "Do you want to share?" she asked, sliding her plate in his direction.

"Thank you, no," he said, but he was not smiling.

"Why not?"

"I've already eaten my breakfast."

"So have I. But you can have breakfast again. You can have breakfast as many times as you want to, can't you, Grandma?"

"Of course you can!" said Delia. She came over and joined them at the table. "Your grandpa, however, is a one-breakfast sort of person."

"You're not Mommy's real daddy, so you're not my *real* grandpa, are you?" Eloise asked Bob, who was looking at his newspaper again.

"Well—" began Delia.

Eloise turned to her and asked, "What happened to Mommy's daddy?"

Delia looked at Meredith, as if hoping she'd answer, but Meredith had no intention of answering. She'd managed to avoid telling Eloise much about her father so far, and what had happened to him was not something she felt like explaining, and it was certainly not a subject for breakfast waffles. She watched her mother's face as she struggled to come up with something. What Delia settled for was "He's no longer alive."

Eloise poked at Bob's newspaper. "So I guess even though you're not my *real* grandpa, you're my grandpa now," she said.

When he didn't respond, Delia reached across Eloise and tapped his arm. "Bob?"

He looked up. "Yes," he said. "Whatever you say."

Crisis averted. Or merely postponed.

"I'll be done teaching before lunch," said Delia, obviously relieved to change the subject. "I know Eloise is eager to see the animals, and we can go out then."

"Your grandma teaches violin," said Meredith. "The students come to the house."

"I know that," said Eloise. "You don't have to tell me."

"If you like, I can give you a violin lesson too," said Delia. "We still have your mommy's old quarter-sized violin. It would be just right for you now."

Meredith hadn't expected this. "Mom?"

Eloise spun around to look at her. "You played the violin?"

"I didn't have a choice."

"Your mommy was very talented, but she gave it up," said Delia.

"Mom!" Meredith was angry now. But her mother didn't seem to notice. "We can have a lesson tonight," she said.

"No!" Meredith said.

Delia looked surprised, then held up her hands in surrender. "OK, dear. Whatever you want. I've got to go get ready for my students. Sorry I'm not free to do something with you now."

"We're quite capable of entertaining ourselves," said Meredith.

Upstairs, Meredith dug out a hairbrush to do Eloise's hair.

"Want a ponytail?" she asked.

"No!"

"Well that's good," said Meredith. "Since I don't think we have any hair elastics."

Eloise pointed to the top drawer of the dresser. "There's some in there."

"How do you know?"

"I looked," said Eloise. "This morning."

"Find anything else of interest?"

Eloise opened the drawer and pulled out something to show her. "What's this?"

"A key chain."

"But what's *this*?" Eloise tapped the gnarled, furry thing that dangled from it.

"A rabbit's foot."

"A real rabbit's *foot*?"

Meredith nodded.

"Was it *dead*?"

"Well, yeah. Pretty disgusting, isn't it?"

"Then why do you have it?"

"An old friend gave it to me."

"Who?"

"His name is Wylie."

"Why'd he give it to you?"

"It's supposed to bring you good luck."

"How?"

"Beats me," said Meredith. She took the rabbit's foot from Eloise and held it in her closed hand. She wasn't ready to think about Wylie, but now that was impossible. She hadn't let him know she was back, but he'd find out from Evan soon enough. And then what? She placed the rabbit's foot back in the drawer and pushed the drawer closed, tight.

"I want to go see the animals," said Eloise.

"Later, when Grandma's done teaching. And it will be warmer out, then. We'll do some drawing now."

Downstairs, Meredith got out paper and colored pencils and set things up for Eloise at the dining room table. She settled herself in the armchair by the window and started drawing in the sketchbook she'd brought with her. Eloise sharpened all the pencils, then arranged them by color across the table before she began drawing too.

"I wish you wouldn't always draw me," Eloise said after a while.

"I'm not," said Meredith. She held up the sketchbook to show Eloise the sketch she'd been doing of the vase of dried flowers on the sideboard. That was the good thing about drawing inanimate objects: they didn't demand anything emotional from you. They were just there, and when Meredith sketched them she could enter a calm, uncontroversial zone.

~

The downstairs bathroom was off the hall in the front of the house. After Eloise used it, she crept towards the music room. The sliding wooden door was shut, but she could hear the lesson going on inside. Someone was playing "Twinkle, Twinkle Little Star" on a violin. She stood and listened.

"What are you doing here?" She turned quickly. Bob was coming up the hallway towards her.

"Nothing."

"Nothing will come of nothing."

Eloise stared at him.

"It's what King Lear says to his daughter, Cordelia."

"Oh."

"*King Lear*, Shakespeare's greatest play." Bob paused. "You have heard of Shakespeare, haven't you?"

"I guess," said Eloise.

Bob frowned at her. "What became of your mother?"

"She's back there." Eloise pointed towards the dining room.

"Well, keep out of trouble," said Bob. "Both of you."

"What are *you* doing?"

"What am I doing?"

"Uh-huh."

"I live here," he said.

"I know *that*. But what are you doing?"

Bob scowled at her. "Where does a question like that come from?"

Eloise shrugged. "My head, I guess."

"Well, that's reasonable. The answer, Eloise, is that I was coming here to check on you. I didn't want you bursting in on your grandmother's lesson."

"I wouldn't do that!"

"Well, that's a relief. If I had known, I would have saved myself the trouble of investigating." He turned and walked back down the hallway.

Eloise stayed in the hallway a while longer. There was the sound of a piano now in the music room. First it was just the piano playing, and then the violin played too. She liked to play the piano at her house, using one finger, all the way from one end of the keyboard to the other. And she liked to play a whole lot of keys at the same time with all her fingers, even her thumbs, but she couldn't do that when her father was home. One time when he was there her father had shouted upstairs to her mother, "Get Eloise to stop that banging," and her mother had shouted back, "You're the one who's down there!" and when Eloise hadn't stopped right away her father had slammed down the lid of the keyboard, and Eloise had pulled her hands back just in time.

~

3

After the third lesson was over, Delia stood for a moment in the music room, watching out the window as Nathan, a Book 1 pupil, followed his mother to their car. She would have tried to reschedule the Saturday-morning lessons if she'd known Merry was coming, but it had turned out she was happy to have these few hours in the music room, this time away.

Nathan looked back at the house and waved wildly when he saw her, banging his violin case into the half-open car door. Delia waved back. Nathan invariably played too fast, got the bowing mixed up, forgot the repeat, but he took such pride in his efforts that Delia enjoyed teaching him more than the previous student, Kaitlyn, who perfectly reproduced Bach's Bourrée, her face frozen in joyless concentration. Nathan's mother, unlike Kaitlyn's mother and the other parents who believed their children were musical prodigies, was simply grateful if Delia was able to get him to stand still for the lesson.

The music room was the old front parlor, and students entered through the sunroom, a Victorian-era addition to the side of the house. It was architecturally unfortunate, but a useful place for them to leave their coats and shoes. Delia taught in bedroom slippers, and some kids brought their own, which they called their Suzuki slippers. Parents, in their stocking feet, sank back into the oversized old sofa to take their notes, and—the fathers in particular—looked somewhat tamed when shoeless. The music room was large enough to accommodate Delia's baby grand. The Steinway was one of the few things she had left from her father, and more of a presence than he'd ever been. He'd been a composer who worked in the film industry, and while he was in Hollywood, she and her mother remained in their New York apartment. Presumably it was so she could have continuity in school, but even as a child she sensed there was more to it than that. Her father had been successful without being famous, and one of his songs, "Way Over There," had been a hit in his time. No one remembered it now.

Teaching in her home had been fine while Bob was still working at the hospital, but once he retired it was a problem for both of them. Although the music room's heavy door did a reasonable job of muffling the sound of little kids playing little violins, Bob, aggrieved, ostentatiously retreated to the back part of the house as soon as what he called "the onslaught" began. Even if he was not actively complaining, Delia sensed his resentment. He was resentful that she hadn't retired yet, and she found she was resentful that he had. She'd gotten used to having the house to herself all day during the week—not just while she was teaching, but while she was practicing or reading or doing anything. It was a big house—especially for just two people—but somehow Bob always seemed to intrude. All his annoying little habits, which she'd been barely aware of before, irritated her now: the way he cleared his throat, the way he scratched the back of his ear, even the way he slit open the mail and rattled the pages before stuffing them into the recycling basket. Delia knew she was being unreasonable, yet knowing didn't help how she felt. It was like that with a lot of things, wasn't it?

Delia was gathering the music scattered across the piano, when the sliding door to the front hall opened, and Bob, as if summoned by her thoughts, stepped in. "Done for the day?" he asked.

She nodded.

"Good, I wanted to catch you for a moment before lunch."

Delia looked up at him. "Yes?"

"How long are they staying here?"

"I don't know."

"Have you asked her?"

"Bob, I can't just ask her!"

"Well, someone has to."

"They've barely been here!"

"I just want to know what we're in for."

"In for? I love having Eloise here. And Merry."

"Let me restate that then. What *I'm* in for. I know you love having them here, but it's never easy. Not with Merry. And I have to live with the fallout."

There was some truth to this, and although Delia wasn't ready to concede that now, she placed her hand on Bob's forearm and said, "It will be OK."

"You don't need to invite Kat over as well," said Bob.

"Kat wants to come."

"Of course she does. She always does!"

"I thought you didn't mind having Kat come over."

"Of your three children, Kat is the only one who's sensible and predictable. I appreciate that. But I do not look forward to sitting down for dinner with Kat and Merry together."

"They'll be fine," said Delia.

The look on Bob's face made it clear he was not convinced.

Delia found Eloise and Merry in the dining room. Eloise was drawing at the table without something to protect the surface, and Delia stopped herself before she said anything. The table still bore the imprint of the stick-figure person that Merry had done as a child. Merry, curled in the armchair, sketching, looked like the girl she had once been—skinny, with her scraggly hair obscuring the side of her face so that Delia had an urge to tuck it back over her ear. When Merry was young Delia had never been able to get her to clip it back properly, although she'd bought her an assortment of hair accessories—headbands with flowers and barrettes with Scottie dogs. Eloise's hair was similarly unkempt. A genetic flaw?

"I'll go make us some lunch," Delia said.

"We already ate. We're going outside now."

"Oh." Delia looked at her watch. It was just a little past noon.

"I was hungry," said Eloise.

"After all those waffles?"

"Eloise is always hungry," said Merry. She got up from the table and closed her sketchbook.

"Would you like second lunch?"

"Nope," said Eloise. "I want to go see the barn and the animals."

"I'll join you out there, soon as I get some lunch for your grandpa."

"Bob still can't get his own lunch?" asked Merry.

"I need to eat something too," said Delia.

"Didn't you want to see my picture?" asked Eloise. She held up the piece of paper she'd been working on.

"Of course I do," said Delia, quickly, and leaned down to admire it. Eloise had drawn a row of girls with hair down to their waists. They each had their name and age written below them.

"They're all princesses," said Eloise. She laid the drawing on the sideboard before she and Merry went outside.

Bob came into the kitchen behind Delia. "What's for lunch?" he asked.

Delia opened the refrigerator door and scanned the contents. "There's leftover meat loaf for sandwiches. I would have made something else for Merry and Eloise, but they've already eaten." Delia set the meat loaf on the counter and got out bread to slice. She turned to Bob.

"You know there's no reason you can't make lunch for yourself." When Bob didn't say anything, she added, "Not to mention you could also make lunch for me once in a while."

"I thought you *liked* making lunch."

"Not always!"

"Sorry you're feeling out of sorts, but—"

"I'm not out of sorts. It's just that—well, since I was teaching this morning, the least you could do would be to make lunch."

"You're the one who insists on teaching. No one's making you."

"That's not the point."

"Every time Merry comes for a visit you get all stirred up about things."

Delia laid down the bread knife and turned to Bob. She thought about this. "Maybe so."

"Why do you let her do this to you?"'

"Because I never know how to handle her. I keep feeling I'm failing her as a parent."

"She's a grown woman, Lili!"

"That doesn't mean I don't still worry about her."

"You know what your trouble is? You think you can control things, but you can't. You can't control Merry, you can't control Kat, and you can't control Evan. But you keep on trying."

Delia closed her eyes for a moment. "Hug me, Bob. I need you to hug me."

Bob came over and put his arms around her waist.

"That's a pathetic hug. I need a real hug."

He moved his arms so they encircled her back and drew her close. "Better?"

"Yes."

Bob slowly released his hold. "So, are you going to find out what's going on?"

"I will," she said, quickly. "At least I'll *try* to find out what's going on, but you know Merry. It's not always easy to get to the bottom of things."

"I do know Merry," said Bob. "At least I once did." He squinted at her. "You're not hoping that I can do anything about this are you?"

"No, Bob. No hope of that!"

He touched her shoulder. "Hey, Sweetie, sarcasm does not become you."

"I wasn't being sarcastic, Bob. I was being resigned."

"I guess that's an upgrade then," he said. He smiled at her and tilted his head, waiting for her to smile, too, and eventually, she did.

Delia's first marriage had ended because of a dead dog, and her second marriage—her marriage to Bob—had begun because of one. Phil, her first husband, had been unsympathetic about her caring for their geriatric dog, and called her "overly emotional" when it died—the very quality that had brought her together with Bob. They'd first met when she'd come to pick up heartworm medicine for her dogs, and Bob was standing by the counter at the veterinarian's office, clutching a sheaf of papers he'd just been handed. He was a hefty man, with a face that Delia later described as "sorrowful."

"You don't have to take his ashes, of course," the receptionist was saying, "but most people do. And you might change your mind later on. We'll call you when they come in."

He'd stuffed the papers into his jacket pocket, then stepped away from the counter and just stood there.

"Was he old?" Delia had asked him.

It was clear he hadn't noticed her before this, but her question didn't seem to faze him. "Old, but not *that* old," he said. "Now that I'm old myself I have a different perspective on it."

The man looked as if he was her age, and she didn't consider that "old," but she said, instead, "It's never easy to say goodbye to a pet."

"I suppose not."

"Would you like a hug?"

The man gave a small laugh.

Delia laughed too. "You probably think I'm a bit crazy, offering a perfect stranger a hug—"

"Unusual, perhaps, but not crazy."

"It's just when I saw you standing there and guessed what you were going through, you looked as if you needed a hug, and you seemed as if you were alone, so I just thought I'd offer and—" She looked up at him, the question on her face.

"Do you do this often?"

"Hug people? I guess it's instinctive. I'm part Greek. Greeks hug. It's not personal, it's more just the way we are."

"In that case, it's excusable."

"Excusable, but not desirable?"

"Depends on the circumstance."

She held out her arms. "What was your dog's name?"

"Morrow," he said softly, and he leaned towards her to accept her embrace, his jacket open so they were chest to chest. He bent his head so the side of his face rested on her shoulder, and she could feel his crying. Her hands met around his back. He smelled of woodsmoke.

When they moved apart he said, "Thank you." She thought he might wipe his eyes with this jacket sleeve, but he didn't.

"I hope your wife won't think my behavior inappropriate. That is, if you have a wife."

"I don't. I did at one time, but I don't now."

"Well, that's a relief," she said. "Oh dear, I don't mean it the way it came out."

This time he laughed aloud.

"Well at least I got you to laugh," she said.

"And you? Do you have a husband who would find your behavior inappropriate? Unless he's Greek, of course, in which case, as you claim, it would be expected."

"I did at one time, but I don't now. And he wasn't Greek." They stood there, not speaking for a moment. Then she said, "I was going to propose that we go somewhere for a drink. Or a cup of coffee."

"I had a similar thought," he said, "but you beat me to it."

It was only when they were sitting across from each other at a diner not far from the vet's that they realized they didn't even know each other's name.

Delia put on her old down jacket and went out to the barn with Merry and Eloise. The barn was built into the side of the hill, with the stable on the lower level, opening into a fenced yard. The upper floor was spacious, with a hayloft at one end. The barn was quiet and peaceful. It had been the reason Delia had wanted them to buy the property years before—though they'd had no animals and no need for a barn whatsoever. And Bob, in spite of his reservations, had gone along with her. She loved the soft, almost ecclesiastical light, the way the beams had been pegged into place rather than nailed, the enterprise of the spiders whose webs spanned the corners, the nests of the swallows, gone now but who would return, as they did year after year. Once they got some animals, she'd found the smell of manure and hay and straw comforting, as was the gentle murmur of their movements and their chewing when they were brought in for the night.

"Can I climb up here?" asked Eloise, although she was already halfway up the ladder to the hayloft.

"Just watch out for splinters," Delia called out.

Merry wasn't paying attention to Eloise. She was looking all around, as if she was taking stock of things. She was wearing only a lightweight jacket, and she rubbed her arms and stomped a little to keep warm. "You wouldn't consider selling this place, would you?" she asked.

"Not I, but as you heard, Kat is working on Bob to think about it."

"She said she'd like to get you and Bob to move into one of those senior communities."

"When did you talk to her?"

"She called me a month or two ago. She wanted me to be on board. She wanted us to present a united front."

"And your brother?"

Merry laughed. "She implied he was on board, but my guess is she hasn't talked to him. She thinks Evan's an obstructionist. He doesn't listen to Kat."

"And you do?"

Merry laughed so hard she broke into a cough. "Not if I can help it!"

Delia stepped back so she could see up into the loft better. Eloise had stretched out on a hay bale.

"You've never really appreciated Kat."

"Appreciated her? Come on, Mom! It's hard to appreciate Kat!"

Delia sighed. "You've never been fair to her."

"Fair to Kat? You think she's ever been fair to me?"

"She loves you, Merry!"

"Oh, please," said Merry, and she started up the hayloft ladder. She looked back at Delia. "Coming?"

It had been a long time since Delia had gone up to the hayloft. She had no trouble climbing the ladder; it was getting herself up onto the floor of the loft that was the problem. "Swing your knee up, Mom," said Meredith.

"My knee doesn't swing the way it once did," said Delia.

Merry reached back and offered her a hand. "Here, grab on."

"I'm not sure I can do this," said Delia, but she took Merry's hand, lifted her leg, and managed to hoist herself up.

"See, you did it! You're not as decrepit as you think you are!" said Merry. "But promise me you won't climb up here on your own."

"I don't like thinking of myself as decrepit," Delia said. She sat down next to Merry and leaned back against a bale of hay while she caught her breath.

"You OK, Mom?"

"Don't look so worried, Sweetheart," said Delia. "I'm fine."

"I'm going to go get Moosie," said Eloise. "He wants to come up here too."

"Want me to come with you?" asked Merry.

"No. I can get him myself. I want you to wait right here for us."

"OK," said Meredith. She turned to Delia. "How do you manage the hay?"

"The farmer who delivers it—you know Henry, up the road?"

"Yeah, of course I know Henry."

"He and his son heave it up here. Bob comes up and pushes down some bales as we need them."

"Good old Bob!" said Merry. "Glad he's useful for something."

"He's more than useful," said Delia.

"OK, Mom," said Merry. "No need to act injured on his behalf."

"You know, it would be nice if you expressed a little bit of gratitude now and then. Bob's always been extremely generous to you, and—"

"I'm not big on gratitude," said Merry.

"You might make an effort," said Delia. "He's been more generous to you than your own father ever was."

"That's a pretty low bar."

"When Eloise asked about him I wasn't sure what to say—I didn't know what you'd told her about him."

"Not much. What's there to say? That he was a shitty father? That once you split up I rarely saw him?"

Having Merry state it this way hurt. Delia put her hand on top of Merry's. "I'm sorry, Sweetheart," she said.

"Not your fault, Mom!"

"I meant I was sorry that he wasn't there for you."

"Hey, not a big deal," said Merry, although Delia remembered her refusing to go to her elementary school's parents' open house that fall when Phil had moved out. "And I had you being there for me," said Merry. "More than two parents' worth, at least."

Delia, surprised by Merry's words, took this in. The smell of the hay was soothing. She started to settle back and close her eyes, but she knew Eloise would be returning soon, and it seemed like a good moment now to talk with Merry. She sat up quickly. "I love having you and Eloise here," she began. "How long do you think you'll be able to stay?"

"No idea," said Meredith.

"Is Josh going to come and join you here?"

"Mom! Where have you been? You just don't get it, do you?"

"Well, Sweetheart, you haven't really explained what you—"

"Explained? I have to *explain* things to you? I can't just come here with Eloise. I need to go into all the reasons and—"

"You don't need to go into the reasons—I just want to be able to help you—"

"That's what you always say! Can't I just be here, without you grilling me?"

"I'm just trying to—"

"Here's Moosie!" cried Eloise as she came running into the barn. Cutting Delia off and saving them both.

4

Meredith held Eloise's hand as they went around with Delia to say hello to the animals. The three donkeys—Clementine, Myrtle, and Tulip—were in the field beyond the barn, with Falstaff, the horse, tired and old, but not dead yet. In the chicken coop there were a number of newcomers to the flock. There had been two ducks the last time they'd been here, but apparently the fox had made off with them while the so-called guard dogs were lounging by the woodstove indoors. Eloise burst into tears when she heard about the fate of the ducks, but Meredith reminded her about the little kits waiting in their den for the mommy fox to bring them something to eat. "Just the way you do," she added.

"But we don't eat ducks," Eloise pointed out.

"It's the way of nature," Merry said somewhat brutally, and then, seeing Eloise's face, felt like shit. "Maybe Grandma will get some ducks again," she said. "And reinforce the henhouse." She looked at her mother.

"Of course," said Delia.

"Did the fox scare the donkeys?" asked Eloise.

"No. The donkeys are a lot bigger," said Delia. "And they're tough."

"If the fox can't get more ducks, what will the little foxes eat?" asked Eloise.

Meredith immediately had an image of the mother fox with a bloody rabbit dangling from its mouth, but she said only, "Oh, the mommy fox will find something. She's very resourceful." She smiled at Eloise. "I'm going in to get my phone so I can take some pictures," she said and, seeing Delia frown at her while she pushed her cell phone deeper into her pocket, added quickly, "And use the bathroom. You be OK out here?" she asked Eloise.

"Of course she'll be OK," said Delia. "She's going to help me brush Falstaff and the donkeys."

Meredith wiped her shoes on the mat inside the back door, but she didn't bother taking them off. Her mother had gotten excessive about this shoeless business. She stepped into the kitchen and looked out the window to check that Eloise hadn't decided to follow her. Eloise was holding Delia's hand as they were walking back to the barn, presumably to get the brushes, the dogs close at her heels. It was a relief to see Eloise happy. Wasn't this one of the main reasons she'd come back here? A lot in her life was uncertain, but Meredith knew she could count on her mother to bestow on Eloise the abundant, unconditional love that Josh had never offered her.

Meredith went into the dining room and sat sideways on the armchair by the window, her legs over the armrest. She took out her phone and called Evan.

"This a good time to talk?" she asked when he picked up.

"I'm in the car," said Evan, "so I may lose you. But go ahead."

"Are you alone?"

"Does it matter?"

"No. But, yeah, I guess. It's different talking to you if you're with someone."

"So what's up?" Evan asked.

"I'm at Mom's. And she's invited Kat to come for dinner tomorrow. And I need you to come too." Meredith sloughed off her jacket and scrunched it behind her on the chair.

"Why?"

"To protect me."

"Against Kat?"

"Against Kat and Mom when they team up against me."

"Is that what you call it? Wait—did you say you were at Mom's?"

"I got here yesterday."

"Just you?"

"Eloise is with me."

"Not Josh?"

"Nope. I'm done with Josh."

"Oh," said Evan. He was quiet for a moment, then he asked, "For real this time?"

"Oh yeah. For real."

"Have you let Wylie know you're back?"

"No. And for your information, Wylie doesn't have anything to do with it."

"No?"

"No!"

"OK. Just wondered. What did Mom have to say about you and Josh?"

Meredith leaned forward and straightened the armrest cover that her leg had pushed aside. "I haven't told Mom yet."

"And you want me to come to dinner to act as referee when the shit hits the fan?"

"Something like that."

"Merry. It's not easy for me to just pop over there for dinner. I don't live nearby. I have a life!"

"You're less than two hours away. An hour and a half, if you're the one driving."

"I don't know," Evan began.

"Things are shot to hell. I wouldn't be asking if I didn't need you."

Evan sighed. "So, you'll let Mom know you invited me?"

"No—not that."

"What am I supposed to do? Just call up Mom and invite myself?"

"No, I'll ask Mom to invite you. She'll like that. All her kids together. But I'm not going to tell her I called you."

"Merry!"

"Please? You'll come?"

"Well, all right. Maybe."

Merry was about to say "Love you," but everyone said that all the time now, whether they meant it or not. It had become a standard way of ending a call. "Thank you" is what she said.

There was a soft cough at the doorway. She turned quickly, startled. Bob was standing there.

"I'm sorry I alarmed you," he said. "But you hadn't seen me sitting in the kitchen, and I was unable to exit in time, and I'm afraid I inadvertently heard you on the phone."

Meredith's hands went automatically to her chest, as if she was blocking her phone from observation. "How much did you hear?"

"Most of it," said Bob.

"You heard that I've left Josh?"

"That part. Yes, I heard."

"I'm sure Mom has been going crazy wondering what's up. So now you can tell her soon as you get a moment alone with her."

"Do you want me to tell her?"

Meredith turned around fully and sat forward in her chair. "Of course not."

"Then I won't."

"You won't?"

Bob sighed. He pulled out a chair at the table and sat down. "I find myself in an awkward position. I like to be open with your mother, and I'm uncomfortable withholding information from her. But I don't feel comfortable sharing private information—in this case, yours—that I was made privy to by accident."

"Mom will find out eventually," said Meredith. "It's just that I'm not up to talking with her about it now. She'll want to know *why*. And she'll keep badgering me until she gets an answer, but she won't be happy with my answer."

"I can understand that."

Meredith studied Bob's face. "You never liked me, did you?"

"I didn't like you much when you were a teenager. It was difficult to like you then, even if I'd been so inclined. I'd married your mother in spite of her having children, not because she did."

Bob hadn't liked her, but he had rescued her that night when her car had run out of gas on her way home from a party at Wylie's house, a party she wasn't supposed to go to. She'd told her mother she was at a girlfriend's house instead. She'd called home and prayed that Bob would answer the phone, and he had. He didn't tell her mother where the car was, or that she had irresponsibly neglected to fill the gas tank. "Why are you being so nice to me?" she'd asked him, and he'd replied, "I'm not nice as much as self-serving. I don't like witnessing your mother's distress and your rows. I'm not happy about being dishonest, but it's clearly a price I have to pay on occasion to keep a little peace in this house."

"And do you like me now?" Meredith asked him.

"I'm open to the possibility."

"And Eloise?" she asked cautiously. "Do you like her?"

"Eloise takes some getting used to." It was impossible to tell from the expression on Bob's face how seriously he meant this, and at first Meredith was hurt, on Eloise's behalf. But maybe it was true. In fact, Eloise's own father had never really gotten used to her. Or rather Josh had never gotten used to being a parent, which amounted to much the same thing.

Meredith stood up. "Is it OK with you that Evan will join us for dinner tomorrow?"

"I don't have a problem with Evan," said Bob, "even if he is accompanied by one of the many young ladies your mother finds entirely unsuitable as a prospective daughter-in-law. And as long as Kat doesn't bring Roger's two troublemakers," said Bob, as he got to his feet as well, "casualties may be kept at a minimum."

"I thought she'd managed to have the boys bundled off to prep school."

"That she did. But though their mother has custody, there's always the danger they may turn up now and then."

"What about Roger?"

"In my experience, Roger usually is able to come up with an acceptable excuse for avoiding Sunday dinner with his mother-in-law."

Meredith didn't mind if Roger came with Kat—in fact, he sometimes had a neutralizing effect on Kat—but she hoped that Evan wouldn't be bringing anyone. But she could hardly ask him not to. It would be enough if he showed up.

~

Eloise loved Falstaff, and she loved the donkeys: Tulip, Myrtle, and Clementine. She loved them so much she forgot about everything that had happened—not forgot, exactly, because it was there still, but just set it all aside in the place where she didn't have to think about it: leaving home so suddenly she didn't have time to find her favorite sweater, the one with the duck; her mother's shouting and snatching her arm; the way her father's face looked, all tight and angry-sad; the way the airplane bounced in the air as if they were real bumps in the sky; and her mother yanking her thumb from her mouth and then flinging it back, and saying "Oh forget it, whatever," and her mother crying but saying she wasn't.

The donkeys had their winter coats still, long and bristly, but soft and white under the belly, and Eloise pressed her face against them and inhaled their wonderful, warm smell. Their eyes were enormous and nearly black, and when she looked into them she could see her own reflection, so she was in their eyes, part of them. And they looked into her eyes and saw themselves.

~

When Meredith returned to the field, her mother was showing Eloise how to saddle up Falstaff.

"Grandma's going to give me a ride!" cried Eloise.

Meredith reached down to tighten the cinch belt for the saddle. "You have to pull this tight," she said. "Falstaff doesn't like it, so he puffs his belly out."

"Then why do you do it?"

"So the saddle won't slip around. We don't want you to be riding him upside down."

"I'd like to ride upside down!" said Eloise.

"I don't think Grandma would approve," said Meredith. She lifted Eloise up onto Falstaff and adjusted the stirrups. She handed the reins to her mother.

"Have fun," she said.

"The saddle at the ranch had something to hold on to," said Eloise.

"That was a western saddle, this is an eastern saddle," explained Meredith. "Western saddles have a pommel in front, but it's not really for holding on, it's for tying a rope to if you're roping cattle."

"I held on to it," said Eloise. "But only sometimes."

Meredith leaned back against the fence and watched her mother walking Falstaff around the field. Eloise bravely let go with one hand and waved. Meredith had missed having a horse. She hadn't had a chance to go riding in California—just that one time she'd persuaded Josh to go on a family vacation at a dude ranch. They took a trail ride with a group up in the mountains. It had been a hot day, and Josh, who hadn't wanted to go in the first place, had gripped the pommel with one hand and swatted flies with the other. When she'd galloped off in a circle and come back into line again, he'd said, "No need to show off."

"I'm not showing off," she'd said, but she had been. They hadn't even gotten to the place where there was the big overlook, when Josh said, "OK, I'm done with this. I'm ready for a drink; let's go back," but Meredith had refused. One of the two guides had to go back with him, and he'd been pissed that Meredith hadn't come with him too.

"This was a special outing for Eloise," Meredith said afterward. "You wanted me to drag her back just because you decided to bail from the trail ride so you could have a beer?"

"Maybe I thought *you'd* come back with me, and we could have a drink together."

"What, and leave Eloise out there on the trail ride without me?"

"There was a guide along. That's what you were paying them for."

"I can't believe you'd think that was OK!"

"If you were so worried about Eloise, then yeah, you'd 'drag' her back with you."

"Maybe it was a special outing for me too. Maybe I was happy to get a chance to be on a horse again."

When Eloise was done riding, Meredith stopped Delia from taking the saddle off Falstaff.

"I'll take him out for a while," she said.

"Around the field?"

"I thought I'd head down the road a bit."

"He's an old horse, Merry!"

"Come on, Mom, he's not that old."

"I'll go find your helmet."

"Screw my helmet," said Meredith. She lowered the stirrups, checked the cinch, then swung herself easily up on Falstaff's back.

"When will you be back?" asked Eloise.

"I'm just going for a little ride," said Meredith. "I'll be back soon."

Her mother took Eloise's hand. "Let's go back to the house," she said. "Your Aunt Kat is coming to dinner. We can make a cake for dessert."

"What kind of cake?"

"What kind of cake do you like?"

"Cake with pink icing."

"I suppose we could do that," Delia said. Meredith saw her give Eloise's hand a squeeze. "Sure, Honey. Why not?" Typical grandma indulgence.

Meredith gave a little click, nudged with her knee, and Falstaff did her bidding and started off. Meredith looked back at her mother walking towards the house, swinging Eloise's hand.

~

Back at the house, Eloise found Bob sitting in the wing chair in the little room he called his study.

"What are you doing?" she asked.

Bob looked at her over his glasses. "What does it look like I'm doing?"

"Reading."

"That is, in fact, what I'm doing. Rather it *was* what I was doing before you asked."

"What are you reading?"

Bob held up the book so she could see the cover.

"What does it say?"

"Don't they teach you to read in the school you go to?"

"Yes, but not words like that." She tapped the book cover.

Bob pointed at the words as he read them. "*Caucasian Prayer Rugs*."

"What's it about?"

"It's a book about prayer rugs, just as it says. The Caucasus is a region where they were made."

"The rugs pray?"

Bob looked annoyed. "No, the rugs are where people get down on their knees to pray. We don't do any praying around here, but there are people who do." He pointed to the rug on the floor. "That happens to be a very fine Kazak prayer rug from the turn of the century. I keep it in here so the dogs don't defecate or vomit on it. They have a propensity for choosing the antique rugs for that."

Eloise knelt down on the rug on the floor. "Do you pray like this?"

"More like this," Bob said, and he leaned forward, head down, arms stretched straight out in front.

"What are you doing?" asked Delia as she came into the room. Bob sat up.

"I'm praying," said Eloise, arms out in front of her, head down.

"Bob!"

"Don't worry, Delia, experiencing the rituals performed on nineteenth-century prayer rugs is unlikely to damage the psyche of even the most sensitive child."

Eloise sat up. Delia looked as if she was about to say something to Bob, but instead she said "Come on, Eloise. I've gotten the ingredients all lined up, and you can run the mixer."

Eloise looked from Delia to Bob.

"Go run the mixer," said Bob, and he shooed Eloise out of the room.

~

Meredith circled the field at a gentle trot, then took Falstaff out on the dirt road. She'd heard that little quaver in Eloise's voice when she'd asked, "When will you be back?" so she didn't want to be gone for long, but God, it felt so good to be out here! She urged Falstaff into a canter, and felt the wind tangle her hair. For the first time she felt freed of all the stress that had been gripping her for days. When she got back to the barn, Meredith took the saddle off Falstaff and rubbed his sweaty back. Faithful, uncomplicated Falstaff! She pressed her cheek against his soft muzzle, then kissed him flat on the nose. As she walked towards the house she felt cleansed—well, maybe that was putting it too strongly—at least unburdened.

When her mother had married Bob, the last thing Meredith had imagined was that they would end up buying a place like this. She knew her mother had always harbored fantasies of owning an antique house and a farm, but she'd never expected Bob would go along with her. She hadn't thought of Bob as a man who compromised easily. The fact that he had done so had shown Meredith how much he was in love with her mother—something that both surprised and reassured her.

She hadn't expected to fall in love with the farm, but she had. The place was like her—scruffy and unconforming, unlike the suburbs she'd grown up in, the world of well-maintained kids who lived in well-maintained houses with neat lawns. She had few friends, but it didn't matter on the farm. She wasn't lonely, as she'd been. She had Falstaff; she had this huge barn, this open land. She could escape here and have a sense of things under her control when nothing else was. If she was lonely, it didn't show. But she wasn't lonely, not when she was here. Places can save people, as well as people can. The farm had saved her as a teenager. It could save her now.

In the kitchen she was treated to a scene worthy of Norman Rockwell: a beaproned grandmother tilting a mixing bowl, the creamy batter pouring into a cake pan that a beaproned little girl held steady on the counter.

Eloise didn't notice her standing in the doorway until the cake pan had been safely deposited into the oven. "Mommy," she cried. "We're making a cake for tomorrow when Aunt Kat comes to dinner."

Meredith's stomach clenched. Tomorrow. Sunday dinner! Kat would be coming, and maybe Roger, and Evan. And with everyone here, she'd make her announcement.

Bob suddenly appeared in the kitchen. "Bears knocked down the feeder again."

"Bears?" asked Eloise.

"Black bears, *Ursus americanus*. They're a damn nuisance. It's almost spring, so they've come out of their dens and are hungry and keep going after the seed in the feeder."

"Isn't that for birds?"

"It's intended for the birds, but the bears are ravenous. They'll eat anything."

"Don't scare her, Bob," said Meredith.

"I'm not afraid of bears," said Eloise.

"You should be," said Delia.

"I'm not afraid of anything," said Eloise. Though Meredith knew there were a number of things Eloise was afraid of. Like getting shots, and putting her head underwater at the pool, and the scene in *The Lion King* where the baby lion is lost. "There's only one thing I'm raising my daughter to be afraid of," she said, "and that's politicians." She ran her finger around the inside of the mixing bowl, scooped up a dollop of cake batter, then stuck it in her mouth. "Mmmm."

"You haven't washed your hands yet!" said Delia.

"Handwashing is overrated."

"You've been riding a horse!"

"Not 'a' horse, Mom, Falstaff. Certified germ-free." She took a seat at the kitchen table and drew Eloise close to her.

"Grandma is going to give me a ride again tomorrow," said Eloise.

"That's nice," said Meredith.

Eloise turned to Bob. "Are you going to have a ride too?"

"I don't ride horses," said Bob.

"Have you ever ridden a horse?"

"Years ago. And I will never get on one ever again."

"Why not?"

"I had a misadventure with a horse, and I would prefer not to repeat it."

"You could try again with Falstaff." Eloise turned to Meredith. "Couldn't he?"

"Not on your life," said Bob.

5

"Of course I'll invite him," Delia said when Merry suggested she ask Evan to join them for dinner. She was hoping to invite him anyway, but it was better the suggestion originated with Merry, who was already annoyed she'd invited Kat, and Delia felt she was on delicate ground. She was doing her best to make this surprise visit feel casual. She didn't want Merry to bolt, as she'd done the Christmas when she'd come with Eloise, and Delia had worked to recreate the kind of festivities she'd orchestrated when her children were little. "You always overdo things, Mom," was what Merry had said. "I'm outta here."

Ever since her offspring had fledged, Delia did everything she could to gather them back in the nest. She concentrated on the major holidays: the trifecta of Thanksgiving, Christmas, and Easter. If Easter proved unpromising, she'd shift to its counterpart, Greek Easter, but she seized any occasion for an excuse for a family celebration—birthdays, anniversaries, Bob's retirement, once, even, the arrival of a new donkey. She had limited success, and she was perpetually disappointed.

"Face it, Lili," said Bob, "the diaspora is complete. Your children are gone."

"Gone? Bob, that's cruel!" Delia cried.

Kat had settled nearby, so she could be counted on to turn up dutifully for major holidays, usually with Roger, but Evan, who didn't live that far away, was unreliable. He was always off somewhere—kayaking in Alaska, bicycling in Italy, surfing in Australia. And Merry? From the day she'd dropped out of college and taken off on the back of a boyfriend's motorcycle to join so-called artist friends in Taos, her visits home were irregular and unpredictable. And once she'd settled on the West Coast (Delia called it the Wrong Coast), it was a challenge to lure her back, even though Delia underwrote the travel costs. Merry would never commit herself to coming, and when she did come, she usually showed up only at the last minute. She'd schooled her mother into being grateful for whatever access she could get. This gratitude had intensified once Merry had provided Delia with a grandchild. "Points to Merry!" Evan had cheerfully said, when Eloise had been born.

Delia had accepted the fact that her children had grown up, but she couldn't quite accept that they were gone forever. She liked to imagine they had moved away only temporarily, and somehow, someday, they would relocate nearby, and they'd be reunited as the family unit they'd once been—minus their father, of course, and with the addition of Bob. This was not a fantasy she shared with him.

Delia went into the music room to call Evan, closed the sliding doors to the house, and sank into the sofa. It was a generous sofa, deep enough so that getting out of it required effort and discouraged parents from popping up and intruding on the lesson. Delia didn't often sit here, and it was interesting to have the parents' view across the room, their perspective on her teaching. The sofa, green velvet with a worn nap, was a comforting presence from her past. She'd nursed Merry on this sofa when she was a baby, shooed dogs off this sofa (except for thunderstorms, when they were allowed), and made love with Bob on this sofa. Recently she'd discovered that mice had gnawed a corner, but wedging a throw pillow against the armrest had hidden the damage.

"Where are you, Mom?" Evan asked immediately.

"I'm home, dear."

"But you're on your cell?" At home Delia usually used the landline, but she didn't want anyone to pick up an extension.

Sometimes it was simpler to be honest with Evan. "I needed some privacy."

"What's up?"

"Merry's here for a visit, and Kat's coming for dinner tomorrow, and I thought you might want to come too. I think it would be really nice for Merry—in fact she suggested it."

"You didn't tell me Merry was going to be in town."

Delia shifted on the sofa and pulled her feet up. "Actually we didn't know. She just called us once she was on her way. Eloise is with her."

"But not Josh?"

"No. In fact I'm afraid something's going on between the two of them."

"What did Merry say?"

"She hasn't actually said anything, but I'm worried about her."

Evan laughed. "That's your default position, Mom. When you don't know what else to do, you worry."

Delia was tempted to say something like "Someday when you're a parent, you'll discover that worrying is part of the territory." But Evan didn't appreciate comments about his potential for parenthood. "She doesn't seem happy" is what she settled for. "And Eloise isn't happy either. I mean she's happy to be here, but I think whatever's going on with Merry has unsettled her."

"Eloise is a kid, Mom. She'll be fine."

"I hope so." She waited a moment, then added, "And what about Merry?"

"Merry is—Merry. She'll survive."

"I'm afraid I don't find that particularly comforting."

"I didn't expect you would," said Evan, and he started laughing. And Delia found herself laughing too. That often happened with Evan; his laughter was contagious. He often told jokes, and seemed to have an endless supply of them—especially those dreadful knock-knock jokes—and he remembered them all, a talent which, unfortunately, he'd failed to apply to his schoolwork. He always saw the humor in everyday life, and his buoyant good nature flourished when things didn't go right. When the kids were young and a flat tire had derailed their family outing midway, Evan had said, "Hooray, we can dig into the picnic basket now!" and even Kat, who even as a kid took things seriously, had laughed. When Merry was a little girl he would easily reduce her to fits of giggles. Sometimes she'd wet her pants, and once she choked on a noodle. The banana joke was a favorite. He'd enlist Merry to say "Hey, you've got a banana in your ear," and he'd answer, "I can't hear you, I have a banana in my ear." They'd carry on varieties of this, forever. Kat was not amused, and Delia guessed Evan relished tormenting her.

"When will Evan grow up?" Kat asked, long after it was obvious that Evan had.

With that snatch of laughter bonding them, Delia decided to risk saying "It's been so long since I've had the three of you together, I wondered if maybe this time you could come on your own?"

"Kat isn't dragging the unfortunate Roger with her?"

"I don't know. He's invited of course—"

"And that's different from someone I'd bring?"

"Well, Roger is her husband—"

"And Kirsten is not *wife*?"

Delia had forgotten (or was it repressed?) Evan's latest girlfriend's name and so was glad Evan mentioned it, but the proximity of the word "wife" and the image of Kirsten made her take in her breath.

"It's not exactly that—"

"What then? You don't fancy her tattoo?"

The tattoo—featuring some prehistoric bird of prey that curled up from her shoulder and was clawing her neck—had been distressing, but it wasn't just that. Kirsten had a sulky demeanor, and the only thing she was interested in talking about was bouldering.

"I just don't feel she's quite—"

"It's OK, Mom. You've been spared. I'm dating someone else now."

"Oh." Delia hesitated a moment. "So, perhaps—" Delia was never good at judging the seriousness of Evan's relationships. She was never able to predict their potential for longevity and had no idea what brought about their demise. If Evan had ever suffered rejection, he never gave a hint of it. But of course he wouldn't, not with her.

"Perhaps what?"

"It's just that Merry is home so rarely, and I thought she might enjoy having it be just you."

"I hear you, Mom. And I'll take your suggestion under advisement."

That was as much as she could hope for. "Thank you, dear," said Delia. Unlike Merry, who was usually reluctant to go out of her way to please her mother, Evan always seemed eager to please—not just his mother, but the world in general. He'd navigated his parents' divorce with apparent equanimity (though Delia couldn't keep herself from worrying he may have ignored his true feelings) and had cheerfully accepted her marriage to Bob, unlike Kat, who had been merely stoic about both. He and Bob maintained an amicable relationship because Bob, wisely, had stepped back from any parental role. Bob had been less successful sustaining a position of noninterference with Merry, no doubt because she'd been more underfoot, and—Delia had to admit this—she'd been an antagonistic, resentful teenager.

"What time are we eating?" Evan asked.

"Six-ish. But come earlier, please. Five? Eloise will be so excited to see you—it's been a long time!"

"I have a friend who needs to rehome his bearded dragon. He's passing on all the equipment too. I'll bring it to her as a gift."

"What!"

"It's a great entry-level reptile."

"And what do you think Merry will have to say?"

"She'll be cool."

"And you imagine Eloise will bring a lizard back to California with her?"

"If that's a problem, it can stay with you. Add to the menagerie."

"I don't do lizards," said Delia. "I do only mammals."

"Have you informed your chickens of their new classification yet?" asked Evan, and before Delia could say anything more, he hung up.

Delia sat for a moment and held her cell phone between her hands. It was possible that Evan was teasing her about the lizard. But it was equally possible he'd bring it. She got to her feet and slipped the phone in her pocket.

Merry and Eloise were out in the field with the donkeys. Eloise was brushing Clementine. Delia stood for a moment in the doorway before walking out to them. They looked so much alike: their shape, their posture, their scraggly hair—they were undeniably mother and daughter. They both had thin dancer's legs, Eloise's no fat on them at all, just sinew and bone. Merry's husband, Josh, was short for a man—which may have accounted for some of his personality quirks—and sturdy looking. Eloise and Merry were wisps. Watching them now, Delia felt a surge of such protectiveness for them both, she nearly flew across the field to embrace them. She walked, instead, and hugged Eloise from behind.

Eloise was brushing Clementine's neck. "How come you use people brushes for the donkeys?" she asked.

"I'd bought expensive brushes for them, but they prefer my cast-off hairbrushes, especially the kind with wiry bristles."

"Maybe 'cause they smell good, from the shampoo?"

"I think it's because they like that scratchy feeling."

"So do I," said Eloise, and she used the brush on her own hair.

"Oh, Eloise!" cried Delia.

Merry didn't say anything, just shook her head, and Eloise went back to brushing Clementine.

"I called Evan," Delia informed Merry after a moment. "And he says he'll come."

"Good!" said Merry, and something about the way she said it made Delia wonder if she already knew. She was glad that Merry and Evan were close—that's what a mother wanted for her children, right?—but she sometimes suspected they were planning things behind her back. The business about Kat reaching out to enlist them in getting her to give up the farm had made her feel she'd become an outsider to her own family.

She picked up one of the brushes and ran her hand along Clementine's stubby mane, and along the stripe on her back. "I'll do her tail," she told Eloise.

"Are you going to braid it?" asked Eloise.

Delia lifted Clementine's tail in the air and ran the brush through the rough ends of hair.

"Not much to braid," she said. "Unlike horses, donkeys have pathetic tails, don't they? We'll braid Falstaff's tail if you like."

"OK," said Eloise. "But I think Clementine would like to have her tail braided too."

"All right, Sweetheart," said Delia. "No reason not to try."

6

Meredith, in bra and panties, stood at her bedroom window and watched her sister arrive. Kat was always punctual. Her mother had said something like "around five," but Meredith knew Kat would be there exactly at five, or a few minutes before five, but never a minute after. Roger was driving—so Kat had managed to drag him!—and Kat got out of the car and opened the rear door to get a platter that had been on the seat, leaving Roger to close the car door behind her, which he did. He did not slam it; he closed it conscientiously. So very Roger. Kat was wearing a tailored jacket, and as she walked towards the house bearing her offering, she looked as if she were in a procession.

Kat was one of those people who believed it was important to maintain good posture. She sat upright on chairs; she walked erectly, as if she had a book balanced on her head. Meredith walked nose first, as if she were an animal sniffing her way, or, when strolling, she swung along side to side, shoulders rolling, head lolling. She sat crookedly on chairs, draped herself over armrests, hoisted her feet up on any nearby surface, incorporated available dogs as ottomans. And she never stayed in any position for long. "Stop twitching!" Kat would say to her when they had the misfortune to be seated next to each other.

Kat had disappeared into the house, and Meredith watched Roger approach the front door, then turn to click his key to lock the car doors. What was he thinking? They lived in the boondocks! He gave a nod of satisfaction, then hurried to the house, following his wife.

Meredith wondered what would happen if she didn't go downstairs at all, but Kat would no doubt come rushing up the stairs, invading her bedroom. Meredith could picture Kat looking around the room and holding herself back from commenting on anything—the contents of opened suitcases spread across the floor, clothes dangling from the chair, the unmade bed—before she hugged her. Better to go right down and get it over with. Meredith pulled on a pair of jeans and dug in the suitcase till she found her black sweater. She reached around to adjust her bra, which was pinching under her arm, but it was already on the farthest hooks, so she took it off and tossed it on the pile of clothes. Going braless here was an act of defiance as well as a matter of comfort, and the sweater was thick enough so that her nipples weren't in your face. There was this weird thing about women's nipples—everyone knew you had them, but some people thought you were supposed to hide them behind a layer of foam, while men's nipples could be as pokey as they wanted.

There was a tear at the seam of the neck of the sweater where Meredith had cut out the annoying label. She pulled the sweater on anyway, unclipped her barrette, and shook out her hair to cover the hole. She retrieved the socks she'd worn the day before from her sneakers. The socks—favorites of Eloise's—had howling wolves on them; Meredith had been sent them by a wildlife foundation in appreciation of a donation. It was not clear if the wolves were howling because of the indignity of appearing on socks or as an appeal for additional funding.

Meredith felt she needed to fortify herself for the coming drama, so she put on the pair of dress boots she'd brought—kick-ass boots with pointy toes and nasty heels, a twisted ankle in the making. Screw shoeless house! She'd never wear clothing that wasn't comfortable, but she'd endure perilous footwear if the occasion necessitated it. And considering what she was planning on doing, this occasion necessitated it. She stood at the top of the stairs until the furor in the front hall had quieted as Delia herded Kat and Roger into the kitchen, and then Meredith took in her breath and rushed down the stairs before she could change her mind.

"Here's Merry!" cried Kat when she saw her.

"Yes, here I am," said Meredith, and allowed herself to be folded into Kat's stiff embrace. Embrace accomplished, Kat stood back to give Roger his turn. Meredith and Roger had developed a two-pat greeting, in lieu of a hug, which had served them well over the years.

"We're so happy to see you!" cried Kat, though the "we" was a stretch. Roger rarely looked happy, and didn't do so now. "And Eloise, of course," Kat continued, looking around to smile at her niece. "This is such a wonderful surprise. We had no idea you were coming!"

"I like to surprise people," said Meredith.

"And Evan's coming too?"

"Eventually," said Delia.

"I hope he makes it," said Kat. "It will be so nice to have us all together." Apparently Meredith's husband did not count as part of the "all." Or was this Kat thinking she was being tactful about Josh's absence? "But you know Evan," she continued, "he may not show up at all. He often disappoints people."

"Not me," said Meredith, though the look on Delia's face informed her that her mother shared Kat's view. And what she'd claimed wasn't strictly true. Evan had disappointed her on occasion, too, in the past. Though by accident, not intention; Evan's intentions were always good. Meredith hoped he would not disappoint her now, because she needed him here. Really needed him.

"Look what Kat made," said Delia, as she lifted the plastic top off the platter to reveal a circle of deviled eggs. Their filling was artistically rippled—some trick with a pastry bag?—and sprinkled with paprika, with a parsley sprig posed pertly on top.

"I don't know when you find the time to make things like this," said Delia. Kat always did find time for impressive culinary accomplishments, in spite of a schedule packed with billable minutes. Meredith never had enough time for anything. Not that she'd squander time on making deviled eggs even if she did.

"Not that hard," said Kat, smiling. "I wanted to be sure there would be something vegetarian for Merry." She turned to her. "You're not vegan, now, are you?"

"Not yet," said Meredith.

"I should hope not!" said Delia. "We have chickens laying eggs, after all."

"More eggs than any two old people can consume," said Bob, "so it's a good thing there are violin pupils willing to take some off our hands. A perk of Suzuki lessons."

"There were ducks that laid eggs too," said Eloise. "But the baby foxes ate the ducks." Meredith stepped closer to her daughter and rested her hand on her small head. "Eloise is excited to be here," she said.

"What do you like best about visiting Grandma?" Kat asked Eloise. She had that annoying habit of adults who try to demonstrate their fondness for children by squatting at eye level and talking in a higher voice.

"The aminals," said Eloise.

"An-i-mals," said Kat, enunciating each syllable.

Although Eloise didn't seem to notice Kat's correction, Meredith said quickly, "We call them aminals around here." Eloise was a precocious speaker, and Meredith savored her few childlike pronunciations and strove to protect them, as if in doing so she could prolong her daughter's childhood.

"Do you want to go outside to see them?" asked Eloise.

"Maybe later," said Kat. She was wearing slacks with a crease that Meredith guessed required ironing.

Eloise turned to Roger. "How about you?"

He seemed surprised to be addressed. "I'll wait on that too," he said.

"I'm not going to wait on these," said Bob, and he scooped up one of the deviled eggs and popped it whole, into his mouth. "Want to try one, Eloise?"

"Do I have to eat the gooey stuff inside?"

"Not if you don't want to."

Eloise picked up an egg, pushed out its contents with her forefinger, and stuffed the half into her mouth.

"Smaller bites, please," said Meredith. She did not look at Kat's face.

"Grandpa ate the whole thing," said Eloise, when she'd chewed up some of the egg.

"His mouth is larger than yours," said Meredith.

"But no one's is as big as mine!" cried out Evan, who had managed to arrive and sneak into the kitchen unnoticed. "I am the big bad wolf!" He swept up Eloise in his arms and, as she shrieked and giggled, pretended to gobble her up.

"You made it!" said Kat.

Evan swung Eloise around once and set her on her feet. "Why wouldn't I?" he asked. "Not every day I get to see my baby sister and my favorite niece."

"Am I really your favorite?" asked Eloise.

"My favorite and my only."

"Mommy isn't a baby, though."

"I should hope not!"

"But you said she's your baby sister."

"My bad," said Evan. "What I should have said, then, is my younger-than-I-am sister. As opposed to my older-than-I-am sister, your Aunt Kat." He pointed at her. "I am the middle child, which explains why I have the best disposition in the family."

"What's disposition?" asked Eloise.

"It means he tells stupid jokes that no one finds funny," said Meredith.

"I can't hear you," said Evan, and he held up his hand to his ear.

"Because you have a banana in your ear!" screamed Eloise.

"Oh no!" moaned Kat. "Don't tell me this idiocy has been passed along to the next generation!"

"I'm sure the boys bring home some stupid jokes too." Meredith did not say "Roger's boys"—Kat would find that upsetting—but she could not quite call them "*your* boys."

"Exeter is a humorless place," said Bob. "You don't spend fifty thousand a year to have your kid acquire stupid jokes."

Delia, who was at the counter making the lasagna, turned around, spoon held in the air. A bit of tomato sauce dribbled onto her wrist. "Is that what it costs these days!"

"More like sixty-five," said Roger, soberly. Kat gave him a "keep your mouth shut" look.

"Good thing there are only two kids," said Evan. "A dozen would break the bank!"

"You went to an expensive private school," said Kat defensively.

"Only for a year. And only because I was a fuckup at the public high school and that was the only alternative. And I was just a day student there, unlike my pal Wylie, so I missed out on the fun pranks the boarders did."

"What were the fun pranks?" asked Eloise.

"Careful, Evan!" said Meredith, but she was smiling.

"Oh, like carrying the headmaster's car up onto the front terrace."

"Why didn't they drive it there?" asked Eloise.

"There were stone stairs."

"Wasn't it heavy?"

"They were strong boys!"

"And strong girls," said Meredith.

"Hadn't it been an all-boys school originally?" asked Kat.

"Yeah," said Evan. "They started admitting girls the year before I got there. They needed to improve their academic rankings, and the simplest course was to allow girls in, since they are—"

"Smarter," said Kat.

"No. Better test takers."

Meredith noticed that Eloise had disappeared. The front door was open, and Meredith saw her in the driveway looking into Evan's car; then Eloise ran back to the kitchen.

"Did you forget to bring it?" she asked Evan.

"Forget what?"

"The dragon. Or didn't it fit?"

"Fit where?"

"In your car. But you can bring it in a truck or a trailer. If you don't have a trailer you can rent one. I know because Mommy rented one when her painting wouldn't fit inside the car."

"What are you talking about?" asked Meredith, and she looked quizzically at Evan, then back at Eloise.

"Uncle Evan said he was going to bring me a dragon."

"You mean a stuffed dragon?" asked Meredith.

"No, a real one!"

"But, Honey, there aren't real dragons, anymore."

Eloise squinted, and her chin got all wrinkled, as it did when she was about to cry.

"There are! There are! I heard Grandma say to Grandpa she hoped Uncle Evan wasn't going to bring a dragon for me because it would be a nuisance to take care of."

"Oh dear," said Delia. "I didn't realize Eloise was listening."

"Eloise is right," said Evan. "It is a real dragon. Not the kind that live in fairy tales, but a bearded dragon, which is a lot smaller, so some people have them as pets. A friend has one he may give away. And I did think about bringing it for you, Eloise"—he turned to her now—"but I learned that this particular dragon was afraid of dogs *and* donkeys, so it wouldn't be happy here."

"Dragons aren't afraid of anything!" cried Eloise.

"That's true for most dragons. But not this one. This one is afraid of lots of things. It's a small dragon, not much bigger than a cat." Evan held up his hands to show her.

"What if it couldn't see the dogs or the donkeys?"

"It would still smell them. And the very smell of a dog or a donkey would make this poor bearded dragon hide in the back of his cage and not come out."

"The donkeys certainly do smell!" said Kat, and she gave a little shiver.

"Even to eat?" asked Eloise.

"Even to eat. And that would be a problem, wouldn't it?"

Eloise's face relaxed a little. "I guess."

"How about I take you to visit this dragon sometime? I bet, if you're gentle, it would let you hold it. Would you like that?"

"Uh-huh."

Crisis averted, thought Meredith.

Kat stayed in the kitchen helping Delia with dinner, while Meredith, Evan, and Eloise went out to feed the animals. Meredith traded her dress boots for a pair of old muck boots, but Evan's boots were already farm appropriate. It was unlikely he owned any formal footwear. Bob and Roger had been standing around, drinks in hand, putting up an appearance of conviviality, but Delia, in a brave move—inspired by Kat? Meredith wondered—entrusted them with setting the table, and they moved sheepishly into the dining room, silverware and napkins in hand. Meredith wondered if her mother had a designated seating plan and, if so, hoped she'd be placed next to Evan. She needed him beside her to give her courage for what she planned to do.

It was refreshing to be out of the house, to be away from the scene of potential future conflict—to forget for a moment what she was heading into. Eloise had taken Evan's hand and was leading him to the barn. Meredith came up on his other side and slipped her arm through his.

"Hey," he said. "How are you holding up?"

"I'm just glad you're here." She leaned her head against his shoulder.

Inside the barn, it was so serene and safe Meredith nearly sobbed with relief. She loved the wide plank floors, the imperturbable rafters, the soft darkness. She closed her eyes and inhaled the smell of straw and hay. Her mother had once said she'd fallen in love with the farm for the smells alone, and Meredith understood what she meant.

Eloise instructed Evan in feeding the donkeys, and although he probably knew the drill well, he listened attentively and goofed up—intentionally, Meredith knew—so she had to correct him. Unlike Josh, he was ideally suited to fatherhood.

"You have to hold the carrots this way," explained Eloise, "and don't let your fingers stick out!"

"Like this?"

"No, like this!" shouted Eloise.

Evan pushed up Clementine's lips. "Look at those teeth," he said. "Does anyone brush them?"

"Do we, Mommy?"

"I suppose we could, but not with toothpaste."

Evan leaned down and planted a noisy kiss on Clementine's nose.

"What are you doing?" asked Eloise.

"Kissing her goodnight."

"We should kiss them all goodnight!" cried Eloise, and she started to kiss Tulip goodnight. "Mommy, you kiss Myrtle."

"Myrtle doesn't—" Meredith began, but Eloise gave her an imploring look, so she, too, leaned down. Her lips against the donkey's muzzle—the feel of the soft skin, the tickle of whiskers—reminded her she used to kiss Falstaff goodnight when she was young. She was suddenly a teenager again. Unhappy as teenagers were all supposed to be—but not unhappy the way she was now. Grown-up unhappiness was different. If she could just be a teenager again! But then she caught the wish midair and stamped it out. For then she wouldn't have Eloise, and there was nothing in her life that she wouldn't bear in trade for having Eloise. Shaken by that second of near betrayal, she came behind her daughter, put her arms around her small body, and pressed her lips down on her head.

Dinner was ready when they came back inside the house. The two silver candelabras had been set on the table—in her honor?—and there were little handwritten name cards at each place. Meredith saw she'd been seated next to Eloise on one side and Roger on the other, and quickly switched Roger with Evan, so Evan was next to her instead.

"What are you doing?" Eloise asked.

"Just fixing these."

"Are you allowed to move them?"

"It's a secret," said Meredith and held her finger to her lips. She knew Eloise loved secrets.

Delia's head came around the doorframe. "We're about ready to eat," she said.

"Can I light the candles?" asked Eloise.

"Light them? No, Sweetheart. But you can snuff them out when we're done eating."

"Snuff? That's a funny word!" said Eloise.

"We have a special snuffer," said Delia, and she brought it over to Eloise and demonstrated on the unlit candle.

"Go use the bathroom now and wash up for dinner," said Meredith.

"I don't need to use the bathroom," said Eloise.

"You do need to wash your hands."

Kat had come into the dining room. "You've been touching donkeys," she said.

"So?"

Meredith smiled. She could picture herself saying that when she'd been a kid, hands on her hips, but she turned towards Eloise and said, "Now!" When Eloise was gone for longer than she should have been, Meredith went off to fetch her from the bathroom under the stairs. Eloise had decorated the sink with clumps of white foamy soap.

"What's going on?" she cried.

"It's snow, Mommy!"

Eloise dipped her finger into the foam and put a dollop of soap at the end of her nose.

Usually something like this would have made Meredith laugh, but she was too tense to feel amused about anything now. She snatched a hand towel and wiped Eloise's face.

"Ow!"

"Would you please try to behave yourself!"

In the mirror she saw that Eloise looked as if she was about to cry. Meredith closed her eyes for a second and gave a little shudder. When she opened her eyes she saw Eloise watching her, worried now. Meredith took in a big breath. "OK, Sweetheart," she said. "Time to face the throng." She took Eloise's hand, and they walked together back to the dining room, where the candles on the table were all lit.

"Mom, can we put the dogs outside while we're eating?" asked Kat, but Delia didn't answer her and the dogs scrambled happily under the table and around people's chairs.

"The dogs will make cleanup easier," said Bob.

"Evan, I believe you're sitting over here, beside me," said Delia, as Evan took the chair next to Meredith.

"Nope, I'm right here," he said, and he flourished his name card in the air. Delia looked confused. Meredith was afraid Eloise was about to explain, so she leaned down so their faces were close, and held her finger to her lips.

Kat tapped the silver cup that Delia had set by Eloise's place. "That was mine when I was a baby—" she began to say, then corrected herself, "a little girl. Then it was your Uncle Evan's. You can see his teeth marks on it." She touched a dent in the cup. "Then it was your mother's."

"When you're last in line," said Meredith, "you get damaged goods."

"What does that say?" asked Eloise, pointing to the engraving on the side.

"My initials," Kat said. "K. L. W."

Eloise squinted at the letters. "They're all on top of each other."

"That's the way they do monograms," explained Kat. "It's cursive."

"I can write my name in cursive," said Eloise. "Want to see?"

"Maybe after dinner," said Kat, but she didn't sound, to Meredith, as if she really wanted to. Kat pointed at the candelabra near her. "You know, Mom," she said, "I'd be happy to polish these for you, the next time I'm here."

"Thank you, dear," said Delia, "but we don't use them that much, so I'm not sure it matters."

"You keep them out on the sideboard!"

"Even so. I wouldn't want you to be wasting your time on them."

"You should just give them to Kat, Mom," said Evan, "so she can keep them in shape."

"I'm not asking for them!" said Kat.

"You're not?" said Meredith.

"No!"

"You can have that argument about who inherits the silver when I'm no longer here," said Delia.

"Where are you going?" asked Eloise.

"When Grandma's no longer alive," said Meredith.

"Merry!" cried Kat.

Bob stood up at his seat and brandished the serving fork. "I carved the turkey in the kitchen, and there are two separate platters, one dark meat, one light. I'm passing them around clockwise and counterclockwise."

"Is this a sort of Thanksgiving rerun for the benefit of those who missed the premier?" asked Evan.

"I don't eat turkey," said Eloise. "And Mommy doesn't either."

"That's why there's lasagna," said Bob, "and your grandmother will put some on your plate."

Meredith knew Eloise didn't like lasagna, and she gave her a look that said "Be polite!"

They had just begun the salad course when Kat said, "I'm glad you're here, Merry, so we have this opportunity to be together. We can talk about things with Mom in person."

"Mom is right at this table," said Delia, "so please don't refer to her as if she isn't. What things?"

"Your plans for the future. Now that you have all three of your children here, it's a good time to discuss some of the possibilities."

"Possibilities for what?" asked Delia.

"For some alternatives to this—" Kat waved her hand around the room. "We're concerned about you."

"Are you including me in all this?" asked Bob.

"That goes without saying!" cried Kat.

"And just why are you concerned?" asked Delia. "Bob and I are still very much on our feet."

"Actually," said Evan, "you're both sitting down."

"We're looking to the future," Kat said, ignoring Evan. "We want to be proactive!"

"And who is the 'we'?" asked Delia.

Meredith waited to see if Kat was going to include her in this, but Bob said quickly, "I don't think your mother has found any of those condos particularly attractive."

"It doesn't have to be a condo," said Kat. "It could be a house. Just a smaller, newer house, one level. Not a farm! Not a big two-hundred-year-old house that's tumbling down!" She looked up at the ceiling as if it was about to collapse. Which, to be fair to Kat, Meredith had to admit had once happened.

"This house begs to differ with you, Kat," said Evan. "It's still standing!"

"You haven't answered me," said Delia. "Who, exactly, is the 'we'?"

"All three of us," said Kat.

"So my children have been conspiring against me?"

"I wouldn't call it conspiring, Lili," said Bob, and Meredith saw him lay his hand on her mother's shoulder.

"Evan? Merry?"

Meredith pulled back. This would be the moment to speak, but she couldn't find her voice.

Evan shrugged. "Kat called me. She had some ideas she ran by me, but—"

"We've just been discussing things," said Kat. "We felt it was time for you to be taking some steps to—"

"I wouldn't say that—" began Evan. "I'm not exactly on board with—"

Meredith hadn't realized her leg was jiggling until she saw Evan looking down at it. Her body sometimes acted up, as if it had a mind of its own. She took in a deep breath and let it out slowly, the way she tried to get Eloise to do when Eloise was really upset about something.

"It's because we love you, Mom!" cried Kat. "We can't imagine how you can keep on living here, managing this place, taking care of all these animals."

"I can imagine how," Meredith said. The words came right out without her first forming them in her head. But only Evan seemed to have heard her, so she had to say them again. This time her mother looked over at her.

"I have a little announcement to make." These were the words Meredith had practiced, the words of introduction for what she'd been planning to say, and she spoke louder now. Everyone looked up at her. She pressed against Evan.

"You don't have to worry about the house and the animals, Kat," she said. "I'm planning on staying here, and I'll help take care of everything."

No one said anything. The only noise was Ralph scratching at the door to be let out, and no one paid any attention.

"Whoa," said Evan, after a moment.

"What about Josh?" asked Kat.

"I'm done with Josh," said Meredith.

"Done?" asked Delia.

"Done," said Meredith. She stood up. "I'm going outside." She pushed back her chair, turned to leave, then reached for Eloise's hand. For a terrible moment she'd almost forgotten about her.

7

In the morning, Delia found Evan asleep on the living room sofa, one arm dangling so his fingers brushed the floor. He'd had a lot to drink the night before, and Delia was relieved she'd been able to persuade him not to drive home. He could have slept in the bedroom that had been his, but he'd sacked out on the sofa, instead. The throw he'd appropriated from the back of the wing chair was too short to cover him, and he had pulled it up towards his neck so his feet were uncovered. Although his ski and bike shop offered racks of socks, the ones he wore had sprouted holes in the toes. He was breathing through his mouth, each breath ending in a little gurgle, almost a snore. Delia felt an acute tenderness towards him, as if he were still the little boy he'd once been, and she had to hold herself back from reaching out to smooth his hair off his brow.

It was much earlier in the morning than Delia usually went out to feed the animals, but she'd woken up at five and after an hour of lying in bed, trying to reenter the realm of sleep, she'd given up. She'd crept downstairs, careful not to wake Merry or Eloise, and she tiptoed now past her sleeping son. She threw her work jacket over her pajamas and headed out to the barn. Even the dogs were still asleep and didn't even lift their heads when she left. The donkeys didn't seem surprised to see her appear this early—but they rarely registered surprise. That was one of the things she admired about the donkeys: they preferred regularity, but were philosophically accepting of changes in their schedule. She'd hoped to spend some time with them now, but they were impatient when she was brushing them, even when she was scratching their haunches. They were indifferent to her need for comfort and focused only on what her morning presence meant: breakfast. They thumped their muzzles against the barn door, so eventually she let them and Falstaff out into the fenced yard, and then, because they seemed so expectant, she'd laid out some flakes of hay for them all. The stables could be mucked out later.

She went upstairs into the big, open barn and sat down on a bale of straw. It was barely light, but she preferred the softness of almost-dark to the glare of the overhead lights. The straw was prickly, and she stood up and tucked her jacket underneath her before she sat down again. She kept picturing the end of dinner the night before, the way Merry had swept out of the dining room, dragging Eloise behind her; the way Kat had flung her arms in the air and asked, "What is going on with her?" The way Evan had raised his glass, as if in a toast, then tipped his chair back on two legs—as he did when he was a kid.

"I thought I'd find you here."

Delia wheeled around. Bob, his bathrobe tied crookedly around him, clumped towards her in his rubber boots. She moved over to make room for him, and he sat beside her on the bale of straw. She leaned against him and he pulled up his arm, which had been pinned between them, so he could lay it across her shoulder.

"So," he said.

"So."

"Were you surprised?"

"Not entirely," Delia said. "There was something about the way she was looking around this barn, as if she had designs on the space, that made me wonder. What about you?"

Bob gave a little laugh. "No. Nothing Merry does surprises me."

"Do you think she means it, or is it just an idea she's trying out?"

"Oh, I think she means it, all right. I'm not sure she'll stick to it—Merry doesn't always stick with things—but she seems serious about it for now."

Delia sat up and looked at Bob. "How do you feel about it?"

Bob laughed again. "It's certainly not what I would choose. Living with Merry, and especially with Eloise, will test my good nature. But I'm not sure it matters so much how I feel about it. The question is, how do *you* feel about it?"

Delia was about to say she didn't know how she felt, but she had a barrage of feelings, each well defined, and in conflict with each other.

"The thought of having Merry here—of having Eloise here!—I know she's a problem for you, but oh, Bob, I'd love that. But leaving her husband, abandoning her marriage, her home, her life? How could Merry just do that?"

"By getting on a plane and coming here. She said she was 'done' with Josh, but my guess is that it wasn't a casual 'just' but rather a move out of real desperation."

Desperation? The word struck Delia. She hadn't seen it this way, but Bob seemed to have picked up on something she'd missed. She thought for a moment, then asked, softly, "What do you think happened with them?"

Bob shrugged. "No idea. I guess she didn't say anything to you about it last night?"

"She didn't say anything at all about it. She went out for a walk with Evan once Eloise went to sleep, and she might have said something to him. But she didn't talk to me. She doesn't confide in me, Bob, you know that. None of my children do. Not anymore."

"Hey!" said Bob, and he turned her face around and kissed her flat on the mouth. "Your kids are grown up. You can't expect them to confide in you."

"But Merry never did confide in me. I always wanted her to. When she came home from school when she was little, I wanted to snuggle up with her and have her tell me about her day, but she'd squirm away and run off and tag after her brother or go and play in her room on her own. And when she got older she really did run off. I've never felt I had enough time with her."

"Well, now it looks as if she's back, and you will."

Delia stood up quickly and turned to him. "Oh God, Bob, what are we going to do?"

"What do you mean, what are we going to do? Do we have a choice?"

"We could tell her we want her to go back to California and fix things with Josh."

Bob laughed and shook his head. "Listen to yourself!" he said.

Delia sat back down next to him. She parted the folds of his bathrobe and pressed her face against his chest, the slight hollow in the center, smelling of sweat and sleep. Bob's hand cupped the back of her head. Why was she crying? Hadn't she just gotten exactly what she'd longed for? Her youngest child, her daughter Merry, living back home, and her darling granddaughter, Eloise, living here, close to her too?

In the kitchen, later, Delia found Evan and Eloise at the stove.

"Uncle Evan is teaching me how to make an omelet," said Eloise.

"What?"

"You didn't think I knew how to cook anything, did you, Mom?" asked Evan.

"You need to wiggle the pan to move the egg around," said Eloise, and she took hold of the handle of the skillet.

"Careful!" cried Delia, and she reached to take charge of the pan, but Evan stayed her hand.

"Don't worry, Mom," said Evan. "I've got things under control. Eloise is doing fine."

"I'm making one for me, and I'm going to make one for Mommy when she gets up," said Eloise. "It's going to have cheese and mushrooms and spinach inside. Should I make one for you too?"

"I'm not sure, Honey."

"It doesn't have to have spinach."

"Actually I like spinach," said Delia. "So, since this is a special occasion, having my granddaughter as a chef, yes, an omelet would be very nice."

"Sit at the table, Grandma, and this will be a restaurant, and I'll be the waitress, too, and bring it to you," said Eloise.

"Full service!" said Evan, as Delia sat herself down.

The omelet was surprisingly good, just a little burnt on the edges. "I'm impressed!" said Delia.

"I'm going to be a chef when I grow up. And a waitress too!"

"What about an artist? I thought you said you were going to be an artist, like your mom," said Evan.

"Yes. And a veterinarian!"

"That too?" asked Delia.

"You can be a veterinarian and an artist and a chef and a waitress," said Eloise. "You can be a hundred things all at the same time if you want to."

"Wouldn't that be nice!" said Delia. "Maybe when I get old . . ."

"You already *are* old," said Eloise.

Delia was cleaning up the breakfast dishes when Merry came downstairs. Eloise was excited about making her an omelet, and although Merry had started by saying she didn't want any breakfast, she quickly took in the situation, expressed enthusiasm, and sat at the table as directed.

"Has Kat recovered from having her plans foiled?" asked Evan.

Delia dried her hands on the dishcloth. "I haven't talked to Kat," she said.

"I thought she checked in with you every morning to make sure you were still breathing," said Evan.

"I don't know where you got that idea from!"

Evan gestured to Merry.

Merry, fork in hand, said, "Hey, that's what you told me!"

"Not every morning," said Delia.

"No need to feel defensive about it, Mom," said Evan. "Merry and I are happy that we have a responsible older sister to look after you so we can be spared any guilt about our neglect."

"You think I need looking after?" asked Delia.

"Not I," said Evan. "I think you and Bob are perfectly capable of fumbling along without any aid from your offspring—as long as the donkeys behave themselves—but Kat is a metropolis of concern."

"What's a metropolis?" asked Eloise.

"It's a city," said Merry.

"I don't think this is the moment for this discussion," said Delia, pointing her chin in Eloise's direction in a way that she hoped was subtle enough.

"Well, I don't even know if there's anything more to discuss," said Evan. "Merry's an old hand at mucking out stables. And Eloise is strong enough to carry bales of hay. So you're all set."

"I can carry lots of bales of hay!" cried Eloise. She jumped off her seat and staggered around the kitchen, imaginary bales of hay in both hands.

"What have you done to that child?" asked Bob, as he came into the kitchen.

"I'm bringing hay to the donkeys and to Falstaff!" cried Eloise.

"Time to go upstairs and get dressed so you can feed them for real," said Merry. And as Eloise dropped the imaginary bales and scampered off upstairs, Delia decided not to mention that the donkeys had already been fed two hours before. It certainly wouldn't hurt them to be fed again.

"Wylie's coming over later. OK if he stays for lunch?" asked Evan.

"Wylie?"

"I thought since I was staying over we might as well get together. And since Merry's here we can all hang out some, like old times."

It wasn't that Delia had forgotten about Wylie, or forgotten her fears that Merry had been involved with him, back when she was a teenager. But she hadn't expected him to be turning up now. He lived in the area, she knew, and she'd run into him on occasion, but she'd felt that he'd been safely relegated to the past. She looked quickly at Merry and saw that Evan's bringing up Wylie wasn't a surprise to her. Was something going on with her and Wylie? She felt a little stirring of fear. Was this anything to do with Merry leaving Josh?

"You can always include a friend for lunch," she told Evan. "And we have lots of leftovers from yesterday. What's Wylie up to these days?" she asked, keeping her voice as even as possible.

"I'm not sure what he's *up* to," said Evan, laughing. "Probably no good. But he's still doing photography. Freelance. Commercial."

"Food," said Merry. "He photographs food for advertising."

So she *has* been in touch with him, thought Delia, and the fear settled in her chest. She had a sudden memory of the black-and-white photographs she'd come across that Wylie had taken of Merry when she was a teenager: Merry, naked, posed on a rock by the stream. When she'd confronted Merry with them, Merry had been defensive. "They're art studies. I was nude," she had corrected her mother, "not naked."

"That's right," said Evan. "Portraits of burgers and cornucopias of avocados."

"Is he still married?" asked Delia, cautiously.

"Wylie? No way!" said Evan.

"I'm going upstairs to remind Eloise to brush her teeth," said Merry, and she didn't look at Delia as she left.

8

Meredith hadn't seen Wylie for several years, but even with his hair cut shorter (and by the looks of it, done by a barber rather than himself) and some grey in his mustache, he still looked like the gawky teenager who hadn't gotten used to his newly acquired height, his arms too long for his sleeves.

"How've you been, Merry?" he asked.

"Not bad, and you?" She'd come out to the driveway after Wylie's truck had pulled up. He always used to drive disreputable pickups, their bumpers plastered with so many stickers it looked as if that's what held them together, but this was a new truck, clean enough to drive into the city.

"She prefers Meredith, now," said Evan, then he added, "but around here, with family, she's still Merry."

"Do I count as family?" asked Wylie, and he gave her a smile that seemed a little sad too.

"Sure, why not?" she said. She stepped behind Eloise, put her hands on her daughter's shoulders, and gave her a little nudge forward. "And this is Eloise."

"Hi, Eloise," said Wylie. "I heard about you from your uncle."

"What did he say?"

"He said you were, let me see . . . ten years old?" He winked at Meredith.

"No! I'm seven. But my half birthday will be soon—right, Mommy?" she turned to look back at Meredith. "And then I'll be seven and a half."

"That's a nice age to be," said Wylie. "And I like your name."

"It's the same name as a girl in a book who lives in a hotel. She has a dog named Weenie! Do you have a dog?"

"I have two."

"Beagles!" said Evan. "Just like the old days. Wylie can't get beyond beagles."

"I should name my house that," said Wylie, "Beyond Beagles."

"What are their names?" asked Eloise.

"Toad and Flax."

"Of course!" said Meredith. She took Eloise's hand as they started walking towards the barn and swung it back and forth. "Evan told me you're back living in your old place," she said.

"Nicole got the house we'd built. So, yup, I live in my old place, in the carriage house. I rent out The Heap."

"The Heap?" asked Eloise.

"It's a big house," said Meredith, "so that's a joke."

"Like a mansion?"

It had seemed like a mansion to Meredith the first time she saw it. Stucco and stone and lots of dormers. It was set up on a hill, with a long curving driveway, so you couldn't see it when you drove past. Wealthy people's estates were like that, hidden from the road. Wylie had a hyphenated last name, Bennet-Hopkins, which Meredith had thought sounded fancy. When she'd asked Evan if they were rich he'd said, "I guess so, but Wylie never has any money. I'm always bailing him out."

"Not exactly a mansion," said Wylie.

"Are your parents dead now?" asked Meredith.

"Mom, yes, Dad as good as."

"Sorry," said Meredith. "I didn't know." She looked at Evan, who shrugged and said, "Hey, I would have told you if you'd asked."

"What are you going to take a picture of?" Eloise asked, pointing to the camera around Wylie's neck.

"Wylie's a photographer," said Evan. "He can't go anywhere without his camera."

"If you want to take a picture of me, you have to ask my mommy first and have her sign something. That's what we do at school."

"I'll remember that," said Wylie.

As they walked towards the barn, Ralph came running over to greet him, his tail swatting back and forth. Wylie squatted down so they were eye to eye, and he let Ralph pant in his face. Ralph's tail whipped furiously.

"I think this guy remembers me."

"Don't flatter yourself," said Meredith. "That's Ralph's standard greeting."

"Nah," said Wylie, "look at that tail!" He got to his feet and pointed to the fenced enclosure by the barn. "I see you still have those crazy donkeys."

"They're not crazy!" cried Eloise.

"That's right," said Evan, "it's not the donkeys that are crazy, it's the people who have them," but he saw the look on Eloise's face, and said, "Just kidding, Sweetie. People who have donkeys aren't crazy at all, they're just—"

"Eccentric," said Meredith.

"What's that?" asked Eloise.

"Special," said Meredith. She made little clucking noises as they got nearer to the fence and reached over the fence when Myrtle came close, to scratch her under the chin.

Wylie stood back a little, snapping pictures. Meredith turned slowly back towards him, not smiling until she was looking at him straight on. The clicking of his shutter was a sound from her past. All the photos people took now were on their cell phones, and the artificial click some people added wasn't quite the same.

They walked up the hill around to the door of the main level of the barn. When they went inside, Meredith stood in the center and circled around. "What do you think?" she asked.

"Are you asking me or him?" asked Evan.

"Both of you, I guess."

"It's a lot of space!" said Wylie. "Might be cold. It's still winter. I suppose you could get a heater, though."

"Or move all the animals up here to keep things warm," said Evan.

"They can keep you company too," said Wylie.

"Thanks, guys," said Meredith. "I think I'll leave them in their quarters below. And should I need company up here, the dogs will be enough."

"But are they any good as art critics?" asked Wylie.

"Guess I'll find out."

"What did Mom have to say about your plan?" asked Evan, but as soon as he saw Meredith's face, he added quickly, "Oh, I get it. You haven't put this on the table yet."

"I thought maybe I should think it through a little first?"

"I'll stick around if you need me when you spring it on her."

"Thanks," said Meredith. Of course she needed him!

"How big are the canvases?" asked Wylie.

"Big," said Meredith. She looked around and pointed. "Barn door sized?"

"That's big," said Wylie. "What's your studio like now?"

"That's just it. I haven't had a proper studio. I've shared space in this co-op, but it's never been right."

"You'll have some serious cleaning up to do," said Evan. He pointed to the corners where there were piles of stuff: crates, old tools, broken lawn furniture, and a pedal organ abandoned by some previous owner.

Meredith laughed. "That's where you come in!"

"Oh, no," said Evan. "I don't even clean up my own kitchen, and you expect me to tackle this barn?"

"Just hoping for a little help," said Meredith, and she beamed up at him, a big, fake pleading smile.

"I'll give you a hand," said Wylie. "I don't do kitchens, but barns—well, barns are different." He waved his arm around in a broad gesture, as if he were introducing the barn space to an invisible audience.

"I'll help, too, Mommy!" said Eloise.

"I was hoping you would," said Meredith. She hugged Eloise and kissed her on the top of her head. Whatever doubts she'd been trying to push away were suddenly all gone now. She could picture them, all four of them, brooms in hand, transforming the barn. A fantasy Group Effort. "Aren't I lucky to have you all!" she said.

"You are lucky, Mommy," said Eloise. "You have that rabbit's foot to bring you good luck."

"You still have that?" asked Wylie.

"Uh, yeah," said Meredith quickly.

Evan looked back and forth between her and Wylie, but neither of them spoke.

Eloise ran over and tried playing the organ, but no sound came out when she pressed the keys. "It doesn't work!" she cried.

"The bellows are shot," said Meredith.

Wylie walked over to take a look. He pulled over a crate and sat down to pump the pedals, but even when he pulled the different stops, the organ was still silent.

"Sorry, Eloise," he said.

"What did I tell you?" said Meredith.

"Can we fix it, Mommy?" asked Eloise.

"There are a lot of other things that we have to do first," said Meredith.

"We'll put it on the list," said Wylie.

"I like the 'we,'" said Meredith.

She spotted her old hockey stick in the pile of stuff in the corner and pulled it out. "Look what I found," she said.

"What is it, Mommy?"

"It's for ice hockey, Sweetheart," said Meredith. "I used to play on the frozen pond down the road." She swept the hockey stick in a quick, graceful arc, hitting an imaginary puck across the barn floor. The stroke was as familiar to her as her own breath.

"California hasn't wrecked your style!" said Evan. He turned to Wylie. "Did you know Meredith was a hotshot at hockey?"

"I had a great teacher," said Meredith, smiling at him.

"This one time I was playing with some guys," said Evan, "and they didn't want a middle school kid in the way, and—"

"A girl—they didn't want a girl!"

"That, too," said Evan.

"But Evan made them include me."

"And she blew them away. She was little and sneaky and fast, and she zipped around them and scored more goals than they could count."

Meredith remembered how the sun had set early that winter afternoon, and the sky was aflame with magenta and pink. The frozen pond had a rosy glow. But by the time they were ready to go home, the sun was irreparably gone, and it had grown dark and so cold the air hurt her lungs when she inhaled. She'd sat on a log by the pond beside Evan to take off her skates, old hand-me-downs of his. They were too big, so she wore two layers of heavy socks, which kept her feet warm enough, but her gloves were thin, and her fingers were so frozen she couldn't untie the laces. When Evan noticed, he squatted in the snow in front of her, untied the skates, and pulled them off, and helped her put on her boots. Then he'd taken off his gloves and given them to her to wear as they walked home. She'd pushed her icy fingers down into each of the pockets his fingers had warmed, little cocoons of heat, and her hands stung as they came back to life.

"Hey, are you OK?" Evan had asked, when he realized she'd begun to cry. "Still cold?"

"No, it's just because you're being so nice to me."

Evan had tilted his head and looked at her. "Why wouldn't I be?"

"A lot of the kids at school aren't."

"Well, screw them!" Evan had said.

Eloise took a few swings of the hockey stick, then asked, "Can I go up to the loft now, Mommy?"

"Sure," said Meredith. She watched Eloise climb up the ladder, and she waved back at her before she disappeared into the hay.

"You know, before you go much farther with this studio plan," said Evan, "it might be a good idea to float the concept with Mom."

"You think?"

"Mer-ry! It's her barn—well, hers and Bob's. They might have other plans for it."

"More animals?" asked Meredith, and she laughed.

Evan held up his hands. "Hey, I'm just saying."

"I can rent it from her if that's the problem."

"You're missing the point," said Evan. "When you asked Mom about moving back here, did you mention anything about taking over the barn?"

When Meredith didn't say anything, Evan let out a low whistle. "OK, I get it. But take some big brother advice about this, and at least talk to her. She likes to feel included."

"She has Kat, for that. Kat includes her in everything!"

"Kat's—well, Kat is involved. But she can't help it. It's just the way she is."

"Are you a Kat apologist now?" Her tone was angrier than she intended.

Evan pointed at Wylie. "Hey, we've got company. Let's save the sibling saga for later."

"I don't like to think of myself as company," said Wylie.

Eloise appeared at the edge of the loft. "How come you're fighting with Uncle Evan?" she asked Meredith, when she came down the ladder.

"Don't worry, Sweetheart," said Meredith. "Uncle Evan and I weren't really fighting."

Evan smiled at Eloise. "We never fight," he said, and he came and put his arm around Meredith.

"Time for me to be heading back to work," said Wylie. "Good to see you, Merry."

"What about me?" asked Evan.

Wylie ignored him. He was looking at Meredith. "Let me know when you're ready to tackle this barn, and I'll come help you out."

"Will do."

She and Wylie stood for a moment, just looking at each other, and even when he held up his hand and gave a slight wave, he still stood there, as if he had something more to say, before he turned and walked towards his truck.

After Wylie left, Eloise went back to the house to see the toys Delia had brought down from the attic. Meredith and Evan stood at the barn door and watched her walk along the path.

"Eloise seems quite at home around here," said Evan.

"She's pretty self-reliant," said Meredith, and then she laughed a little and added, "when she wants to be!"

"She's not even afraid of Bob."

"I think she's determined to win him over. She tried with her father, but she didn't have any hope with him. He wasn't home much, and when he *was* home, he rarely looked up from his laptop." Meredith turned back into the barn. "Let's go up to the hayloft," she said.

Evan followed her up the ladder, and they sat together on the edge of the loft, the way they used to, looking out over the open barn space below them.

"Mom's still got a thing about Wylie," said Evan.

"She thinks he led you astray."

"Not me! I already *was* astray. She's always been worried about Wylie and *you*."

"What's there to worry about?" asked Meredith.

Evan laughed. "Mom was relieved when Wylie got married and *really* relieved when you got married, and now Wylie's divorced, and you turn up here, saying you're done with Josh."

"Stuff happens."

"Well, that's what worries her."

"There's a lot that worries her. And you know what? Tough shit. I've got enough to deal with as it is." It sounded harsher than she intended. "I'm just overwhelmed at the moment," she said, in a softer voice.

"If you want," said Evan, "I can stay another night and head home first thing in the morning. Then I'll be within shouting distance if you need me."

"Thanks," said Meredith. And then she added, "Eloise will be thrilled. You're the best part of being here."

"After the animals, that is."

"Yes, of course, after the animals."

"She's one cute kid."

"I know."

"So, everything *isn't* shot to hell, as you put it."

"Did I say that?"

Evan nodded.

"Well, no. Not in that department, at least."

"And look, if you'd like, I can be around a bit more. For her. I mean I don't live that far away."

Meredith squeezed her eyes shut, but not quickly enough. She hadn't cried since she'd gotten here, hadn't cried in a long time.

Evan pulled her close against him. "Oh boy," he said. "I hadn't realized things have been that bad."

It took her a while before she could even nod.

"Want to tell me?"

Meredith wasn't going to tell him. Wasn't going to tell anyone. But the spacious stillness of the barn and the comforting smell of the hay and the soft flannel of Evan's shirt against her cheek made her feel that it was OK.

"I had a miscarriage," she said, and Evan leaned closer to hear her.

"I'm so sorry, Merry. Are you all right now?"

"Yeah, well, not really, I guess. I kind of fell apart afterward. The miscarriage was pretty bad, but what hurt most was that Josh thought it was a big nothing. His words. He said he didn't see why I should get so upset about it, since it wasn't like losing a child. He thought it was inconsistent of me—inconsistent!—to be pro-choice and argue that a fetus wasn't an actual person yet, and then carry on—that's how he described it—as if, in my case, it was."

"Jesus, Merry. That stinks," said Evan. And then he asked, "Does Mom know?"

"No. No one knows. Just you."

And then, because she'd already told him so much, she decided to tell him everything. How Josh had confessed he'd never wanted to have children in the first place, how he'd gone along with it when she'd gotten pregnant with Eloise only because he figured if she really wanted a child and got one, then that would be the end of it.

"And when I said I was leaving and taking Eloise with me, he said, 'Fine with me, take her.'"

"I'd like to punch him in the face," said Evan.

Evan went to bed early that night, and at the insistence of Delia, he agreed to upgrade from the living room sofa to his old bedroom. After he'd gone upstairs and after Eloise was asleep, Meredith waited for a moment when Bob had gone off to his study so she could catch Delia alone in the kitchen. She wasn't quite ready to talk to her mother about the barn, but she knew Evan was right, and she did need to bring it up. Better to just get it over with now that Evan was still here.

Delia was at the counter, spooning batter into a muffin tin.

"What are you making?"

"I thought Eloise might like blueberry muffins for breakfast, and I decided to make them tonight, since she gets up early in the morning."

"You don't need to spoil her, Mom."

"The blueberries are from our bushes!"

"That has nothing to do with it."

Delia smiled at her. "I know what you're saying, Sweetheart, but I don't really think fresh muffins will spoil Eloise, and besides, it gives me pleasure, OK? I like to cook special things for people who'll appreciate it, and I haven't had much opportunity."

"What about Bob? He seems to rely on your cooking."

"Bob is basically indifferent to food. He likes to be fed. But he doesn't care a lot about *what* he's fed."

"I never realized that about him," admitted Meredith.

"I think it may not always have been like this—or perhaps I never noticed. Or maybe it's just something with getting old. There are some things you don't care about that much anymore."

"That's depressing."

Delia didn't respond for a moment while she set the bowl in the sink and ran some water into it. "Not really," she said. "I've gotten used to it. And now that I have you and Eloise here, I can enjoy cooking more."

This seemed to be the moment to plunge ahead and introduce her mother to the idea of turning the barn into studio space, but Meredith couldn't quite find the way to begin. It wasn't like she could just talk about her plan for the barn—the conversation would inevitably move into things that she wasn't up to discussing: the why she was there, the how long she was staying. It would also reopen their many unfinished conversations about Meredith's life and her career and her ambition as an artist. There was no end to it. And Meredith just wasn't strong enough now to take it all on. Maybe in the morning, before Evan left? Meredith was well practiced in postponing things that seemed difficult. For a moment, she envied Kat, who was adept at assessing problems, designing strategies to deal with them, then marching right ahead, shoulders square. And Evan? Evan never seemed to have problems, or rather he never seemed to see problems *as* problems. Life, for him, was just life.

Delia dug in the cabinet beside the stove and pulled out a wire cooling rack. She set it on the counter. "It's too bad that Wylie's marriage didn't work out."

"Well, that's the way things often are."

"Where is he living these days?" Delia asked in a casual way, as if she wasn't really interested in knowing.

"His parents' place," said Meredith, matching her mother's tone.

"That's a huge house. They must be happy to have him back home."

"I doubt it. His mom's dead, and from what he said his dad doesn't have long to go."

"Oh," said Delia. "I didn't really know them, but I'm sorry to hear that. They weren't much older than I am."

"Don't worry," said Meredith. "You're in good shape, so I don't think you'll be checking out anytime soon, in spite of your age."

"Tell my knees that," said Delia.

"Goodnight, Mom," said Meredith, and she escaped from the kitchen before her mother asked anything more about Wylie, and before she could feel guilty about not having said a word about the barn.

~

The next morning Eloise played with the toy barn she'd been given the Christmas they'd been here but hadn't been able to bring home to California. The barn folded open to reveal the interior, and it was filled with animals that had come with it, and three donkeys that Delia had bought extra.

Eloise set the horses, cows, and donkeys around on the rug. When Bob came in his foot knocked over one of the animals. "What the hell is this?" he asked, holding it up.

"That's a cow, Grandpa," said Eloise. "Don't you know what a cow looks like?"

"What I want to know is why is it out here in the middle of the living room floor?"

"It's grazing," said Eloise. "The horses and donkeys are grazing too. Do you want to meet them?"

"Not particularly," said Bob. He walked towards the doorway and shouted, "Delia!" When Delia came rushing into the room, he said, "Did you tell Eloise she could scatter those damn animals all over the living room carpet?"

Delia looked around. "Well, I didn't tell her she couldn't."

Bob held out the offending cow. "I nearly tripped on this."

"Aren't we glad you didn't," said Delia. She handed the cow to Eloise. "Here, dear, better put this one back in the barn for now."

"I don't think the living room is the place for toys," said Bob.

Delia sighed. "It's the nicest room to play in," she said. "It gets the best sunshine."

"Delia, I've allowed the parlor to be taken over by your violin prodigies. Surely the living room can be a place where geriatric residents can walk without risking bodily harm."

Delia took Bob by the arm. "We'll talk about this later," she said, and Eloise knew she meant not in front of her.

Delia knelt on the carpet and started collecting the animals. "Let's play on this side of the room, Sweetheart, while Grandpa is here, OK?"

"Play where you want!" said Bob, as he started walking out of the room. "Don't worry about me. I'm retreating to the safety of my lair."

~

Evan left right after breakfast, and Meredith worked with Eloise on some of the homeschool math material she'd accessed on the internet. She didn't think Eloise really needed to work on math—but she didn't want anyone saying she'd let Eloise get "behind" in school—whatever "behind in school" was.

Delia had egg-salad sandwiches waiting for them for lunch.

"I'm afraid I have some students coming for their violin lessons after school today," she said.

"No need to apologize, Mom," said Meredith. "We've got things to do, also."

"Your mother *should* apologize," said Bob. "She should have retired a year ago!"

"I want to take violin lessons too," said Eloise.

"Mom!" said Meredith.

Delia held up her hands. "Don't look at me," she said. "I didn't say anything to her. I can just show her the violin when we're done eating, and if she really wants to try—"

"I thought we already had this discussion," said Meredith.

"Yes, but it seems—"

"Are you just going to keep overriding my parenting decisions?"

"Why can't I have violin lessons?" asked Eloise.

"This is your doing!" said Meredith, looking at Delia; then she turned to Eloise. "OK. I was going to take you to the playground after lunch, but if you'd rather have a violin lesson, you can do that instead."

"Merry, no need to polarize things this way," said Bob.

Meredith turned to him, but before she could say anything, he stood up quickly. "I realize it was foolish of me to intrude in this domestic matter, so I will depart immediately." And Bob did so.

"I want to go to the playground too," said Eloise.

"We can do violin another time," said Delia, "that is, if it's all right with your mother."

"But I want to do violin, now!" Eloise started to cry.

"Oh for God's sake," said Meredith. "You're too much for me. Both of you!" She turned to Eloise. "Stop crying. Go with Grandma and do the violin, since that's what the two of you want so much, and I'll take you to the playground later. I'm going out for a walk now." She got up from the table, and set her plate and mug on the counter. Her fork clattered against the plate. She walked out towards the field, hating herself for reacting that way with Eloise, and with her mother too. The violin was an old sore point:

That was the problem. It stirred up things she thought she'd gotten beyond, but obviously she hadn't.

Meredith had texted Wylie to let him know she was going to be taking Eloise to the playground, but she hadn't heard back from him, so she didn't know if he'd turn up. If he didn't, she'd be disappointed, but it would be a relief, too, since it was probably a bad idea to see him, right? She had enough complications in her life right now.

But there he was, sitting on a playground bench, his long legs stretched out in front of him, his arms slung over the back of the bench, his camera around his neck.

"Hey there!" he said.

"Fancy meeting you here," Meredith said.

"Fancy meeting *you*."

"You didn't bring your beagles?"

"Didn't know they were required."

"Beagles are never required," said Meredith.

"I'll bring them next time, if you like," Wylie said. He laid his hands on his knees and leaned forward towards Eloise. "What have you been up to?" he asked.

"Don't ask," said Meredith, but Eloise said, "I had a violin lesson with Grandma."

"That's cool!" said Wylie, but he caught the look on Meredith's face and said, "Hey, something wrong?"

"Long story," said Meredith.

"The violin bow has real hair from a horse's tail," said Eloise. "But it's not Falstaff's. It's from another horse."

"I'm sure Falstaff is happy about that. When I was a kid, Eloise, I wanted to play the tuba, but my parents had me take clarinet lessons, instead. I wasn't very musical. Unlike your mom, here. She was pretty impressive on the violin."

"Wylie!" Meredith cried.

"Bet she's still pretty impressive!"

"I don't know," said Eloise.

"Doesn't she play for you?"

"No."

Wylie turned to Meredith. "You don't play anymore?"

"I prefer to squander my talent," said Meredith. She grabbed Eloise's hand. "Come on," she said, "we're going on the swings."

The wood chips on the ground were worn down underneath each swing, where kids' feet had dragged. At the playground they went to in California there was rubber matting that Meredith guessed was supposed to look like grass, but was an unhealthy shade of green. There were a lot of things in California like that. Meredith gave Eloise a push to get started, then she sat on the swing beside her. Wylie sat on the swing next to Meredith, and he swung so high it made the whole swing set shake. He whooped when he was at the top. Meredith started swinging slowly, but then she flew up high and whooped too. God, it felt good!

When Eloise got tired of swinging, she ran across the playground to the climbing structure that was made to look like a castle. She waved when she climbed to the turret, and Meredith and Wylie waved back.

"How are things going?" Wylie asked.

"I lost it with my mom earlier. She browbeat me into letting her give Eloise a violin lesson."

"Didn't realize the violin was an issue," said Wylie. "Sorry about before."

"I didn't realize it still was either. But it brought out all my residual adolescent indignation. That's one of the problems with moving back home."

"I think I know a little about that," said Wylie, and he smiled. "By the way, in case you might be interested, they're looking to hire someone to do framing at the gallery."

"Oh?"

"It's part time."

"Yeah, well, maybe. The point is to have time to paint. And I'm OK for money right now. Though I wouldn't mind having some extra

I earned on my own. I might be interested once Eloise is settled in school here."

"I'll let Maxine, know," said Wylie. "I don't think there's any hurry."

"Maxine? Maxine Strindler?"

"Yeah. Only it's Driscoll now."

"Didn't you go out with her?"

"Yeah, well—"

"One of the many!"

"Not that many. Not like Evan! And I'm still friendly with my old girlfriends."

"But not Nicole?"

"I made the mistake of marrying Nicole," said Wylie.

"I could have told you!"

"Mommy!" Eloise called. She stood at the top of a purple slide that circled down from the play structure.

"Come on down," said Meredith.

"It's scary!" said Eloise.

"Don't worry, I'll catch you," said Wylie. He took his camera off his neck and handed it to Meredith, then he squatted at the bottom of the slide and held out his arms. Eloise sat down cautiously at the top.

"You can do it!" Wylie said. "One, two, three, go!" Meredith watched Eloise take in her breath and push off. She flew down the slide, in and out of view, and Wylie caught her in his arms at the bottom. He lifted her and spun her around before he set her on the ground. "Want to try that again?"

"Yes!"

Every time Eloise climbed up and sat at the top of the slide, she waved down to them. Meredith put the strap of Wylie's camera around her neck. She crouched by Wylie and started snapping. Then she stood up, stepped back, and focused on Wylie.

"Hey, no pictures of me!" he said.

"Why not? You've taken plenty of pictures of me over the years."

"That's different."

"Yeah? Why's that?"

"Because you've got that sly smile." He lifted the strap over Meredith's head and took the camera back from her.

"Sly smile? What the hell is that?"

"Just the way you look!"

"Like this?" she asked, and mugged a series of goofy faces—wrinkled her nose, pursed her lips, batted her eyes—while he snapped away.

"Mommy! Catch me!" cried Eloise, and Meredith squatted at the bottom of the slide. She heard the click of Wylie's shutter while she waited, arms out, for Eloise to fly into her embrace. She held Eloise tight against her. When she turned back to Wylie, he was holding the straps of the camera with both hands, his head tilted to one side. He had stopped taking pictures and was just looking at her.

"Would you like ravioli for dinner?" Delia asked when they got back from the playground.

"What kind?" asked Eloise.

"There's cheese ravioli, and there's lobster ravioli."

"We'll have the cheese ravioli," said Meredith.

"Lobster for me," said Bob.

"Kat got a ravioli maker," said Delia. "She made a batch and froze it, and brought some over for us."

"Why am I not surprised?" asked Meredith.

Delia put Eloise's sauce in a little bowl on the side of her plate, so she could spoon it on herself.

"You don't need to spoil her, Mom," said Meredith.

"That's where you're wrong," said Bob. "Your mother *needs* to spoil people. It's what she does."

Delia ignored him. "If you don't like the cherry tomatoes in your salad," she told Eloise, "just leave them on the side of your plate."

"Eat one, at least," said Meredith.

"Did you have fun at the playground?" asked Delia.

"Yes!" said Eloise, "and Wylie went so high on the swings he almost fell off!"

"Wylie?" Delia looked over at Meredith.

"Yeah."

"He was there?"

"Yeah."

"Oh," said Delia. She looked as if she wanted to say something more, but changed her mind. No one said anything for a moment.

"Would you like to have a bath in my big tub tonight?" Delia asked Eloise after a while.

"Yes!" shouted Eloise. "I'll be a mermaid!"

"As long as you keep the water in the bathtub," said Meredith. "If it gets on the floor, it will soak through to the ceiling downstairs. And then the ceiling will collapse, as it's done before."

"Only once!" said Delia. And Meredith laughed with her.

"Can we go to the playground with Wylie again tomorrow?" asked Eloise.

"We'll see," said Meredith. And she did not look at her mother's face.

~

The bathtub had lion-paw feet with rather menacing-looking claws. It was big enough so Eloise could stretch out and float, her hair fanning out around her.

She was remembering the time she went to the playground with her father because something had happened and her mother had to go to the hospital. Her father didn't go on the swings with her, and although she waved to him from the top of the slide, when she got to the bottom he was busy on his cell phone and not watching anymore. They had spaghetti for dinner, and her father had put the tomato sauce *on* the spaghetti, not next to it, and when she wouldn't eat it he got angry.

"That's what there is for dinner," he'd said, and he told her if she didn't like it, she could eat cereal.

"I want Mommy," Eloise had said.

"Well, she's not here."

"When is she coming home?"

"Probably tomorrow," her father had said, and her mother did come home, but she went to bed. She looked like she was sick, but she was pretending that she wasn't. And it was days before she took Eloise to the playground again.

9

In the morning Delia suggested she take Eloise to the mall to buy her boots.

"She doesn't need boots," said Merry.

"But she has only her sneakers here, and they're getting so muddy," said Delia. She didn't want to get into the subject of Eloise's clothing—what Merry's plans were for retrieving it, or when.

"Well, if you have to!" Merry relented. "But just get them online."

"What size?" asked Delia.

Merry shrugged. "Look at her sneakers, I guess."

Delia put on her reading glasses to try to decipher the size. A twelve maybe? When Merry was a kid Delia would bring her to the shoe store in town, where they'd carefully measure her foot on a metal device, then record it on a card in their files. Apparently no one did that anymore. Delia found a kids-shoe-sized chart online and printed it out. She had Eloise stand barefoot on it so she could measure each foot. Eloise's feet were so small! They looked vulnerable and innocent. The sneakers were only a twelve; the foot chart suggested a one.

Delia touched a red place on her foot. "What happened here?" she asked.

"I banged it."

Delia leaned down and kissed the spot. "That will make it better," she said.

"Oh, please!" said Merry.

"I want cowboy boots," said Eloise.

"We can get you riding boots, if you want to do riding," said Delia. She looked tentatively at Merry. It was hard to know what to say. She was afraid to suggest anything. Especially in front of Eloise.

Merry ignored Delia's comment. "I wondered if I could borrow your car today," she asked. "Some friends I'd like to see."

"Oh, yes, of course. I have no plans to go anywhere, today. You can use it anytime. And there's always Bob's car."

"I wouldn't take Bob's car."

"I'm sure Bob wouldn't mind."

Merry raised her eyebrows.

"Is your friend Allison still living around here?" Delia asked.

"Yeah," said Merry, but she didn't say it in a convincing way, so Delia couldn't tell if Allison was the friend Merry planned to visit. She didn't want to ask Merry whom she'd be seeing, and if she did, it was likely Merry would say it was none of her business. But what was her business anyway? They were in entirely unchartered waters here.

Merry was always private about her life—her weapon against me, Delia thought. When she was a little girl she'd say "I'm not telling!" because guarding secrets was her one source of power. When she'd gotten older she'd grown furtive. Maybe that was the way of teenagers? Merry worked hard to keep things from her mother, while Delia worked to find out about her life. Merry, sullen when questioned, would say "You're always grilling me," and retreat to her room.

Kat, not a typical teenager, was open, never furtive. She no doubt had her secrets, too, but she shared things that were important. Evan wasn't furtive, but he was vague and unpredictable. It wasn't as if he wanted to keep things secret from her, but just that his plans—if he had any—often changed last minute. "You were in Vermont?" Delia would exclaim in surprise. "You didn't tell me you were going to Vermont!"

"Well, it just came up," Evan would say cheerfully. "Jeff had a friend with a place up there, so we went skiing." She didn't quite remember who Jeff was, and wouldn't ask—Evan had an infinite number of friends.

"Will you be home for lunch?" Delia asked Merry.

"Nah, I don't think so. We'll catch something."

"Dinner?"

Merry shrugged. "I'll let you know later. OK?"

"I just wondered if I should cook something—"

"Don't worry about us," said Merry.

"I want to make something Eloise would like."

"I like mac and cheese," said Eloise.

"I'll pick up some boxes when we're out," said Merry. "So you won't have any trouble."

"It's not trouble. And I make it with real cheese," said Delia.

"I believe the boxes *are* with real cheese," said Merry.

Delia's last pupil of the day was Lindsey Klebanoff-Stark. The Klebanoff father had recently split with the Stark mother, but Lindsey bore them both, sorrowfully, in her hyphenated last name. They took turns bringing Lindsey to her violin lessons, but their custody schedule was always in flux, and Delia never knew which parent would turn up. Lindsey didn't need a parent there taking notes for her, but her mother still came in with her and flopped on the velvet sofa, asserting her parental rights and maximizing her time with her only child, though Lindsey was not grateful. Today Lindsey's father had brought her. He sat in his car, talking out loud but out of earshot. If Delia didn't know he was recording memos on his cell phone, she would have taken him for a madman, haranguing himself.

Lindsey's hair today was an unfortunate shade of orange.

"New hairdo," said Delia, since it was clear that Lindsey was hoping for a comment.

"It's tangerine."

Delia looked confused.

"The color, it's called 'tangerine.'"

Delia thought "orange" would have been the fruit of choice, but didn't say so. Lindsey had pierced her nose but had removed the steel ring when it had gotten infected——something that made Delia queasy. It looked like it was finally healing.

"How was school today?" Delia asked, as she regularly did.

Lindsey's usual reply was "Sucked," but today, to Delia's surprise, she said "OK."

"That's good!" Delia said.

"We had a fire drill," explained Lindsey. "I always keep my coat with me, because I hate going to my locker." She smiled. "Everyone else froze."

Delia often had an urge to give Lindsey a hug, but you weren't supposed to do that with students these days—Kat had reminded her about it more than once. She felt that Lindsey needed an expression of affection, especially since once her parents had separated, she seemed even more unhappy than the usual fourteen-year-old. In any case, this was not a time for scales, tonalization, or exercises.

Lindsey had completed Book 7, and Delia had transitioned her to repertoire beyond Suzuki. The trick was to keep her engaged, because although Lindsey didn't practice regularly, she got into it in spurts, and she was good. More important, she seemed to like playing—and there didn't seem to be too many things in her life that she did like doing. Delia felt that adolescents, when their lives were spiraling out of control, needed music. It gave them both structure as well as a place to express themselves.

"You should have become a therapist," Bob had said once, and then he corrected himself. "Actually you are a therapist, though unlicensed, and earning a great deal less than you would have had you chosen that career."

"I seem to do a lot better with other people's offspring than my own," Delia had said. And that was the case. Even her teenage students seemed to like her. Sometimes, for a kid like Lindsey, she felt it was less about the violin lesson than the hour away from her regular life and the company of an adult who was caring but who placed no emotional burdens on her.

"Why don't we try the Vivaldi today?" Delia asked. The duet was bright and optimistic. Lots of lively bowing. "You take the first violin part."

"OK," said Lindsey.

The piece was a conversation: each of them taking turns with the melody, the other, playing in the background, the two of them gloriously together. Delia watched Lindsey let herself get taken up by it, get lost in it. When Merry was Lindsey's age she'd get lost in her music in the same way. Merry was a precocious player and had flown through the Suzuki books, and it wasn't long before Delia had moved her on to a teacher who worked with more advanced students. Merry never liked to play for her family, but when Delia did get to watch her, she saw that almost wild, wordless look on her face.

After Lindsey left, Delia took out the sheet music for Beethoven's Romances. She knew the pieces by heart, but it had been a long time since she'd played them, and she wanted to have the music handy if she needed to refer to it. She played it differently now from when she'd played it as a teenager. She'd been more dexterous then, more nimble with her bow, but now she understood the music better, the complexity of it. The sorrow.

There was a knock on the door, and she turned as Bob came in.

"Sorry," he said. "I thought lessons were over."

"They are. I was just playing, myself."

"I don't want to disturb you."

"It's OK. I'm done."

"Merry called to say they won't be back for dinner."

"Oh."

"Want to play for me?"

"Another time."

Bob looked at her, inquiringly. She put her violin and bow away, then sat on the sofa and patted the place beside her. "Sit with me," she said.

Bob sat down beside her and put his arm around her shoulder. "What's up?" he asked.

"It just seems so—I don't know. I keep worrying about Merry."

"I thought you'd be happy that she's here."

"I am, but everything is so up in the air."

Bob gave a little laugh. "That's the way it always is with Merry, isn't it?"

"I know. But it's different now, with Eloise. Eloise needs some stability."

"You're not her mother, Lili. You can't worry about it."

Delia laughed. "Of course I can!" she said.

Bob stood up and took her hand and pulled her to her feet. "Maybe we could have a little dinner, a deux, since they won't be back to eat with us?"

Delia looked at him, trying to read beyond what he'd said. She laid her forefingers on the side of his cheek. "We do have the house to ourselves now," she said.

Earlier in their marriage, when they were so often too tired to make love at night, they'd catch the moments when they had the house to themselves during the day. When Merry had gone off to college, it had seemed like a luxury to be able to make love anytime they wanted to, but over the years they'd gotten used to it.

"Let's eat later," he said.

Upstairs, their bedroom was still cool. Delia kept on her sweater as she climbed under the duvet. Bob left his clothes on the floor beside the bed. She lifted her sweater and snuggled against his warm body.

"I wonder what time they'll be getting back," she said.

"Uh-uh," said Bob. "We're not thinking about them. Not here, not now."

Merry got home after Delia and Bob had finished cleaning up after dinner. She put Eloise to bed and came downstairs to say goodnight.

"Did you have a good day?" asked Delia.

"Yes," said Merry. And as she saw Delia waiting for more, she added, "Saw some friends. And stopped by a gallery in town. They're looking for someone part time."

"That sounds interesting," said Delia. She wanted to ask if Merry had done anything about enrolling Eloise in school, but thought it would be better to bring that up another time.

Meredith seemed about to say something, then hesitated for a moment before plunging ahead. "There's something I wanted to ask you about," she said. "It looks like you're not using the main part of the barn these days—except for the hayloft—and I wondered if it would be OK—while I'm living here—if I used it as a studio."

"A studio?"

"I'm doing large canvases these days, and it would be great to have space like that."

Delia didn't say anything right away. She wondered if this was the moment to ask about Josh.

"I mean, I'd clean up the barn, and I wouldn't be taking up all the space."

"You're asking me?"

"Yeah."

"You know you didn't ask me about moving back and living here. You just announced it."

"That's different."

"Oh?"

"Mom, you're always insisting I call this place 'home.' You've gotten all teary when I said it wasn't really my home anymore, and you'd said it always would be. So if it's my home, am I supposed to ask if I can live here?"

"Well—"

"Hey, if that's a problem now, let me know. It's not like I don't have any place else to go."

Merry's voice had the tone of the woman who had said "Hey, I'm outta here" that Christmas, just two years earlier. It was the Merry who would just get up and take off, take Eloise with her. Of course it was Merry's home. What was she thinking? Delia gave a little cry and rushed at Merry, her arms out. "Oh, Darling," she said. "Of course it's your home. And, yes, you're right, you shouldn't have to ask. And the barn. Of course, the barn is yours to use too."

Merry stood for a moment, her arms at her sides, and let her mother embrace her and then, reluctantly, put her arms around her mother's back. And Delia felt as if she'd had a narrow escape, as if she had caught the world just before it began tumbling down.

10

Meredith had fed and watered the chickens and was mucking out the stalls in the barn. It was always amazing how just four equines could produce such a quantity of manure in just one night—how the hay that they ate—dry, light, greenish—could be so transformed into moist, heavy brown balls. A magic trick. There was something satisfying about the job, the tangibleness of it. It was an accomplishment you could *see*. And unlike so many tasks in life, once you did it, it was done—at least for the moment. Eloise was in the house, reading with Delia, so Meredith had some time alone now. Rare to have time to herself. She'd finished Falstaff's stall and was working on the donkeys' area when Kat came into the barn.

"Mom said I'd find you here," said Kat.

Meredith hadn't heard the car drive up. She stopped, full rake in hand.

"I didn't know you were coming."

"I just stopped by. I called Mom when I left the office."

"Stopped by? It's an hour out of your way." Meredith tilted the rake over the plastic barrel on the cart so the pile of manure slid into the barrel.

"I had some papers to drop off for Mom and Bob. I'm trying to get them to do their taxes early this year."

"Don't they have an accountant?"

"Of course. But the accountant just does the figures. He doesn't get all the material together for them."

Meredith had never worried about taxes. When she was younger, she had no money to be taxed. And later, when she married Josh, and had some money, he handled all that.

"What about Bob? Can't he do it?"

"Bob is a dear man, but taxes are not his strong point. He's just not interested."

"Who is?" asked Meredith, but as soon as she said that she realized that Kat probably was. The corner of the stall where the donkeys always peed smelled of ammonia. Meredith reached up for the tin can perched on a beam and pried open the lid. The tin had once held Italian cookies; now it held stall freshener.

"Stand back, a minute," she said, and Kat stepped back quickly. She was wearing grey suede boots with sensible heels. Office boots. Meredith held her breath while she sprinkled lime on the pee spot, raising a cloud of white dust. It was treated so it wasn't supposed to cause lung cancer if you inhaled it. But who knew?

"I thought while I was here, we might have a moment together. We didn't really get a chance to talk after dinner on Sunday."

Meredith laughed. "That's the real reason you're here, right?"

"It's not that—"

"Come on, Kat. You might as well be up front about it."

"Well, all right. I had some papers to get to Mom, and it seemed like an opportunity—I did think that you and I needed to talk about some things—"

"Maybe *you* needed to—"

"Merry, you can't act as if what you're doing doesn't have major implications for everyone."

"What I'm doing? You want to know what I'm doing? I'm cleaning the stable and feeding the animals. You can watch, if you want." Meredith dragged over a big plastic bag half filled with wood shavings and dumped them in the center of the stall. She used the rake to spread them around. The wood shavings were raw and fresh, in contrast to the dark, stained floor. The donkeys would love to roll in them. Eloise would probably love to roll in them too. Once, when Merry was younger, she had lain back in a pile of fresh wood chips, inhaled the piney smell, and not wanted to get up. Ever.

"It would be nice if, for once, you were willing to be serious about this—"

"You don't think I was serious on Sunday? Well, guess what. I was."

"Merry, please! I'm sure you were serious. I'm sure you meant it at the time, but—"

"At the time?"

"I realize that you and Josh had a spat, and—"

"A *spat*!"

"And I can understand why you came here to get some distance, to regroup—"

"Regroup?"

"There's nothing wrong with—"

"As I said on Sunday, I've moved back here," said Meredith. "And you know what? It really doesn't have anything to do with you. It's between me and Mom." She went around to the back of the stable and returned with her arms filled with hay. The smell was calming. She clutched the flakes against her chest. It felt good to hold them in front of her, a protective shield against Kat.

"You're wrong," said Kat—a statement that was familiar to Meredith from years before. Only Kat would say something like that, definitive and arrogant! "She's my mother, too, and if you lead her to believe that you're moving back home—"

"I'm not 'leading her to believe'—it's what I'm doing."

"It's what you *imagine* you're doing now—but you won't stick with it. You'll get Mom involved, and you'll derail her plans for selling this place, for moving on—"

"*Her* plans? They're not her plans, they're *your* plans for her. They're what you want her to do, not what she wants to do!"

“I wish you would face reality for a change,” said Kat. “Mom and Bob are getting old. They can’t manage a farm. This is not a viable situation for them any longer—”

“Look at me, Kat!” Meredith tried to keep her voice level. “I’m here. I’m cleaning the stable. I’m feeding the animals. Watch me!” She did not look back at Kat while she laid hay down for Falstaff and then started laying it in three different places in the donkeys’ stall.

“There happens to be a developer one of my colleagues knows who’s looking for projects right now. He’s potentially interested in this property. He’s willing to pay quite a bit for a parcel of land like this.”

Meredith dropped the hay she was holding and wheeled around. “So that’s it! You want Mom to sell this place that she loves and have it turned into—into a subdivision?”

“She and Bob can buy a nice condo or a new, easy-to-take-care-of house closer to town—and have a cushion of money for the rest of their lives.”

“To do what with? They’re financially OK. They don’t need more money.”

“Everyone needs more money when they get old. Do you have any idea what decent nursing homes cost?”

Meredith couldn’t answer this. She could barely talk. She closed her eyes and worked to summon how she had trained herself to be calm when she was angry at Eloise: breathe in through her nose, feel the air move down inside her chest, exhale slowly, through her mouth.

“I was hoping to have a reasonable discussion with you,” said Kat. “I was hoping you’d gained some maturity at last. I was hoping you’d think about Mom, not just yourself.”

Meredith waited to open her eyes until she heard Kat turn to leave. She watched Kat walk towards the house. Kat was stepping around wet areas on the flagstone path, but the back of one of her boots was streaked with mud. Meredith wondered what Kat would be saying to her mother, how she would describe their argument. Then she remembered that Eloise was there, so Kat couldn’t say very much.

Meredith got carrots for the donkeys and stood at the barn door and looked out at the darkening fields. Then she called out, "Tulip! Myrtle! Clementine! Come! Come!" She'd get Falstaff in later. She waved a carrot and made little clucking sounds. Clementine perked up her ears and raised her head. Slowly, she started walking towards the barn, and the two other donkeys followed. Tulip trotted up beside Clementine, then pushed ahead, because Tulip always wanted to be first. Meredith broke a carrot in half and laid it on the pile of hay for Tulip. Tulip was greedy, and you had to be careful hand-feeding her. Meredith leaned down and held a carrot out in each hand, one for Myrtle and one for Clementine.

"Here you go, sweethearts," she whispered. "Here you go."

At night, after Eloise was in bed, Meredith asked Delia if she'd babysit while she went out for a bit. At first she wasn't going to say where she was headed—being vague had always suited her in the past—but she decided she might as well let her mother know she was going to have a drink at Wylie's house. If she treated it as a secret, her mother would think it meant something more than it did.

"Of course," said Delia. "I'm always happy to take care of Eloise." It was clear she was doing her best to appear nonjudgmental.

"May I take your car?"

"You don't need to ask," said Delia.

"You know, I think I should look into getting a car of my own," said Meredith.

"There are two cars here. And we rarely have occasion to use them both."

"Even so."

"Do you have a house key?" Delia asked, which Meredith knew was her way of asking how late she'd be.

"You lock?"

"Well, we do now. Kat thought—"

"Oh," said Meredith. "Of course she would."

"The world has changed!"

"You do have the dogs."

"Have you met the dogs?" asked Delia, and they both laughed. It was a moment that reminded Meredith that, on occasion, she and her mother were able to laugh about something together, that they weren't always adversaries.

Delia took a key from the row of hooks in the closet. "You might as well just keep this," she said.

The key was on a piece of burlap string, a remnant from string that had been used to bind bales of hay. There was something endearing about it—the fact that her mother would save the string after the bale was cut, find a use for it. No one she knew back in her life in California would do something like that. Meredith slipped the key into her bag.

Meredith didn't intend to start up anything with Wylie. But she wasn't going to rule out the possibility either. She didn't like to rule things out. She didn't trust herself to know what she wanted, or what she might want someday. She barely trusted herself to know what she didn't want.

The carriage house had only a yellow light outside by the door, but The Heap had floodlights illuminating the front entrance and the circular driveway, where the tenant's ostentatious car looked as if it were on display. She hadn't been inside The Heap in years—maybe since high school? Some big party where she'd tried to seem older than she was, but when Evan had spotted her hanging around in the butler's pantry with some friends of Wylie's who were doing lines of coke, he'd come and grabbed her by the arm and pulled her away. She'd been furious with him and relieved too.

Both The Heap and the carriage house were half timbered, stucco, and stone. The stones were the size of cantaloupes. The windows were small and mullioned. "Baronial gnome style," Wylie called it.

In contrast, the carriage house inside was a white open space. The beagles, Toad and Flax, greeted Meredith enthusiastically when she arrived, and Wylie let them out as she came in. Wylie stood back and let Meredith look around. Sparse modern furniture that probably was designer and cost a lot. The living room had a work area on one side, and a sleek little kitchen on the other.

"When did you renovate this?"

"When Nicole and I split up, I took off for a while, but ended up coming back here and moving in with my folks, used this as a workspace. But you know how that is."

"I'm finding out," said Meredith.

"I renovated this so I could live here too. Put in the kitchen."

"Nice," said Meredith, and she meant it.

"After my mom was gone and my dad had checked out, I thought I might move back into The Heap, but it's kind of—"

"Big for one person?"

"That, and hasn't been updated since the turn of the century. It's not likely I'll have a sit-down dinner for sixteen in the dining room. I'd keep stepping on the button under the table to summon the maid to clear the dishes, and no one would turn up."

"You found someone to rent it?"

"New Yorkers," he said. "It's all furnished, hasn't been touched. They love the old stuff. They come up for weekends. Want to see upstairs?"

Meredith hesitated for a second. She guessed the bedroom was upstairs. She was curious, but she didn't want to be curious.

"Sure."

She followed Wylie up the spiral staircase. The ceiling upstairs was low, and the walls sloped in around the dormers. The windows were narrow, with diamond-shaped panes. Like a church. The floor was wide-board pine, newly sanded. She did not want to look at the bed, but it was impossible not to. It was a big white presence in the room, with a pile of oversized pillows, and a puffy comforter that looked like snow. She wanted to flop down onto it on her back and make snow angels. She wondered if Wylie always had the bed made like this, or if he had tidied things up for her.

"Nice floors," she said.

"Had a hell of a time getting the old paint off," said Wylie.

Meredith followed Wylie down the staircase. It was a relief to be back downstairs.

"I'm afraid I can't offer you anything fancy to drink," said Wylie. "But I can open a bottle of wine."

"That would be nice," said Meredith.

"I cut way back after the OUI," he said, and then, when he saw Meredith's face, he said, "Evan didn't tell you about that?"

"No."

"Yeah, well. I had kind of a hard time when Nicole took off. Evan tell you about that?"

Meredith shook her head.

"My drinking was—how shall I put it?—excessive. I totaled the car."

"And you?"

"Nothing much. Airbag scratched up my face, some"—Wylie touched his cheekbone—"and I slammed the brake so hard I did in my ankle. Had to hobble around on crutches for a while. So pissed with myself I couldn't bear to be around me."

"That would be a trick," said Meredith.

Wylie poured them each a glass of wine and put some cheese and crackers on a wooden plate. He set it down on the coffee table in front of the sofa. The table was a single piece of thick glass, the top curving over to form the sides, as if water had splashed up and over and frozen in place. The sofa was grey with a stainless steel frame. Meredith sat at one end and wondered if Wylie would sit next to her, but he sat at the other side.

"Well, here's to the return of the native," he said, and he lifted his glass.

"You too," she said. Who would have guessed that both of them would end up back here, in their old town, living in their parents' place?

"I took your suggestion and stopped by and talked with Maxine. I'm trying to decide if I'd want to work for her, so I'd like your input."

"I don't know her that well."

"Wylie, you slept with her—didn't you?"

Wylie held up his hands. "Not saying I did, but even if I did, that doesn't mean I'd know what she'd be like to work for."

"I'm not sure this is a good time for me to take on a new job—but since this came up, I thought I should at least look into it."

"Well, one thing about Max is she's connected to everyone in the arts community around here—such as it is—so that might be useful for you. That is, if you want to be part of the arts scene, or maybe you just want to be working all on your own?"

That was a point. Meredith wasn't going to miss a lot of things about her life in California, but she would miss her friends—her artist friends, not the couples friends that she and Josh had socialized with. Not that any of them were Josh's friends. He didn't really like to socialize at all, and she'd had to drag him along.

"How are you fixed for money?" Wylie asked. From anyone else it would have seemed intrusive.

"I'm OK. For now at least. And if Josh and I sell the house, I'll be set for a while."

"What's the house like?"

"Nothing special. And the lot is like .001 of an acre. Around here it wouldn't be worth much, but it's California, so it will probably go for something ridiculous."

"What does Josh do? I forgot."

"He was at Google, then went with a friend to a start-up."

"I can never understand that stuff," said Wylie. "I mean I hear the terms, but I never know what these guys actually do. Stare at a screen. Peck, peck, peck at a keyboard?" Was it possible that Wylie was jealous?

Meredith laughed. "Something like that," she said.

The cheese plate was in the center of the table. Wylie leaned forward and scooted over one seat and sat down next to her. He sliced some pieces of cheese and laid them out on crackers. He held the plate up to her, and she took one, before he took one for himself.

"I never expected you to end up with a guy like Josh," he said.

"What *did* you expect?"

"Someone with more hair."

"Maybe when I was in college I went out with guys like that, but when I was in high school? Actually I didn't really go out with guys when I was in high school. Not that I didn't want to. I just wasn't the kind of girl guys paid any attention to."

"Yeah, right!" said Wylie. "I remember you going around in some short little skirt—"

"Everyone wore short little skirts back then."

"Shaking your ass and flirting with your brother's friends—"

"I did not flirt!" Meredith punched Wylie playfully on the shoulder. He grabbed her wrist. For a second they sat there, not moving. His thumb pressed against the soft place under the heel of her hand. She could feel her pulse throbbing. She wondered who would speak first, but neither of them spoke. Wylie lowered her hand to her knee and slowly loosened his fingers. When his hand was free he reached up and cupped the back of her head. She wanted to fall forward against him, have him hold her in his arms. She wanted to be held. It had been so long since she'd been held!

"I'm not sure we should be doing this," she said, finally.

"We're not doing anything," said Wylie.

11

Delia found Bob in the stable's tack room, drill in hand.

"It's time someone added more hooks here," he said. "You bought coats for the donkeys, but you didn't make a place to hang them. Doubling them on the existing hooks doesn't work; they are constantly falling off." Bob pointed to the pile on the floor.

"Aren't the donkeys lucky to have you looking out for their interests."

"Lili, you are conflating affection for donkeys with an interest in maintaining order in this area of the barn."

"I had a thought about the auction we're going to tomorrow," said Delia.

"Uh-oh," said Bob, and he laid down the drill. "I can tell from the tone of your voice it's probably something I won't like."

"Why don't we take Eloise with us tomorrow?"

"Why would we want to do that?"

"She's never been to an auction. I think she'd enjoy it."

"And? I know there's something else behind this."

Delia hesitated for a minute, then she said, "Meredith mentioned she could use some time on her own to 'do things.' So I thought it would be nice for her to have Eloise come with us."

"You're thinking 'do things' means have time to talk on the phone with Josh and work out a reconciliation?" asked Bob.

That had been what Delia was thinking, but she was reluctant to admit this to Bob. "Well—maybe."

"Delia, you can't keep hoping that Meredith will do the things you'd like her to do. It's never worked out that way."

"Please, Bob. I just want to give her the opportunity to—"

"I'm going to this auction to look at the rugs. I don't want to have Eloise underfoot."

"She won't be underfoot, I promise. There are a lot of things there that will interest her."

Bob sighed. "All right," he said after a while, "but I'm not agreeing to this because I expect Meredith will solve her marital difficulties in our absence, but because I—"

"Love me?" asked Delia.

"That too," said Bob.

Meredith seemed happy about the plan, and Eloise was excited, though she said she'd go only if Moosie came too. Delia was afraid she might change her mind about going, and was relieved when Eloise hopped into the car and set Moosie on the seat beside her. She lowered the window and cheerfully called out, "Goodbye, Mommy," while she waved. Meredith, standing in the driveway as they pulled away, looked small and left behind, and Delia was tempted to run back and give her a hug and wish her good luck.

When they got to the auction house, Eloise didn't want to leave Moosie in the car. "You deal with this," said Bob. "I'm going ahead."

Delia turned back to Eloise and began to reason with her, but she could see it was hopeless to try to get her to part with Moosie now.

"Moosie wants to buy something today," said Eloise.

"At auctions, you can't just buy something," explained Delia. "If you bid on it, you may win and get to take it home with you, but there may be other people who want it too."

When they got inside the auction house, Delia found Bob, on his hands and knees, examining a rug. He stood up and dusted off his hands on his jacket. "Some nice Kazaks here," he said. "It will depend on what they'll go for."

"You already have a lot of rugs," said Eloise.

Delia laughed. "That's just what I tell your grandpa."

"You can never have too many rugs," said Bob.

"Like the ones in the book you showed me?"

"Exactly."

"At our house we got new rugs downstairs, but it was just plain and all the same color."

"That," said Bob, "is carpeting, not rugs."

Delia left Bob with the rugs and took Eloise around to show her the other auction lots. Delia loved antiques, the dazzling variety of things humans had created. Everything here had once belonged to someone, had maybe even been loved. Delia had Eloise pose in front of an antique sleigh and texted the photo to Meredith with a note: Eloise is having a great time. How are things going there?

Eloise was drawn to the dolls, which were slumped together on a Victorian sofa, some in fancy outfits, some without a shred of clothing. To Delia's surprise Eloise picked out a small doll in a faded dress. She had blue glass eyes that looked unnervingly real. "Can I get her?" Eloise asked.

"That's the kind of doll you look at but not play with," said Delia.

"I would play with her!"

There was a crack on the side of the doll's bisque head that had been poorly glued, and her legs dangled loosely. "She's not in very good shape," said Delia.

"That doesn't matter," said Eloise. She ran her finger along the crack. "She got broken here, but it doesn't hurt her anymore." She tilted the doll back, so lashless lids covered the eyes, then back up again so the blue eyes stared straight at her. "She can really see me!" cried Eloise.

Bob waved them over to chairs in a row near the middle.

"Time for us to take our seats," said Delia. "Want to sit on my lap so you can see better?" she asked.

"I want to sit on *Grandpa's* lap."

"Bob?"

"Well, all right," said Bob.

Eloise placed Moosie on her vacant chair, then climbed on Bob's lap. "Can I hold the card with the number?"

"Too dangerous," said Bob.

"Oh, for heaven's sake," said Delia.

Bob handed the card to Eloise. "Give it back to me when I ask you, and don't hold it up for any reason. The auction is about to start."

Eloise looked confused. "But nobody's bit on anything," she said.

"This is an auction house, not a restaurant," said Bob. "It's 'bid,' not 'bit,' which is what we're about to do now. Which is why that card you're holding is dangerous. If you raise it by accident, you might end up bidding on something we had no intention of acquiring."

When they started bringing the rugs out, Bob reclaimed the card from Eloise. "Ridiculous," he said to Delia, each time he dropped out of the bidding. He finally won the bid on a small Karabagh.

"How nice," Delia said. "You got a rug you wanted."

"It would have been a lot nicer if I could have gotten it for less."

Delia took out her cell and checked her messages. There was no update from Meredith, except a heart emoji in response to the photo of Eloise.

"Look, Grandma," cried Eloise, pointing. "They're bringing the dolls over."

"No wiggling!" said Bob.

When the auctioneer came to the doll Eloise had liked, Eloise looked at Delia. "Please! Can't I get her?"

"Sorry, dear," said Delia.

"What do we have for this nice little doll?" the auctioneer asked. "Do I hear twenty-five? Do I hear twenty?" Delia was surprised the bidding was starting so low. Most of the other dolls had gone for more than a hundred dollars, some for several hundred. But antique dolls were like antique rugs; you had to know about them to tell what they were worth.

When no one said anything, the auctioneer held the doll up a little higher. "What will you give me for this charming doll. Has some condition issues, but worth investing in repairs."

"Please?" Eloise begged.

Delia shook her head.

The auction room was very still. Delia saw Bob's hand fly up in the air. "Ten," he called out.

"I hear ten," said the auctioneer. "Anyone give me twenty? Do I see twenty?"

No one moved.

"Ten to the gentleman on my left," said the auctioneer. "Do I see fifteen?"

"Fifteen," someone called out.

"Back to you," said the auctioneer, turning towards Bob. "Do I hear twenty?"

Delia thought he was done with bidding, but then he said, "Twenty."

"Twenty-five?" asked the auctioneer to the woman who had bid fifteen, but she shook her head. "Sold for twenty, to number—"

Bob held up his card. "To number eighty-seven," said the auctioneer. When the runner brought the doll to him, Bob gave her to Eloise.

"Well," said Delia, "that was a surprise. Thank Grandpa, Eloise."

Eloise held the doll up in front of Bob. "Thank you, Grandpa," she said in a little voice. "I'll call her Sofia."

"Sofia?" asked Delia.

"She's a girl in my old school. I had a playdate with her, but Mommy said I can't go to her house again."

"How come?"

"Because her mommy wasn't home when Mommy came to pick me up, just a babysitter, and she hadn't told Mommy ahead. Mommy was angry."

"I see," said Delia.

"Daddy said she was sessive."

"Sessive?"

"Excessive," said Bob.

Delia checked her cell phone again. There was nothing more from Meredith.

They were well on their way home when there was a cry from Eloise in the back seat.

Delia turned around quickly. "What happened, Sweetheart?"

"Moosie's not here."

"Pull over when you can," Delia told Bob.

"What?" Bob asked, but he pulled off the road.

"Where did you last have him?" asked Delia.

"Back there!" cried Eloise, and she pointed in the direction they'd come from.

"At the auction house?" asked Delia. "Are you sure?"

Eloise nodded. She was crying now, with little hiccups at the end of each breath. There was no point in Delia reminding her she'd been told to leave Moosie in the car. She couldn't be angry at Eloise; she was just angry at herself for not insisting about Moosie.

"I guess we better go back," Delia said to Bob.

"We're not going back!" said Bob. "We're halfway home."

"Bob!"

"We'll get her another moose," said Bob.

"I don't want another moose," cried Eloise. "I want Moosie."

"Bob—"

Bob didn't say anything. He pulled back onto the road and drove farther along. Then he made a U-turn. Delia put her hand on his shoulder. "Thank you," she whispered.

Bob waited in the car while Delia and Eloise went back into the auction house. The auction was over, and the rows of grey folding chairs were dismally empty, except for a paper cup and some crumpled-up napkins.

"Let's ask at the desk," Delia said, but then Eloise spotted a brown shape on the floor, under a seat. "Moosie!" she cried, and she ran to scoop him up.

"Must have slipped through the back of the chair," said Delia.

"Any luck?" asked Bob, when they got back to the car.

"Found," said Delia, and she pointed at Eloise, who was clutching Moosie against her chest.

"Thank God," said Bob. "Peace is restored."

~

When they got back to the house, Eloise heard her mother say to her grandma, "I was expecting you an hour earlier!" but her grandma didn't tell her they'd had to go back to get Moosie. When her mother saw Sofia she said, "You got her an antique doll?"

"She fell in love with it, so Bob bought it for her," said her grandma.

"*Bob* did?" Her mother laughed.

"Eloise named her Sofia," said her grandma, "after a child whose mother you apparently didn't approve of."

"What did you tell Grandma?" her mother asked.

"Nothing," said Eloise. "I'm going upstairs!" She took Moosie and Sofia with her. She propped Sofia on the window seat, and she crawled into her mother's big bed with Moosie. The pillow smelled like her mother's shampoo. Eloise held Moosie against her chest. The time she'd left him in the booth at the restaurant, her father had said to her mother, "We're not going back! You told Eloise not to bring it, and you gave in when she made a fuss. It's time she learned to take responsibility for things." But her mother had him wait in the parking lot and ran back to get Moosie for her. Eloise held Moosie tighter, and since no one was there to see her, she put her thumb in her mouth. She would never forget about Moosie and leave him behind again.

~

Delia waited for Meredith to come down to the kitchen after she'd gotten Eloise to bed, and she busied herself unloading the dishwasher while Meredith made herself a cup of tea. When Meredith was done, Delia asked, "How did things go while we were away?"

"What things, Mom?"

"You'd said you had things to do, and I was hoping you were able to accomplish them."

"Well, yeah, I got some stuff done," said Meredith.

"Stuff?"

"Yeah. Stuff," said Meredith, as if that put an end to it. Delia wasn't sure how to bring the conversation around to Josh without Merry getting angry, so she started with a safe subject. "I think Eloise had a good time, today," she said.

"Seems she did," Merry said. "I hope *you* had a good time having her along. I knew you wanted to bring her, but I wasn't sure she'd want to go—but she was OK, wasn't she?"

"Just fine," said Delia.

Meredith pulled the tea bag out of the mug and dropped it into the sink. "I gather Bob got himself yet one more rug he didn't need, so the trip was a success, right?" She pointed to the living room, where Bob had laid the rug out on top of others on the floor. "At least this one isn't as threadbare as some of them." She picked up the mug of tea. "I'm heading up to bed now. Goodnight, Mom," she said, without giving Delia a chance to bring up the subject of Josh.

In the morning Delia put on her cleats before she and Bob went out on their walk. March was the fickle season. The dirt road had frozen and thawed and turned to mud and frozen again.

"You're just wearing boots?" she asked Bob.

"Looks like it, doesn't it?"

Delia shook her head. "Kids can fall and bounce back, but not us, Bob."

"Sounds like a lecture from Kat."

"It's not only Kat. I just heard about someone I'd gone to college with. She tumbled down the stairs, cracked her head, and died. Just like that."

"I don't think cleats would have protected her," said Bob.

The dogs had free run of the farm, but they liked their walks too. When Delia called out "walk" they came flying towards her, wriggling in the ridiculous way dogs have and wagging their tails. It had been too long since either of them had been to the groomer, and their fur was decorated with leaves, twigs, burrs, and other, less-pleasant evidence of farm life. That was the downside of dogs with long fur. That, and shedding, which Ralph did in abundance. Juno did not shed; she just matted. On walks, Juno ambled along contentedly beside them, but Ralph tended to get into trouble, so Delia put him on his expandable leash. Perversely, he seemed to relish the constraint and ran happily in front of them, zigzagging back and forth across the road.

Delia loved walking along the dirt road, but always shuddered when they passed the titanic-sized new house where the owners had slashed down all the trees, then set a rock bearing a brass plaque with the house's name, Mountain View, at the entrance of the driveway. Ralph sniffed at the rock, then lifted his leg on it.

"Good dog!" said Delia.

Farther along the road they stopped, as they often did, at the edge of a field, and looked out across the valley.

"I got a moment to speak with Meredith last night," Delia said, "but I have no idea if she talked to Josh while we were away yesterday. I asked her if she'd had a productive day, and she said she got some stuff done—nothing more. By the way, she didn't thank us for taking Eloise; in fact, she seemed to think she was doing us a favor allowing Eloise to go with us."

"Did you really expect Merry to thank you?" asked Bob.

Ralph found some enticing smell on the side of the road, and Delia had a hard time dragging him away. She tried, unsuccessfully, to get Ralph to heel as they continued along the road, but "heel" was not a command that either Ralph or Juno felt obliged to obey.

"Kat thinks Merry's going to pick up suddenly and head back to California, that she's not serious about moving here—or rather that she thinks she's serious, but it's just a whim."

"Maybe you should stop listening to what Kat thinks," said Bob.

"I listen to her, but that doesn't mean I agree with her. In this case, though, she may be right. Merry seems to be making plans for staying here—she's talking about turning the barn into studio space—but I'm not convinced she's committed to being here. She hasn't done anything yet about enrolling Eloise in school. So it's hard to predict what she's going to do."

"What do you want her to do? Stay or go back to California?"

Delia stopped walking and turned to Bob. "Here's my dilemma. I want her here, but I also want her to be with her husband—"

"Because she's supposed to be with her husband?"

"No! How can you think that?" Delia looked at Bob straight on. "I want her to be with her husband because I want Eloise to grow up with two parents and—"

"Your children didn't."

"It wasn't my choice!"

"I thought it was."

"Only because living with Phil had become impossible."

"Maybe that's the case with Josh."

"But we don't know that. She can't just run off when she has some disagreement with him—she can't just abandon her life there!"

"No?"

"Well she can, but she shouldn't."

"*Shouldn't?* What are you saying?"

"I don't know," said Delia. "I just don't know."

They turned off to the left and took the road that circled back around. It was a rough farm road, hardly a road at all.

"And then there's Wylie," said Delia.

"What about Wylie?"

"Do you want her to end up with Wylie?"

"What, you think there's something going on with them?"

Delia thought about this for a moment. It was hard to separate what she thought was going on between them from what she was afraid might go on with them if Merry stayed around longer. "Merry has been infatuated with Wylie since she was a teenager."

"If I recall she was infatuated with all of Evan's friends," said Bob, "all of them unsuitable for a variety of reasons, including being too old for her."

"There has always been something more with Wylie—I'm not sure what."

"You never liked him. How come? He always seemed relatively harmless to me. Especially compared with some of the other young men Merry attached herself to."

"I don't know. I just didn't trust him."

"Didn't trust him or didn't trust Merry?"

Delia laughed a little. "Either of them."

"You still don't trust Merry, do you?"

That was a question that Delia had not wanted to confront. Loving your child was entirely separate from trusting your child. Delia had always believed that Merry's core moral values were intact, but in some situations Merry had shown that her judgment was—well, impaired. Delia hadn't really trusted Merry since she became a teenager, but it made her sad to admit this to Bob—and to herself. "I guess I don't," she said.

"She is grown up now, though, isn't she?"

"I'm not sure," said Delia, and she felt frightened as soon as she said it. The future seemed precarious.

Ralph discovered a redolent pile of leaves along the side of the road and started rolling in it. Delia had to tug on the leash and drag him out. When Juno was about to roll, too, Bob hauled her off by her collar. Delia kept Ralph on a short leash until they were far enough past the leaf pile. It had been a relief to forget about Merry for a moment, but as soon as the dogs were under relative control, the problem was back, in full force. "I feel so conflicted!" said Delia. "I want what's best for Eloise, but I hate to think of her living five thousand miles away."

"Three thousand miles."

Delia turned on Bob. "Could you at least try to be sympathetic?" She gripped Ralph's leash and walked fiercely ahead.

Bob hesitated a moment, then caught up with her. He put his hand on her shoulder. "I *am* sympathetic. I know you love having Merry and Eloise here. And I know you're afraid Merry will take off again."

Delia looked up towards the sky. The tree branches were a tangle of black lines across the blue. That was it. She was afraid Merry would just pick up and leave. She had trained Delia in the past to expect that. And Eloise would be gone, and it would be a long time before Delia got to see her again. But wasn't it best for Merry—and, especially, for Eloise—to be with Josh, back in California? Delia didn't know what she wanted. She looked at Bob.

"Until I find out what the problem is between Merry and Josh, I feel helpless. What do you think I should do?"

Bob didn't offer an answer for that right away. A dead tree branch had fallen across the road, and he dragged it off and laid it along the side.

"If you need to know what's going on with Merry and Josh, you have only one recourse, and that's get Merry to tell you."

"And if she won't?"

"Then that's that. You know, Lili, this is Merry's life. You have to stay out of it. You just have to let things take their course."

"You mean I should just wait?" asked Delia.

"Yes."

"I'm not very good at that."

Bob laughed. "I know," he said. "But I don't think there's anything else you can do," he said.

"Would you try talking with her?"

"Are you kidding? No way I'm venturing into that minefield!"

In the afternoon Delia found Merry out in the barn, sanding the top of an old worktable. Merry had set up Eloise in the living room with her iPad to watch what Delia thought was an inane cartoon that featured puppies who ran a detective agency, which gave Merry and

Delia an hour to talk. Delia had planned to begin by saying something like "Bob and I have been concerned that," but decided it wiser to keep Bob out of it.

"Is this a good moment to talk with you?" she began.

"What do you mean, Mom?" asked Meredith. "You talk to me all the time."

"I meant talk with you without Eloise—"

"Oh," said Meredith, and she put her sanding block down, "one of those cheerful little conversations about your ultimate demise, like who inherits the silver Kat hasn't already laid claim to?"

"No—it's about you."

"What about me? Short version, please. I've got stuff to do here. As you can see."

"I wondered if you'd had a chance to talk with Josh yesterday while we were at the auction—"

"Josh? I didn't talk with Josh. I haven't talked with him since I left LA."

"Didn't you let him know you and Eloise got here safely?"

"I texted him, Mom. That's it."

"Hasn't he called you?"

"Frankly, that's none of your business. But to get you off my back I'll tell you. No, he hasn't called me. And I'm certainly not going to call him. The ball's entirely in his court. Not that I want to talk to him if he does call me."

"I thought that maybe he was going to be coming out here—"

"You thought wrong, Mom."

"But what about Eloise?"

"What about her?"

"I just wondered about Josh—about his not seeing Eloise, about her not seeing him."

"Mom, you don't get it, do you?"

"I guess I don't. Which is why I'd appreciate you telling me what's happening. Was Josh"—Delia wasn't sure how to phrase this—"involved with—"

"If you're asking me if Josh has been fucking someone else, the answer is no—nothing like that!"

"Then what is it?"

"I've already told you more than you need to know. And frankly, Mom, it's really not your business, it just isn't. Get it through your head. It has nothing to do with you."

"But it does!"

"Why?"

"Well, you're here!"

"So that's what it's all about? If I'm living here, I'm required to confide in you about every detail of my private life?"

"No, it's—"

"I get to live here—in a house which, may I point out to you, you insist on claiming has always been my home—and the cost of doing so is that I have to confide in you about everything? Satisfy your curiosity? That's kind of a hefty price, isn't it?"

"Nothing like that! I'm your mother, so you can hardly blame me for wanting to know what the situation is with you and Josh."

"You're not going to let this go, are you? So, to get you off my back, here's the current situation: I'm here in Massachusetts. Josh is in California. Got it?"

"But why?"

"Mom, you claim you care about my feelings, but you don't act as if you do. Maybe this whole thing hasn't been a lot of fun for me. Maybe it's painful to talk about it. If you want to know why Josh isn't here with me and why he isn't calling me, maybe you need to ask him. I'm done talking about this. Done. Finis. I need to look after my own mental health. If you ask me about this again, I'm going to have to pack up and take Eloise and leave."

"I'm so sorry that you've been hurt!"

"Mom. Stop! I'm so done talking with you now. I'm going back to the house." Meredith took off the denim apron she'd been wearing and flung it over the back of a chair before she left. Delia stood there for a moment in the empty barn space. The top of the worktable had been coated with a film of wood dust. Delia ran her finger along the edge, leaving a smooth line through the sandings.

In bed at night, Delia lay on her side, close to Bob, and described her conversation with Merry.

"I never really liked Josh," she said, "but I thought he was good for Merry."

"Good for, or good to?"

"Both. But he's not being good to her now, is he?"

"Doesn't seem that way," said Bob. "But what do I know?"

"After I talked with Merry I called Josh, but just got his voicemail, and I didn't leave a message."

"Calling Josh was probably not a good idea," said Bob. "Merry would be furious. And if you got him, what would you say to him, anyway?"

"He's my son-in-law. I should be able to discuss this with him! Something's happened between him and Merry—he's hurt her in some way—though apparently it's not infidelity, at least she says not—and she's waiting for him to make the next move. She's not going to be the one to contact him—you know Merry, Bob. So he's the one who needs to take the initiative for making things right."

"And you're going to call him and tell him that?"

Delia sighed. "I was actually relieved he hadn't answered, when I called. You can't really talk about something like this on the phone. I think I need to just fly out there and talk to him face to face. If not for Merry's sake, for Eloise's sake."

Bob got up on his elbows. His face was barely visible in the dark. "That," he said, "would be a really bad idea."

"But it may be the only thing I can do."

While she was getting breakfast started the next morning, Delia sent Eloise out to gather eggs. She lined the egg basket with a blue cloth napkin. The henhouse had been designed so you could access the laying boxes from the outside.

"Remember to close the little doors and hook them when you're done," said Delia.

"I will," said Eloise. "And you don't have to remind me."

Delia smiled. Eloise might be impolite, as Bob had pointed out more than once, but Delia thought spirit was important, especially in a girl. Though that might be sexist.

"You should wear your jacket!" she called as Eloise ran off.

"She doesn't need to wear her jacket," said Merry, who had come down to breakfast in an old sweatshirt that looked vaguely familiar, with a surfer on the front. Evan's probably?

"Good morning, Sweetheart," said Delia. "I'm making toast. Do you want some?" She was going to be careful not to make any reference to the conversation from the day before.

"Sure, why not," said Merry.

Bob lowered his newspaper. "It will be cold by the time the eggs are ready."

"I don't think so," said Delia. "I'll keep it warm in the oven."

"Your mother is a resourceful woman," said Bob.

Delia set a jar of honey on the table. "This came from the Bruckners, up the road. Their niece, Amelia, is the girl who came by to ride Falstaff when you weren't here."

"I know where the Bruckners live," said Merry. "Kyle Bruckner was on my bus. I thought they gave up on bees. That winter when everything froze. Including the bees."

"They had all the equipment, so they started up with them again."

"Kyle was a yo-yo champ," said Merry. "A real oddball. I think he went to some college in Canada and stayed there. Lucky Canada." She helped herself to a teaspoon of honey from the jar.

"That's supposed to be for the toast," said Delia.

"It's not bad," said Merry. She licked the spoon and laid it on the table.

Delia leaned down to get a bowl from the cabinet for scrambling the eggs, but stood up suddenly when she heard Eloise screaming. Eloise burst into the kitchen and ran to Merry.

"What happened?" cried Merry, as she gathered Eloise on her lap.

Eloise was sobbing incoherently. Delia squatted beside her. "Are you all right, Darling?" she asked.

"I'm handling this, Mom," said Meredith, and she swiveled on her chair, turning Eloise's face away. Delia wanted to touch Eloise, but didn't dare.

Eloise looked all right, though. She didn't look like she'd been hurt.

"What happened, Baby?" asked Merry. "Tell Mommy."

"Harriet is all icky. She has no head!"

"Oh God," said Delia, and she got to her feet. "Bob, it's the chickens."

She ran outside, not bothering to grab her jacket. Bob ran beside her.

The chicken coop was a scene of carnage. Terrified chickens were squawking and flapping their wings. Harriet, a sweet Orpington chicken, lay in a gory pool, and what was left of Luna, a Plymouth Rock, also headless, was strewn beside her. Agnes, a bloody wound on the back of her neck, quivered, pathetically, on the floor of the henhouse. Agnes was an Ameraucana. She wasn't Delia's favorite chicken, but she laid beautiful blue eggs.

"Let's get her to the vet," said Delia. She pulled off her apron and wrapped Agnes in it. "My poor darling Eloise saw all this!"

Bob ran inside to tell Merry where they were headed while Delia got into the car with Agnes. She found a towel on the floor and pressed it on Agnes's neck. The towel was used for the dogs, but it would be better than nothing. She tried to think of soothing words for Agnes while they drove to the veterinary clinic, but couldn't come up with anything, so she made soft clucking sounds.

Dr. Sprucer, the vet who'd been there back when Delia and Bob had met at the clinic, was retired, and the practice had been taken over by his younger associate, Dr. Pruzniak. "I don't think it makes sense to try saving this chicken," she said.

Delia spoke as evenly as she could. "Agnes is a beloved pet. We'd like you to do whatever you can."

"I can't tell you what the cost of this might come to."

"The cost doesn't matter," said Delia.

In the car, driving back to the farm, Delia said to Bob, "Dr. Sprucer would never have suggested we euthanize Agnes."

"Dr. Sprucer may have wanted to propose such a thing, but he knew you well enough not to. You do realize, Delia, that chickens are—well, chickens. People eat them."

"Not ours," said Delia.

Merry was still sitting in the kitchen with Eloise on her lap when they got home. Eloise had stopped screaming; she was whimpering now. She didn't lift her head when Delia went to kiss her.

"I'm so sorry, Darling," said Delia.

"What was it?" asked Merry. "A fox?"

"Couldn't have been," said Delia. "The henhouse door was still closed. Must have been a weasel."

"But how did it get in?"

"Probably right through the chicken wire," said Bob. "They can squeeze through holes this big." He held up his forefinger and thumb in a circle. "Got to redo the fencing. We'll need to get some hardware cloth."

"I don't want to be here anymore," said Eloise. "I want to go home."

"I'm very sad about Harriet too," said Delia. "We'll have a little funeral for her, OK?" She wasn't sure if Luna should be included, but decided this was not a good moment to mention her.

"I don't want to," said Eloise. "I want to go home. Now."

The words stung. Delia looked up at Bob. He shrugged. "I better go clean things up," he said.

"Thank you," whispered Delia. At times like this she felt enormously grateful for Bob. She could clean up manure, dog poop, and vomit, but she was useless when it came to corpses. They didn't have a cat on the farm, because cats sometimes brought their owners slain mice, and they didn't use mousetraps, except for the humane catch-and-release kind. Bob could handle dead mice—dead anythings, including, it seemed, even dead and mangled pet chickens. He could handle gore. One of the advantages of having gone to medical school.

"Do you want some breakfast first?" she asked Bob. Obviously, it was not going to be eggs.

"I'll pass," said Bob.

"What would you like, Sweetheart?" Delia asked Eloise. "You can have toast with honey. Or I can make you oatmeal with maple syrup."

Eloise didn't look up.

"I don't think Eloise wants anything," said Merry.

"What about you?" Delia asked Merry. "The toast is warm in the oven. Oh, and I got your kind of Greek yogurt." Delia started towards the refrigerator.

"Mom, lay off about the food, will you? Nobody is up for breakfast right now. Eloise and I are going upstairs."

Eloise clung to Merry as they walked out of the kitchen. She wouldn't look at Delia, as if she felt Delia was responsible for what had happened in the chicken coop. Delia could hear her voice as Merry and she went upstairs. "When can we go home?" she asked. "I don't like it here. I want to go home."

12

Meredith had never encountered a live weasel and didn't know much about them, so she stayed up late researching them on the internet. She found a wealth of contradictory information—some villainizing weasels and some aiming to rehabilitate their image—and decided that the view that weasels were inherently vicious and killed for sport was a male projection.

Eloise didn't want to talk about what had happened to the chickens, but Meredith thought they probably should. In the morning she cuddled with Eloise on the window seat and showed her a photo of a relatively cute weasel, sitting on its haunches with its paws held up against its white chest.

"It looks like the ferret named Archie we saw when we went to the Oakland Zoo, doesn't it?"

"Archie wouldn't hurt Harriet," said Eloise.

Meredith wasn't so sure about that, but let it go and instead talked about Nature, with a capital *N*, and the food chain, and how some wild animals—like weasels—were carnivores, which meant they ate other animals to survive.

"It's not like the animals on the farm," she told Eloise. "We feed the donkeys and the dogs and the chickens, but wild animals have to find food all on their own—for themselves, and for their babies too."

"But why did the weasel want to eat Harriet? She was our pet!"

"It didn't realize Harriet was a pet—it couldn't tell the difference," said Meredith, although she was quite sure that pet status wouldn't confer protection on any chicken.

Eloise hadn't wanted to go anywhere near the henhouse, but Meredith thought it was important to face that too. Eloise clutched her hand as they went out to feed the surviving poultry. Bob had cleaned up the crime scene in front of the henhouse, and the chickens, with their short memories, seemed unperturbed by the previous day's trauma. There were advantages to having small brains. Bob had run new hardware cloth around the sides of the chicken's yard and patched a hole in the henhouse. Meredith thought he should have secured it all earlier to prevent the tragedy, but she had to admit that you didn't really worry about weasels until one made an appearance. It was like a lot of things in life. She pointed to the new wire. "See, we don't have to worry about the chickens anymore because Grandpa patched the cage so a weasel can't get through."

That was a mistake. Eloise cried, "Is the weasel still here?"

"Oh no," said Meredith quickly. And in spite of everything she'd read to the contrary, she said, "That little weasel was scared away by the dogs and won't be coming back ever again." A total fabrication, since Ralph and Juno were totally inept at scaring away anything.

"But I still want to go home," said Eloise. "I don't like it here."

They were not going back to California, but Meredith wasn't up to discussing it now. Dealing with the untimely demise of two chickens was stressful enough.

"We're going to Uncle Evan's next week, remember? You're going to see all the cool things in his store: skis, kayaks, canoes—"

"Can I go in a canoe?"

Meredith had no idea, so she resorted to that most useful of parental responses, the word "maybe."

"Will we see the dragon?"

"The what?"

"The dragon Uncle Evan was going to bring me but didn't because it was afraid of dogs."

"Oh, that," said Meredith. She had hoped Eloise had forgotten about the dragon. "I'll have to ask Uncle Evan about it."

After Meredith had read enough about the unpleasant relationship between weasels and poultry, she'd spent time researching how to help a child heal from trauma and loss. The psychology-heavy babble was a lot of horseshit, but maybe it would be good to have a chicken memorial ceremony, as her mother had suggested. She introduced the idea to Eloise while they were mucking out the stable. Eloise insisted she didn't want to have a funeral for Harriet and Luna, but Meredith lured Eloise into the project by hunting for stones for the chickens' graves. She took Eloise down to the stream at the far end of the donkeys' field. Clementine followed along with them, but stayed up on the hillside to watch while they selected some flat, relatively smooth stones. Now and then she nibbled, disconsolately, at some dried grass. It was peaceful by the stream—just the sound of the water rushing along to somewhere. It was so insistently not California.

Meredith took Eloise to the crafts store in town, and they bought acrylic markers designed for rock painting. The markers claimed to be not only outdoor quality and waterproof but also ecofriendly, which meant what? That when the paint proved not to be really waterproof it wouldn't harm the organic garden?

Bob had buried the chickens in the Dead Pet area by the perennial bed. Meredith knew that somewhere, under the weeds, two dogs, a duck, a gerbil, and a squirrel that had gotten hit by a car, were interred. Their graves were unmarked, though, and Meredith wasn't sure who was where.

"Can we dig them up and find out?" asked Eloise.

"I don't think we want to do that," said Meredith. "We'll just decorate stones for them too."

"Like with flowers?"

"Flowers would be perfect."

"What were their names?"

"One dog was Tully, the other was Prince. The duck was Anna. The gerbil was Uncle Evan's. He'd named him Webster."

"And the squirrel?"

"He didn't have a name. You can make one up for him."

"What did he look like?"

What he had looked like was squished. Meredith had been in high school at the time, but when she saw its bloody corpse in the road she'd run screaming into the house. Bob had buried it near the dogs. "They'll appreciate the proximity," he'd said.

"Grey and furry" is what Meredith told Eloise.

"I'll call him Furry, then," said Eloise.

Meredith wrote down the names of all the animals so Eloise could copy the spelling. Eloise ran out of space for "Harriet" on the stone she'd chosen, and when she reached the *i* she burst into tears.

"Why not use a second stone for the rest of the letters?" said Meredith, and she placed another stone next to the first to show her. "Harriet's really special," she said, "so she deserves two stones." She watched Eloise's face while Eloise, lips clamped, brow furrowed, was trying to decide how to react.

"All right," said Eloise, at last. Thank God, thought Meredith.

Once she had been sold on the idea of a funeral, Eloise got excited about the preparations, just as Meredith had hoped. Eloise wanted to make cookies, so Delia dug out the cookie cutters for her. They didn't have a chicken-shaped one, but they had one with a dog, one with a donkey, and several heart-shaped ones. Eloise covered the cookies with pinkish sprinkles, the safe, organic kind. Eloise made invitations for Meredith, Bob, and Delia, and one for herself. The front had a drawing of a chicken with the word "Harriet" written next to it, and an arrow pointing to the bird.

"Since when do we have funerals for chickens?" Bob asked, but Meredith saw her mother give him a look.

"Would you like some music at the ceremony?" Delia asked. "I can play something on the violin."

"Yes!" said Eloise.

"Something sad or something happy?"

"First something sad. Then something happy," said Eloise, and Meredith felt that was a good indicator that Eloise hadn't suffered irreparable harm.

Eloise wanted flowers, so Meredith drove with her to the supermarket, which had a florist section. She wished Eloise had thought of it when they'd been in town earlier, but didn't say so. Eloise selected a bunch of pink and yellow flowers, and Meredith also indulged her in a helium balloon, which said Happy Birthday, but that was OK because Eloise liked the colors.

"Can we get ice cream?" asked Eloise.

"Doesn't Grandma have some?"

"Just the kind that has prosciutto in it."

"Prosciutto?" Where did Eloise pick up that word?

"Those green nuts."

"Oh, pistachios! Well, all right," said Meredith, "you can pick out something else. But let's be sure to get chocolate too."

As they were heading to the checkout lines, a voice called out, "Meredith, is that you?" Meredith turned around to see a woman with a cart full of groceries and a toddler in the baby seat. It was a friend from high school, well not a friend really—Meredith didn't have many friends then—but a girl who had liked Meredith for no reason Meredith could imagine, in spite of the fact that Meredith had never particularly liked her. Names spun in her mind, but she spotted an embroidered letter *N* decorating the woman's canvas shoulder bag, and she had it just in time.

"Nora!" she said, her voice hitting the same pitch of enthusiasm as the woman's had when calling out her name, to compensate for the delay.

"Are you home for a visit?" asked Nora.

There were several ways to answer that. Meredith settled for a sort of semiaffirmative murmur, and asked "And you?"

Nora laughed. "I live here! Not far from my parents. Free babysitting! You know how it is. I've got four kids."

There was nothing to say except "How nice."

"This is Theo, my youngest," said Nora. Theo stared in an unsettling, adult way.

"This is my daughter, Eloise," said Meredith.

There was an uncomfortable moment when Meredith imagined Nora was about to ask if she had any other children, but Nora said instead, "Hi, Eloise!" and then, noticing the balloon, asked, "Is it your birthday, Honey, or are you going to someone's birthday party?"

Too late to steer her off.

"It's a funeral," said Eloise. "For Harriet and Luna."

"A what?"

"A funeral. That's because they're dead," said Eloise.

Nora looked at Meredith.

"They're chickens," said Meredith.

"They *were* chickens," said Eloise. "But now they're dead. The weasel got them."

"Oh dear," said Nora. "I'm so sorry."

They stood there after that, not saying anything, and were rescued by Theo, who had decided to try climbing out of the baby seat.

"I guess I should be moving along," said Nora. "I haven't even gotten to the cereal yet. If you're here for a while, why don't we get together?"

"That would be nice," said Meredith. Had she really used the word "nice" twice in the past two minutes?

It wasn't until she was paying for the flowers and ice cream she realized that she and Nora had neglected to exchange contact info. Not that she would ever want to get in touch with Nora. But as soon as she'd thought that, she suddenly felt acutely lonely; the supermarket seemed vast and too bright. Aside from Wylie, whom else did she know around here? It might be nice—that word, again!—to have another mother to talk with. She thought that maybe she should run back down to the cereal aisle, and she and Nora would laugh together when they realized their mistake. But maybe it hadn't been a mistake. Maybe Nora hadn't really wanted to see her again. Maybe Meredith had been wrong. Maybe Nora had never really liked her at all.

Agnes was retrieved from the veterinarian's in time for her to be able to attend the ceremony for her less-fortunate colleagues. She had an ugly wound on her neck that Meredith found revolting, but strangely Eloise didn't seem to mind. She cradled Agnes in her arms while Delia played the violin—fortunately it was an unseasonably warm day—and had Meredith hold her only while she laid flowers by the painted stones. Her eulogy consisted of two words: "Goodbye, chickens."

Agnes had to be kept separated from the flock, since chickens were a nasty bunch and would go after an injured member, so she was brought into the house. Fortunately, the dogs had been raised with chickens and were indifferent to them. Bob helped Meredith lug a dog crate to the kitchen from the barn. It had never been used for the dogs because Delia felt it was cruel to imprison them, and it seemed unlikely that Agnes would make use of it either. Eloise preferred to carry Agnes around, which was fine with Agnes, who was a lazy chicken.

"I want her to sleep in my bedroom," said Eloise—Eloise had her own bedroom now, next door to Meredith's—but Meredith quickly said, "Absolutely not," before her mother had an opportunity to say "Yes."

The weather had cooperated for the chicken memorial ceremony, but turned uncooperative the next day. First it rained, then it got cold, then there was freezing rain, followed by sleet. The next morning some wispy bits of snow made tentative appearances.

"We might get some more snow tonight or tomorrow," said Delia while they were eating lunch.

"Unlikely," said Bob.

"I wouldn't say unlikely," said Delia. She tapped her iPad, where she'd just consulted the weather report. "63 percent chance of precipitation."

"Precipitation does not mean snow," said Bob.

"I'd love to have snow," said Meredith. "I've missed it."

"You should have been here in January," said Delia. "We had more than enough snow in January."

"Well, I wasn't here in January, but I'm here now," said Meredith. She turned to Eloise. "Maybe we'll be able to build a snowman!"

"I wouldn't count on it," said Delia.

"Mom! First you predict a snowstorm, then you deny us a snowman?"

"I'm sorry I mentioned snow at all."

"I want to build a snowman!" cried Eloise.

"You shouldn't promise her things," said Delia.

"I'll promise her anything I like," said Meredith. She looked at Eloise again. "Sweetheart, if there isn't enough snow for a snowman, we'll make something else, just as much fun."

"Like what?"

"Like—" Meredith closed her eyes for a second, struggled to come up with something, then said, "How about costumes for the donkeys? We'll have a parade!"

"Can I make a costume for Agnes too?"

"Of course," said Meredith.

After she tucked Eloise in bed that night, Meredith found Delia and Bob reading in the living room.

"Mom, are you OK with babysitting while I go over to Wylie's house for a while?"

"But it's snowing!" said Delia, pointing out the window, where, indeed, some of the lackadaisical snowflakes of the afternoon had gained momentum.

"There are snow tires on the car, aren't there?"

"Yes, of course, but it's been a long time since you've driven in snow."

"I'll be fine, Mom."

Bob looked up from the Sotheby's rug auction catalogue, where he was making notes on a recent sale. "It's like riding a bicycle," he said to Delia. "It comes right back to you." He turned to Meredith. "Though I wouldn't suggest biking anywhere tonight."

"They might not sand till morning—" said Delia.

"You know, Mom, if you don't want to babysit, I won't go anywhere."

"Of course, I'm happy to babysit, anytime—" Delia began.

Meredith cut her off. "Good," she said. "Don't wait up for me."

Meredith kicked the snow off her boots by the door when she came inside Wylie's house, then sat on the bench in the hall and took them off.

"I needed to get out of there," she said when she was settled on Wylie's sofa, glass of wine in hand. "My mother keeps forgetting I'm not a teenager anymore."

"You're not? That's a relief," said Wylie. "Now I don't have to worry about you as jailbait."

"I've never been jailbait!"

"Ha!" said Wylie. He poured himself a glass of wine and sat beside her.

"The trouble with being back home is that I end up acting like a teenager again. I fall right back into that attitude, and I can't stop myself."

"I remember that attitude you cultivated: snarky and sarcastic."

"I didn't cultivate it. It came naturally. And you liked me for it, didn't you?"

"In spite of it," said Wylie. He pushed the pile of magazines to the side and stretched out his legs on the glass coffee table. "So what's your strategy for surviving living there in the future?"

"Get my studio set up in the barn and spend most of my time there."

"Or here?"

"I don't know about that!"

Wylie ran his forefinger around the rim of the wineglass and then took a long sip. "Can you afford to get a place on your own?"

"No problem. For half of what we get for our little three bedroom when we sell it, I could buy a mansion here—maybe not a mansion like The Heap, but something four times as big as what I had in California—and a lot nicer. The real estate market out there is crazy."

"So why not buy a house here, then?"

"I suppose I could, but I don't really want to. There are reasons for living on the farm. I mean that was the plan."

"You had a plan?"

Meredith laughed and poked Wylie in the side. "Of course I had a plan! My plan was to save my mother's farm, introduce my daughter to the pleasures of rural life, and, at the same time, pursue my career as an artist."

"Yeah, right."

"OK, so I didn't exactly have a plan when I started out, but I did have a guiding concept, an image to inspire me."

"Meredith tilling the soil. Eloise on horseback, or donkeyback. Meredith, brush in hand, capturing the light."

"Yup. You nailed it."

"You told me a weasel did in the chickens, so that kind of undermines that farm idyll, doesn't it?"

Meredith gave a little shudder. "Yeah, well it was a reality check, for sure. Nothing like some mangled, bloody chickens to remind you about the downside of rural life."

"But in spite of what happened, you're still here."

"I'm still here."

"Nice for your family."

"So they say. Well, not all of them. Kat's not happy. I've upended her plans to get Mom and Bob to sell off the farm and move into something she calls age appropriate."

"Screw Kat!"

"My sentiment exactly."

Wylie stood up. "Would you like some dinner?"

Meredith laughed. "It's nine o'clock!"

"Some of us dine fashionably late."

"Some of us have a seven-year-old. 'Fashionably late' doesn't work." She followed Wylie into the kitchen. "What do you have against Kat?"

"Me? Nothing. I hardly know her. She always came across as someone who took herself seriously, someone who *decided* it was important to take herself seriously. No nonsense. It's a great defense mechanism."

"Against what?"

"Against the possibility men might view her in a sexual way. You know how it is with some women? They're scared guys will notice they have tits."

"Since when did you get to be a specialist on women?"

"Not a specialist. Just a keen observer." Wylie took a container out of the refrigerator. "I'm heating up some spaghetti alla puttanesca," said Wylie. "Will you have some? I didn't add the anchovies."

"Ooh, puttanesca. Sounds fancy."

"Puttanesca, from *puttana*, meaning whore."

Meredith remembered that now. The recipe in her Italian cookbook had used the term "ladies of the night."

"You made it?"

"Yes, I made it. Why do you sound so surprised?"

"Just didn't know you cooked."

"You think I'm like Evan? Pop a frozen burrito in the microwave and call it dinner?"

Meredith shrugged.

"I actually like to cook."

"OK. I'll risk it then."

Wylie made dressing for the salad and handed Meredith silverware and paper napkins to set the table, and matches to light the candles. The silver candelabra—twice the size of her mother's—had five curving arms to hold candles, and one in the center. No doubt a Bennet-Hopkins relic from the dining room in The Heap. The dogs' silver water bowl was probably a serving bowl from there too. The napkins were cocktail sized and had *W*'s embossed on them.

"These napkins are for martinis, Wylie, not spaghetti."

"Someone gave me a pack of them. I'm using them up."

"Even so."

Wylie turned the two napkins Meredith had laid on the table upside down so they were *M*'s rather than *W*'s. "Better?" he asked.

Funny that their initials were the reverse of each other that way. Meredith turned Wylie's back right side up, so there was an *M* and a *W*. "We'll need at least three per person, judging from that sauce," she said.

The dinner was surprisingly good, and there was a diminutive carrot cake for dessert.

"A freebie from a photo shoot," said Wylie. She'd forgotten for a moment that he photographed food for a living. "Want some coffee now or later?"

"I'm kind of full now," said Meredith, "so maybe later."

They carried their plates over to the kitchen counter. She looked outside the window. The snow had picked up. She should think about going, but she wasn't ready to leave.

"Another glass of wine?"

That might be a mistake. But so what. "Sure," she said. It was a good wine, probably expensive. She didn't care about pedigree—that had been Josh's department—she just liked wine that tasted good, and "fine wines" didn't necessarily taste better. It was like that, too, with violins. Their value was based on the name of the maker, not necessarily their sound. She settled on the sofa and took the throw that was folded over the sofa back and spread it on her lap.

"Cold?" asked Wylie.

"It takes a while to adapt after years of exile in California."

"I'll make a fire."

Wylie's woodstove was sleek and modern, not like the hefty, old-fashioned ones at the farm.

"It's got a special low-emission catalytic converter," said Wylie. "Heats the whole house. Evan got me into these stoves when I was renovating this place."

"Sounds like him."

Wylie got the fire going and laid the big leather gloves by the hearth. He took more time doing it than necessary, placing them carefully side by side, his back to her. He sat down beside her again, but it was a few moments before he said anything.

"I asked Evan if he thought you were going back to Josh."

"What did he say?"

"He said no, he didn't think so."

"Did he say why?" Meredith was afraid to ask—afraid that Evan might have talked about her, afraid she'd lose her trust to confide in him, and if she didn't have Evan, whom would she have?—but she asked anyway.

"No. Want to tell me?"

"Not something I want to talk about now."

"That's OK," said Wylie. He got up and poked at the logs in the fire. They didn't need poking, but he did it anyway. He picked up his wineglass when he sat down, but he didn't take a sip. "Are you going back to Josh?" he asked.

"That's not my plan."

"Are you still in love with him?"

"In love?"

"Semantics. Do you still love him?"

It wasn't just semantics. "In love" would be an easy "no." "Love?" That was harder. "In love" was a rare and ephemeral state of being. It was exclusive and canceled out everything else. "Love," on its own without the "in," was more substantial and general. It was also more complicated. It could coexist with a lot of other feelings. Even hate.

"No," said Meredith. She wanted to say the word, wanted to hear herself say it out loud.

"You did once, though, right? I mean you married him."

"Yeah, sure. At least I thought I did."

"What about him, does he love you?"

"Did once. At least I thought he did."

"But then—?"

"Hey, you want the whole sad history?"

"Only if you want to tell it," said Wylie.

"Maybe sometime, but I'll take a pass tonight." She wanted to be here, in this room, watching this fire. She didn't want to be thinking about Josh, about having once loved him—wondering if she ever really did, wondering if he had ever really loved her. But she couldn't help asking Wylie, "What about you? Are you still in love with Nicole?"

"No way! Kind of a mistake, the whole thing."

"She's remarried, right?"

"Evan tell you?"

Meredith nodded.

"Nice to know he's been keeping you informed, so you don't have to rely on gossip."

"I never rely on gossip."

Wylie put on some music, and Meredith leaned back against the sofa. She didn't usually like jazz, but it was OK to listen to it now. It was slow and meandering. The kind of music that was fine for watching a fire. When she listened to classical music—even now, years after she'd given up playing—she thought about what the composer was up to, anticipated what was coming next. Jazz was more like the sounds of nature—water rushing in the stream, wind stirring the pines, squirrels foraging in the leaves—she just let it happen.

She and Wylie didn't talk, just sat shoulder to shoulder, letting the music find its way, letting the logs settle down next to each other, close, but with enough space so the flames could creep between them, circle around.

After a while, Wylie got up to add more logs to the woodstove. He flipped on the outdoor lights and looked outside. "The snow's really picked up," he said. He sat back down beside her. "You're welcome to spend the night here if you like."

"Thanks, but I don't think that would be a good idea."

"Too soon?"

It wasn't too soon, not really. In some ways it felt as if it was something that might have happened—perhaps even *should* have happened—a long time before. But what she said was "I'm sorry, Wylie, but I'm not there yet."

Wylie tilted his head and studied her. His face had a contemplative, almost-sad look, a way she hadn't seen him before. "I don't think I'm there yet either."

"Are you just saying that to make me feel more comfortable, or do you really feel that way?"

"Some of both, I guess."

She wasn't sure if she believed him. But maybe she did. It was OK, either way. "I guess I should be going, then."

"You OK driving?"

"I think so," she said. She hadn't had that much to drink, had she? Mostly she was just tired. It was that soporific fire and the music, soporific too. She looked at her cell phone. "Shit, it's 12:45."

"I'll help you clean off your car."

When she stepped outside Meredith was surprised by how much snow had fallen, was falling still. The snowflakes were plump and ungainly, oversized like the artificial snow in a TV Christmas special. Her car was entirely engulfed. And where had the wind come from? There hadn't been any wind when she got here. How long ago was that? Just a few hours.

Wylie found the snow scraper in the back of the car. "Start up the engine and turn on the heater," he said. "I'll work on the outside."

The snow was fluffy, rather than icy, so it wasn't hard to sweep off, but it was coming down so fast and so densely Wylie could barely keep up with it. The windshield wipers struggled to keep the windshield clear.

Wylie came around to the driver's side of the car and thumped on the window. Meredith tried to open it, but it was stuck. She had to open the car door to hear him properly.

"You know, Meredith, I don't like the idea of you driving back in this. The plows haven't come up this way."

"I don't have any choice, do I?"

"It might be wise to stay here."

"I need to go," said Meredith.

"It won't have to be anything, your staying over. I'll sleep upstairs, you'll sleep downstairs."

"That's not the problem. I need to be back. I really do. Goodnight, Wylie. And thank you for dinner."

Wylie leaned in the car and kissed her goodbye. Snow fell from his hair onto her shoulders. "Text me when you get back."

"Will do," said Meredith, and she slammed the car door. She felt much more alert now. She felt fine about driving. Wylie stood to the side of the snow-covered driveway, and Meredith started to back up into the turnaround. The wheels spun. She went forward again, then put the car into reverse, but this time she got no farther and the wheels spun more. Wylie ran around and tapped on her window.

"You're just digging yourself in. Try turning more sharply."

She went forward, then pulled back around too quickly and her back tires must have gone off the paved part of the driveway and they sank into a drift. Now she couldn't go back or forward. Wylie tried pushing, while she accelerated, but the car didn't budge. He came around again and opened the car door.

"This isn't working. I think you're going to have to stay here tonight. We'll get you hauled out in the morning."

"I can't stay, Wylie. I have to get back for Eloise."

"Your mother will take good care of her."

"She'll wake up, and I won't be there in the morning, and she'll be scared."

"Your mother will explain."

"It's not the same. Eloise expects me to be there. She needs to be able to trust that I'll be there. Her whole life has been torn apart. I have to be there for her."

Meredith fell against the steering wheel. She hadn't cried like this in so long—hadn't cried like this when she left Josh and her home and everything behind, hadn't cried like this even when she lost the baby.

Wylie knelt in the snow beside the car seat, and she unbuckled her seat belt and turned so she could lean against his chest. He let her cry until she was exhausted with crying.

"We'll take my truck," he said. "It will do OK in the snow. I'll drive you home, and we'll deal with your mother's car tomorrow." He took her arm and helped her out of the car. His truck was in the garage. It had no snow on it at all, but it was even colder inside the cab than it was outdoors. Her fingers were too cold to get the seat belt to click in, so Wylie leaned over and did it for her.

There wasn't a single other car on the road. It was hard to tell where the road had been. The snow had obliterated everything. Wylie drove slowly, but the snowflakes flew vertically towards them, attacking the windshield. It made her dizzy to watch them, but she couldn't not watch them.

When they reached the house, Wylie pulled close to the side door and waited until she got inside. Ralph didn't stir as she came in. Juno looked up, thumped her tail twice, and went back to sleep.

The lights were on in the living room. Delia was sitting in her soft armchair, slumped to the side, her feet propped up on the hassock. Her book had fallen from her hands. She had obviously tried to wait up for Meredith, though Meredith had told her not to, but had fallen asleep. Meredith wondered if it was kinder to wake her to let her know she'd gotten back all right, or kinder to let her sleep. She should have called her mother when it got late, but she hadn't gotten to it. It wasn't that she was deliberately inconsiderate, but that she hadn't been paying attention to the time, and hadn't been thinking about her mother and how she was no doubt worrying as the snow got worse. She didn't want her mother to be waiting up for her and didn't want her to be worrying, but the truth was, she didn't have the emotional energy to take her mother's feelings into account right now. She had Eloise to worry about. And herself. That was already too much. The small light was on in the hallway, enough light so Meredith could make her way upstairs. She was about to go up the stairs, then stepped back to the doorway to the living room to turn off the lights. She reached to flip off the light switch, but stood there for a moment, first. Her mother—with her head flopped forward, her chin pressed against her chest, her left hand dangling off the armrest—looked like a child sleeping.

"I'm home," Meredith said, and when her mother didn't wake up, she said, again, more loudly, "I'm home," then added, "I'm sorry, Mom."

Delia stirred and sat up.

"I made it home, Mom," said Meredith, and she ran upstairs.

In the morning, after they'd had breakfast, Meredith went to play in the snow with Eloise. Wylie said that once the roads were cleared, he'd come by in his truck to pick her up so she could get her car. But the plow hadn't ventured out to their part of town yet, and the roads were hidden under the snow, as white and untraveled as the fields around them. Meredith loved this feeling of being cut off, of being in this white, timeless place.

Eloise helped her make paths in the snow for the donkeys. Falstaff didn't mind just tromping through the snow, but the donkeys, especially Clementine, were more finicky. They'd go back and forth in one narrow path all day rather than venture into untouched snow, so Meredith and Eloise stomped trails from the stable to the far fence and back around.

She and Eloise were building a snowperson when Bob came out and started trudging towards the barn. He was not an outdoor person and was fond of describing winter as an unfortunate mistake of nature.

"Hi, Grandpa," Eloise cried out, and before Meredith could stop her, she'd made a snowball and thrown it at him. Fortunately it landed several feet in front of him.

Bob stood looking at her for a moment; then he bent to scoop up snow for a snowball. "My turn to get you!" he said. Eloise shrieked—Meredith couldn't quite tell if it was delight or delight laced with fear—and bobbed up and down. Bob's snowball went far afield and hit Meredith in the shin.

"Guess I'll need to practice later," he said. He gave Meredith a little salute and continued on his way.

"Time to make snow angels!" said Meredith. She feared Bob's humoring of Eloise would be short lived. She lay back in the snow and showed Eloise how to fan her arms and legs, and how to stand carefully so the angel's dress was not rumpled. Eloise made a snow angel beside her, so their wings brushed each other.

"Make another one, Mommy!" said Eloise.

So Meredith flopped back down in the snow. She lay there before moving her arms and legs. She had forgotten how wonderful it was just to let yourself go, to fall into the soft whiteness. She looked up at the sky. It was impossibly blue, with clouds that looked like snow, themselves. Clouds imitating snow or snow imitating clouds.

Maybe this was what was wrong with California. There was no snow.

Josh was someone who didn't mind the lack of snow. He'd grown up in California, so he never missed it. But she'd missed it. She moved her arms up and down, moved her legs side to side; then she pressed deeper into the snow. For the first time she felt a kind of certainty that she had hoped to find, had skittered near but not quite achieved. And now she did. She felt as if she could sink right down through the snow into the earth itself. As if she was really home at last, where she was supposed to be.

Now, all that remained was figuring out everything else.

Wylie picked up Meredith the next day to go get her car. The inside of his truck was warm, and there was the comforting smell of the coffee in the mug in the cupholder between them. Meredith leaned back against the headrest.

"I heard you're heading up to Evan's place tomorrow, " Wylie said, as he pulled out of the driveway.

"Yup, can't wait," said Meredith. "I really need to get away from here."

"What happened?"

"Nothing new. Just the same old. More so. I'd like a T-shirt that says: I AM NOT A TEENAGER ANYMORE."

Wylie laughed. "A lot of people would like a shirt like that. You could make a fortune selling them on Etsy."

"I'll keep that in mind."

"I was wondering if you'd like me to give you a ride up to Evan's."

"I'm all set," said Meredith. "My mother's impounded the Bobmobile for me. Apparently the tires on his car are better than hers."

"Thought you might like to have someone do the driving for you."

Meredith sat straight up and turned around to look at Wylie. "Wylie, you're talking to someone who successfully navigated the LA freeway. I can certainly manage the back roads around here."

"It's a long trip, so just thinking you might want some company—I know you've got Eloise with you, so I'd keep her entertained if you want to do the driving. And I wouldn't be encroaching on the family reunion. I'd hang out with Jay when we got there."

"Jay Rosen?"

"Yeah."

"What's he doing there?"

"He works there. He's the bike guy."

"If Evan employs all his old friends, it's a wonder he stays in business."

"Evan's doing just fine. What? You want him to sell out to some chain like EMS?"

"The two of you always stick up for each other, don't you?"

"Someone has to," said Wylie.

They were both quiet for a while. When they got to Wylie's place, he pulled up next to Delia's car, but he didn't open the door of the truck right away.

"Sure you don't want me to come along?"

For a minute Meredith imagined driving along the road with Eloise and Wylie—the three of them singing dumb songs like "A Hundred Bottles of Beer on the Wall," or more Eloise-appropriate songs like "Baby Beluga"—like one of those happy sitcom families. But maybe she needed to do this trip with Eloise on her own.

"No, I'm good," she said, and in response to the look on Wylie's face she reached out for his hand. "Another time."

He gave her fingers a little squeeze. "Sure," he said.

"Maybe we can get together Sunday."

"I've got to meet a client in New York. But soon, OK?"

She'd almost forgotten that about Wylie—the fact that he had a career, and he had to fit her in around other things—that he wasn't always just there. "OK," she said.

When they got to Wylie's house, they worked together to clean the snow off Delia's car and dig it out from the snowbank. In the sunlight, the snow, which had seemed so treacherous before, seemed tame now. Meredith was able to back out on her second try. She lowered the car window halfway. "Hey, Wylie, did Evan put you up to it?"

"Put me up to what?"

"Offering to drive me up to his place."

Wylie stepped closer to the car. "Why do you want to know?"

Meredith lowered the car window all the way. "Just wondered."

"He does look out for you, Merry."

"Yeah, I know that. But was this his idea?"

Wylie shrugged. "Not exactly."

"I sort of thought so," Meredith said. She leaned against the window frame, and snow stuck to her hair and the side of her face. She was not surprised when Wylie reached out and gently brushed it off.

"Safe travels," he said.

At breakfast the next morning Eloise informed Bob, "When we visit Uncle Evan today, I'm going to ride in a canoe."

"In this weather?"

"Eloise, I said there were canoes at Uncle Evan's store," said Meredith. "I said maybe you could *sit* in one, but—"

"OK. *Maybe* I'll ride in one. Are you coming, too, Grandpa?"

"I don't think so."

"Then I'll make you a card." Eloise went to the closet in the hall and returned with paper and colored markers.

"Eloise, finish your cereal!" said Meredith.

"I will. Later."

"There isn't much later. We're leaving soon."

"I'm doing this now," said Eloise, and Meredith recognized her own voice from the past. No point arguing with Little Meredith! She smiled and let it go.

Eloise showed her the card when she was done making it. On the front of the folded paper she'd written: FOR GRANDPA FROM ELOISE. Inside she'd drawn a heart and a chicken wearing a large hat. She presented the card to Bob.

"What's this for?" he asked.

"Because we're going away. So you won't be lonely."

"I see." He pointed to the chicken. "And what's this?"

"It's Agnes."

"Isn't she accompanying you today?"

Eloise turned to Meredith. "Can Agnes come?"

"No," said Meredith. She turned to Bob. "Thanks a lot!"

"Are you going to be back for dinner?" Delia asked.

"Not sure," said Meredith.

"I'll pack you some lunch."

"We'll be fine, Mom. If Evan doesn't have anything, we can go out to eat."

"I don't think there are any decent restaurants around there—"

"They'll manage, Delia," said Bob. "They're not going to the Arctic."

But when they left, Delia handed Meredith a stuffed grocery bag.

"I said we didn't need anything, Mom!"

"I made sandwiches for lunch, just in case," said Delia. "And there's some food for Evan, and snacks for Eloise for the car."

"We don't need snacks, Mom, it's less than two hours from here."

"*I* want snacks!" said Eloise.

"Of course you do," said Delia. She hugged Eloise and kissed her several times.

"Enough!" said Meredith. "We're going away for just a day!" She hurried out of the kitchen before her mother could attempt to embrace her too.

It was a week since it had snowed, and the snow had melted in the field. In the yard by the barn, where Falstaff and the donkeys liked to stand around, there was now just mud. But as Meredith drove north, the landscape whitened, and snow banked the road. It felt wonderful to get away from the house.

The plow had left piles of snow at the sides of the parking lot of Green Hills Outfitters, but the snow by the entrance door was slush. Eloise stomped in the puddles.

"Enough!" said Meredith.

When they went inside, Evan hugged Eloise and lifted her in the air. When he started to swing her around, her feet kicked a revolving rack of gloves. He set her down and gave Meredith a big hug and lifted her off her feet too.

"Evan!" she cried out, laughing.

The store was small—no bigger than when Meredith had seen it years before—and it seemed even more packed with stuff: skis, boots, bikes, camping and mountain-climbing gear. She put her arm around Evan and gave him a hug. "A boy surrounded by his favorite toys," she said.

Ruby, the black lab dozing on the dog bed by the counter, had been a puppy when Meredith had last seen her. She was grey around the muzzle now. She lifted her head, and her tail beat a slow thump, thump, but she didn't get to her feet.

"Does Ruby sleep here at night?" asked Eloise.

"No," said Evan. "At night she goes home with Jay. She's really his dog."

Jay, who'd been working in the back, came out to say hello. He still had his fuzzy reddish beard, but the hair on his head was thinner now.

"How are you doing?" he asked Meredith.

"Just fine!" she said. "How are you doing?"

"Your brother works me hard, but I'm surviving."

"Are you the friend with the dragon?" asked Eloise.

"Dragon?" Jay looked at Evan.

"That's a different friend," said Evan. "And we'll see it next time you come. OK?"

"OK," said Eloise. She waited a moment, then asked, "Uncle Evan, why don't you have a dog of your own?"

"I travel a lot, so I'm not always around to take care of it."

"You could take it with you."

"Not the places Uncle Evan goes," said Meredith.

"Want to see what we've got in the dog department?" asked Evan. He brought them over to the other side of the store. Meredith picked up some rubber dog boots and flipped the tag so she could read the price.

"Seriously?" she asked Evan.

"You'd be surprised what people will spend to get the best for their dogs."

"Can we get backpacks for Juno and Ralph?" Eloise asked.

"Can you imagine trying to get Ralph to wear a backpack!" asked Meredith, laughing.

"Juno would wear one," said Eloise.

"Then I'll bring one for her when I come to visit next time," said Evan, "and we'll go for a hike. Which one do you like?"

Eloise picked one that was bright orange.

"The deluxe model, of course!" said Evan.

"What are you going to put in the pouches?" asked Meredith. She was laughing again.

"You'll see!" said Eloise. "Where are the boats?"

"Not the season for them yet, so they're in storage," said Evan.

"Can I see them?"

"Another time," said Meredith, but Evan said, "Let's go and check them out in the warehouse."

The building in back was a new addition. It was cold and lifeless. Evan flipped on the lights, and they buzzed, as if they'd been holding back for a long time. The canoes were stacked against the walls, and when Evan started to pull one down, Meredith said, "You don't have to do this, Evan."

"Hey, why not?" He gave Eloise a paddle and showed her how to use it. "Imagine you're in the water!" he said. "I'll take you out on the lake by my house, sometime, so you can paddle for real."

"Can we go now?"

"It's frozen now. People aren't canoeing, they're ice fishing."

"Ice fishing? Can I see?"

"Sure! Why don't we grab some sandwiches, Merry, and go to my place for lunch. I can take you out on the ice."

"Mom has already provided us with sandwiches. Not to mention food to bring to you."

"Big surprise," said Evan. "She thinks I'll starve on my own. She doesn't believe I can cook anything for myself."

"Did you know that Wylie's quite a chef?" said Meredith.

"I hear you've been seeing each other," said Evan.

"Not really—just hanging out a little."

"I thought that was in the cards."

"What cards?" asked Eloise.

"Just means something that was likely to happen," said Evan.

Meredith had been to Evan's house only once since he'd bought it. It had been built as someone's vacation cabin, and he hadn't done much to change it. The room downstairs had a little kitchen along one wall and sliders opening onto a deck. There was a bedroom upstairs with a mattress on the floor. Even Eloise couldn't stand in the sides because the roof sloped down. Meredith flopped down on the mattress. The window went from ceiling to floor, so she could look out across the lake, which was all white, as far as she could see. She could imagine why Evan would want to wake up here and watch morning come across the lake.

"What does Mom think of this place?" she asked.

"The one time she came out here, she climbed only halfway up the stairs and looked around, and when she came down she was smiling in that way of hers when she wants you to know how much she loves you and she isn't going to say anything but she sure as hell wishes you'd grow up."

"I am quite familiar with that smile," said Meredith.

"But aren't you grown up?" asked Eloise.

"Not if I can help it!" said Evan.

"Like Peter Pan!"

"Where does she get these things?" Evan asked Meredith.

Delia had made egg-salad sandwiches for their lunch, which unfortunately brought up the subject of the chickens.

"I was sorry I wasn't able to make it to your memorial service, Eloise," said Evan. "But I had to work that day."

"I painted stones for them, and you can see them when you come, but you can't see the flowers because they dried up."

"Agnes, the injured chicken, is now living in the house," said Meredith.

"Bob must love that."

"Oh, he does for sure."

"Can't wait to see Kat's face when she finds out!" said Evan, and he and Meredith started laughing, and Meredith knocked over her bottle of ginger ale. There was no sponge, so she used a pile of paper napkins to wipe it up.

When Evan's phone rang, he looked at it but didn't answer.

"Guess what?" he said. "That was Kat." And he put his phone back in his pocket.

"Wonder what she wants."

Evan shrugged. "Who knows."

"Probably wants to tell you about our tiff," said Meredith.

"What's a tiff?" asked Eloise.

"It's when people argue about something."

"Oh, I thought it was something pink."

Evan laughed and then asked, "What was the gist of it?"

"She's pissed because I've upended her plans to get Mom to trade in the farm for a condo. She thinks I'm going to abandon ship and move back to California after leading Mom to believe we're staying here. I told her we *are* staying. We're here for good."

"Aren't we going back home to California?" asked Eloise.

"Shit!" said Meredith. How had she forgotten she hadn't explained all this to Eloise yet?

"Oh boy," said Evan.

Meredith took Eloise by the arm and tried to get her to sit on her lap, but Eloise pulled away.

"Here's the thing, Sweetheart," she said. "We're staying with Grandma and Grandpa on the farm. It's where we're living now."

"How come?"

"Because Grandma and Grandpa really want us to stay, and they need us to help take care of Clementine and Myrtle and Tulip. And Falstaff. And the chickens."

"I can take Agnes to California with me!"

"No, Sweetie, Agnes is a—a Massachusetts chicken—she wouldn't do well in California." Meredith reached to touch Eloise, but Eloise stepped back. "That's why I took you to see your new school. And you liked it. Remember?"

"I liked my old school."

"You liked the playground at the new school, right? That purple slide that went round and round?"

"Is Daddy going to come here too?"

"No," said Meredith. "Daddy is going to stay in California. And then he's going on a trip."

"Oh."

Meredith patted her lap. "Come, Sweetheart," she said. But Eloise wasn't ready to sit on her lap.

"How about we go out on the lake and see what the ice fishermen have been up to?" Evan said. Eloise let him take her hand.

Meredith blew out her breath.

The lake was huge and perfectly flat. Wind blew across and stirred up the surface so it almost looked like it was snowing.

"Are there polar bears?" asked Eloise.

"Not here," said Evan. "But there are deer and foxes and coyotes. You don't see them often, but I know they're around because they leave their tracks."

"What's that?" asked Eloise. She pointed to a tent far out in the middle of the lake.

"That's where the ice fishermen go to get out of the wind. They aren't there now, but let's check out some of the holes they've drilled nearer to my house." He took Eloise's hand.

"Don't go too close!" cried Meredith.

"It's OK, Merry, it's almost the end of the season, but the ice is still solid."

The ice did seem solid, but you could never tell. Meredith looked out across the lake. It was desolate, not a single living creature in sight. And not a single color, anywhere out there. Eloise's bright-pink jacket was like a color that hadn't been invented yet.

"Damn," said Evan, "there goes my phone." He pulled it out and looked at the screen. "Kat again."

"Maybe you should answer it," said Meredith.

"I don't feel like talking to her now—rather, I don't feel like listening to her. If it's anything important, she'll text."

"How do the fish swim in the ice?" asked Eloise.

"They don't," said Evan. "They swim in the water that's under the ice. The fishermen drill a hole and drop a line down, with bait. Then when a fish bites, they pull it up through the hole."

Eloise lay down on the ice and looked in the hole. "Where's the water?" she asked.

"It's frozen over," said Evan, "with a layer of new, thinner ice." He poked at the bottom of the hole with a stick, and when the ice broke through, he swished the stick around to enlarge the hole.

"Can you see the water now?" he asked.

"Yes!" said Eloise. She started to put her finger down, but Meredith shouted, "Eloise, no. You'll get your glove all wet."

Evan had his phone out again. "It's a text from Kat."

"Everything OK?"

Evan was scowling as he read it.

"What's up?"

"Something about Mom not being there when she called, and Bob finally letting her know that Mom had gone off to—" He looked up at Meredith.

"What?"

"Kat thought I should know that—"

Meredith grabbed the phone from Evan's hand and read the text. "What the fuck!" she screamed.

"Maybe it's nothing—"

"Nothing? Why do you think she'd be going there."

"I don't know, Merry."

"Well, give one good guess!"

"Just calm down, Merry."

"I can't believe this," cried Meredith. "I can't believe she'd do this."

~

Eloise wanted to ask what it was that her grandmother had done, but neither Meredith nor Evan noticed her. It was as if they'd forgotten she was there. She poked more with the stick Evan had used, and made the hole even bigger. She took off her glove and lowered her hand into the hole. Would the fish nibble at her fingers? The water was so cold it burned.

When they got back to the farm that night, her grandmother wasn't there.

"You shouldn't have let her go!" Meredith screamed at Bob, but Bob just said, "I'm not in charge of your mother. She does what she wants to do."

"Well the least you could have done was let me know she was planning on going!"

"I didn't know she was actually going to leave."

"I just can't believe this," said Meredith. "I just can't fucking believe this." She brought Eloise upstairs to bed, but she didn't read her a story. Instead she put on an audiobook, *Ramona the Brave*, that Eloise had already heard on the plane when they'd come here, but she didn't say anything because Meredith was so angry. Eloise hugged Moosie to her. She wondered where her grandmother had gone and why it made her mother so angry. Was it because her mother was afraid her grandmother was never coming back?

13

Delia was buoyed by her sense of purpose on her ride to the airport, but the doubts that she had been keeping at bay began to stir as soon as the plane loosened its hold on the ground, and it was too late for her to call off the trip. She'd always been a fear-filled flier, but she'd brave anything if she was doing something to help one of her children, and she was stoic while the plane—somewhat shakily—gained its cruising altitude. She'd hoped to distract herself with conversation with the man sitting to her left, but he quickly immersed himself in a sheaf of papers. He was making notes in the margins with a red pen. A professor, no doubt—bald, with a fringe of grey hair, and tufts of hair sprouting from his ears.

The terrain below was a reassuring patchwork of farmland. Somewhere, down there—maybe even right below her!—was her own white house and red barn. Reduced by distance so small they would be invisible were her chickens, dogs, donkeys, husband, and even Falstaff, who was fifteen hands high and weighed half a ton. Thinking about the animals was comforting, but the thought of Bob was upsetting. She hadn't asked for his help with travel plans because she didn't want him implicated in what she was doing. He was going to have to deal with Meredith when she got home from Evan's and learned about Delia's trip. He'd been resigned in the face of her determination, and when she was getting ready to leave had said only, "Oh, Lili, I wish you weren't doing this."

"What kind of a mother would I be," she'd asked him, "if I didn't do everything I could to help one of my children?"

"I'm not convinced this will help Merry—" he began, but she'd cut him off.

"I'm aware of that, Bob, but I'm going to at least try. It's the best I can do."

"Merry won't be happy about it. She's not someone who likes to accept help from anyone—and especially not from her mother." The look he gave her was sobering, but she'd done a good job of convincing herself of the necessity of her mission, and said, "It's for the best, you'll see." Then with her hands on his cheeks she had pulled his face down close so she could kiss him full on.

As clouds began obscuring the landscape, the misgivings that Delia had been struggling to ignore kept growing. In spite of an Agatha Christie mystery with a tantalizing surfeit of suspects, and a glass of Malbec that had survived the indignity of being canned, she confronted the possibility that Bob was right that Merry would not appreciate her help. By the time they'd crossed the Mississippi, the great divide of the country, the sense of purpose that had fueled her initially abandoned her completely. A series of air pockets left her stomach queasy and her heart pounding. If the plane suddenly dropped out of the sky and plunged to the ground, it would be a judgment, and Merry's grief at her mother's demise would be offset by her conviction that Delia's punishment was deserved.

When the plane started jittering and the "fasten your seat belt" notice came on again, Delia tapped the arm of the man sitting beside her, and was reassured when he turned towards her with a kindly expression on his face.

"Excuse me," she said, "but would you mind very much holding my hand?"

He capped his pen, clipped it to his papers, and took her hand. "No problem," he said, and he chuckled. "As long as you have your husband's approval." Was there something about her that projected "married," or was it just the customary ring on the finger of the hand she had extended?

"For hand-holding during turbulence, yes. Though not, I'm afraid, for the trip itself."

"Oh? Why's that?"

"I'm going to deal with a family matter. And he would prefer I not interfere. But I'm—"

"The interfering type?"

Delia had been going to say that she was concerned, rather than "interfering," but she laughed and said, "Well, I suppose so. But the good kind."

"You really think there's a good kind of interference?"

"If your intentions are good."

The man actually laughed. "The road to discord is paved with good intentions."

"I'm hoping to avoid discord, but I'm trying to help my daughter. Do you have any children?"

"Two. Grown up, so the word 'children' doesn't quite apply."

"Then you might understand—I mean my daughter is grown up, but—"

"Still requires your help?"

"Maybe not *requires* but—"

"Appreciates it?"

"Actually, I'm not sure about that," Delia admitted.

"But you're going to help her anyway, whether she wants you to or not."

"If you put it that way!"

"How would you put it?"

Delia paused for a moment. She couldn't come up with a way to put it that made it sound OK. "Sometimes our children don't appreciate our efforts at the moment," she offered, "but they do, later."

"A consoling supposition, I suppose. But parents have so much at stake emotionally they're incapable of accurately predicting how their offspring will respond. And if they expect appreciation, they'll be disappointed more often than not. At least that's my opinion."

"Based on personal experience?"

"Personal experience, observation, and the lessons of literature." So, he was most likely an English professor.

"But when you love your child—"

He interrupted her. "There it is, the age-old justification for all sorts of meddling!" He laughed. And to be polite, Delia laughed also. But his words troubled her, and a disconcerting memory from years before, when Evan was a little boy, came to her just then. She'd been sitting with some other mothers on benches in the park, watching their children play. It was a rough outdoor space, with rock outcroppings and low-branching trees. The other mothers were chatting, not really watching their kids, but Delia was the kind of mother who rarely took her eyes off her own child. The boys—yes, they'd all been boys—had broken off sticks from dead branches on the ground and brandished them as they engaged in battle. They were climbing on the rocks, shouting, and thrusting their weapons at each other's faces. Delia had turned to the other mothers, but they were oblivious to the dangers. Delia had leaped to her feet and run across to the knot of kids and snatched the sticks from their hands.

"I'm confiscating these," she'd told them. "They're not safe to play with."

One red-faced boy, who'd clung to his stick before Delia wrested it from his hand, screamed out, "Mommy!" And as Delia pulled Evan away, the group of mothers rose in unison, blinking in surprise and outrage. She'd flung the sticks at their feet. "You can let your children poke each other's eyes out," she'd said, as she'd dragged Evan away. He'd been mute with rage. Years later he'd asked, "How could you *do* something like that?" And she'd answered, truthfully, that it wasn't something she'd thought through; it was just her instinctive, natural defense of her child.

The seat belt sign turned off as the plane regained its solidity. "OK now?" he asked, and he released her hand.

"Yes, thank you so much."

"Let me know if you require similar assistance at landing."

"Thanks, but I should be all right. Once an airport's in sight I figure if the plane's in trouble, there's a runway to land on and a waiting rescue crew."

"A comforting thought. I'm Leonard, by the way, in case you want to know whom you've been holding hands with." *Whom.* An English professor for sure.

"Delia," she said.

Delia texted Bob to let him know she'd arrived intact, but waited to call him till she got to the hotel. The lobby decor was a style now called "mid-century modern," though it had been simply "modern" when she'd been a girl. Her room had a dizzying pattern of parallelograms on the carpet and a dizzying view of the airport and the city beyond. She kicked off her shoes and plunged onto one of the two queen-sized beds. The white sheets and blanket were pulled tight as a drumskin. Had a human being actually managed to make the bed this way?

"I'm here," she told Bob. "They had a shuttle bus from the airport."

"Everything OK?"

"As OK as I can be when I'm in a room eight stories up that overlooks runways and highways and has a window that doesn't open. How are things there?"

"Kat found out where you were going and called Evan, who told Merry."

"How did Kat find out?"

Bob sighed. "She called to talk with you, and I put her off, but she was persistent. You know Kat—"

"So you told her?"

"What did you want me to do? Say you'd gone off on a vacation to a spa—for massage, meditation, exfoliation, whatever the hell they do at places like that?"

"No, but—"

"But what? You didn't give me a script. What did you expect me to say? You took off and left me to handle the fallout from all three of your kids."

Bob rarely expressed anger this way. Delia rolled to her side. She wished she could be there with him in person, so she could touch him, so it wouldn't be just their voices. "I'm sorry, Sweetheart," she said. "I was so intent on getting out of there, I had to just rush ahead and not think about it too much, or I would have lost courage. I'm afraid I just left you with the mess. Was Merry upset?"

Bob gave a laugh. "What do you think?"

"I'm so sorry."

"She's angry with me, as well. She thinks I should have stopped you."

"Oh, Bob!"

"She tried calling you, but you didn't answer."

"I can't talk with her now."

"You'll have to talk with her, Lili. You can't not talk with her!"

"I will, when I'm home. In person. But I don't have the stamina for it now. And I'm not answering calls from Kat or Evan. Just you."

"For that I should be grateful?"

"Oh, Bob, I am sorry, but I had to do this. What else could I do?"

There was silence at Bob's end of the phone.

"What else was there?"

"You really want an answer to that?"

"If you're just going to tell me I should stand by and do nothing and watch Merry get hurt and watch Eloise's life turned upside down, and not make an attempt to get Josh to do what he needs to do to—"

"Not my choice of words, but that would be the general intent."

It felt cold in the room. Delia laid her phone on the stack of pillows and yanked at the covers to free them. Bob's voice, muffled, called out, "Delia?"

She crawled under the covers and picked up the phone, held it against her cheek. "I'm here. I needed to get into bed. I was cold."

"Cold?"

"The air-conditioning's on too high."

"I'm sure you can figure out how to adjust it."

"I'm not sure I can figure out anything."

"You're just tired."

"Oh, Bob. What have I gotten myself into?"

"I don't know, Sweetheart. I tried to dissuade you. But I wasn't very successful."

That was true. Bob was a gentle dissuader, unlike Phil, her husband number one, who'd go to battle over things he didn't like her doing, things both small and large.

"Do you still love me?"

"Dumb question, but I'm afraid I do."

"And do you forgive me for this?"

"I'm not the one you should be asking."

"Will she?"

"For future peace in this household—if this *is* a household—I certainly hope so."

It had been years since Delia had been apart from Bob at night, and she didn't want to end their conversation, but although it was only 9:45 LA time, it was after midnight her time and Bob's time, and he had to get up in the morning to let the dogs out and feed the animals. The distance from Bob seemed crueler because of the time difference. They were not only apart, but time itself had separated them. When she ended the call, she felt as alone as she ever had since she'd been a small child. What came back to her, with frightening clarity, was a night when her parents went off to a concert and left her home with a new babysitter who was studying at the dining room table and wouldn't read her a goodnight story or kiss her goodnight. Her bedroom was at the end of the long, dark hallway, and she'd had to walk all the way back there alone. When she passed the door to her parents' bedroom she'd looked in; the bed was neatly made with the bedspread you weren't allowed to sit on, and her mother's perfume bottles were all arranged in their semicircle on the dresser top, and it was so still and silent she wondered if maybe they would never come back, if maybe they were dead.

There was an abundance of white towels in the hotel bathroom, and an abundance of hot water when Delia filled the tub. She unwrapped one small soap and scooped up the other soaps and the diminutive bottles of shampoo and lotion to bring back for Eloise. She sank into the water and closed her eyes and tried not to think about what she'd gotten herself into. But that was impossible. Her plan had been to call Josh in the morning, say she was in town and would like to drop by to speak with him when he came home from work. But what exactly would she say? She didn't particularly like Josh, but since he was her daughter's husband and the father of her beloved granddaughter, she'd always treated him with conscientious courtesy. But she'd never talked with him about anything important or anything personal. She'd never really talked with him about anything at all. It was a mystery to her why Merry had married him. He was a man who didn't like animals, the outdoors, music, or art—all things Merry loved. He had few hobbies, except for running, which he did in a kind of determined, passionless way. He seemed incapable of creativity or spontaneity, two things Merry excelled at.

"I'm afraid she's marrying him as a kind of default," she'd told Bob before the wedding. "She decided it's time to get married, and he's the guy she happened to be dating at the time."

"You're forgetting sex."

Was Josh sexy? Perhaps, if your taste ran to husky men with curly dark hair and crafty eyes. But Merry had dated men of all types. It was better not to think about all of them.

"At least she's marrying someone who has his head on his shoulders and his feet on the floor," said Bob. "So now you can stop worrying about her."

"You think mothers stop worrying about their children once they've attached themselves to a serviceable spouse?"

"Serviceable!" Bob laughed. "Do I qualify?"

"On occasion," said Delia, and she'd kissed his shoulder.

When she got into bed, Delia stayed on the side she would sleep on at home, with Bob. The pillows were all overstuffed. She batted one down best she could and turned off the light. She expected to be worrying about what she was going to say to Josh, but as she lay in bed she realized her anxiety about facing Josh was just a distraction from what was really troubling her. It wasn't the difficulty of her mission that was the problem; it was that she'd taken this up as a mission at all. Even in the optimistic scenario that her meeting with Josh went well, it would certainly damage her fragile relationship with Merry. Her coming here conveyed she didn't respect Merry, that she didn't believe Merry was capable of running her own life. And even if Merry really needed help, was it wise for Delia—uninvited—to jump in to help her? If Delia was, as her seatmate Leonard had suggested, "the interfering type," the fact that her intentions were good wouldn't matter to Merry at all.

The pillow was still too plump, and Delia pushed it to the side and stretched straight out. But the bed felt too flat, and her lower back twinged. She sat up and pounded on the pillow, then lay down again.

She should have listened to Bob. She should have paid attention to her own misgivings, those feeble little warnings she'd managed to ignore. She didn't know what Merry's marriage was really like, didn't know what was behind Merry's decision to leave, and yet she'd rushed in, hoping to help make things work out. She'd acted impulsively, instinctively protective of Merry and Eloise—and hadn't taken a critical look at what she was doing. It was a mistake coming here. The whole thing was a mistake.

Delia got out of bed and went to the window. There were lights everywhere, disrupting the darkness—lights on buildings, highways, cars. The stars didn't have a chance. She longed to be home, to be standing at her open bedroom window, looking out at the sweet darkness, tasting the night air.

An interfering person. That's what Leonard had suggested she was. Yet that's how she'd viewed her own mother. "Stop interfering!" is what she had screamed at her that afternoon, decades before, when her mother had said, "You have three children, Delia. You can't leave your marriage!" And when her mother had offered her sad little smile and said, "It's because I love you," she'd wanted to smack her. Smack the smile. She'd turned and run out of the room, and behind her back she could hear her mother's voice, as she followed close behind her. "Listen to me!" she'd cried. And Delia had flung her head around and shouted, "I'm not going to listen. I can leave Phil if I want to. I'm not staying married to please you!"

"Delia, it's for your own good, believe me, I know," her mother had pleaded.

"You don't know what's good for me! You have no idea!"

"Oh, Delia," her mother had said and shook her head as if an enormous sorrow had befallen her, a sorrow of such magnitude that Delia could not possibly comprehend. Sorrow that Delia was foolish and ignorant, and her mother, in her great wisdom, knew what was best for her, and yet Delia was ignoring her warnings and doing something not only self-destructive, but something that would irreparably harm her three children.

And what had made it worse wasn't her mother's infuriating arrogance, her mother's rectitude, but the fact that there was a small part of Delia that was afraid her mother was right.

But her mother hadn't been right. It had all worked out in the end. Delia had survived. Her children survived. Her mother had not understood her unhappiness and had not appreciated the courage it had taken her to change the course of her life.

Delia felt shaky now, as if the upper part of her body was off-balance and she might topple over. She pressed her hand against the window frame to steady herself and closed her eyes. Oh, God! Had she not understood Merry's unhappiness? Had she not appreciated the courage it had taken Merry to change the course of *her* life?

Delia stumbled back to bed. She'd call in the morning and see if she could get an earlier flight back home. There was no reason for her to stay here any longer. She couldn't undo the fact that she'd come here, but the sooner she was home, the sooner she could explain, try to make things right.

She thought she would never be able to fall asleep, but she must have because she woke, hours later. Her phone had been turned off, but it had been buzzing and buzzing, a stream of missed calls. She called Bob.

"Evan's trying to reach you," he said. "Call him."

Delia sat up in bed. "Not now, Bob. I'm not ready to talk with Evan."

"He's there, Delia, in the hotel."

"What do you mean he's in the hotel?"

"He's downstairs, in the lobby."

"What!"

"He flew there last night—early this morning—to see you."

"I can't believe it!"

"Well, you better believe it."

"Did Merry send him?"

"I don't know."

"Oh, Bob! What have I done?"

"Just get back to Evan now. I'll talk to you later."

Evan had been waiting in the hotel lobby. Delia had just enough time to throw on some clothes before he was at the door of her room. He set his container of coffee down on the bedside table so he could hug her with both arms.

"What are you doing here, Honey?" she asked.

"What are *you* doing here?"

"First—did you have breakfast yet?"

"Oh, Mom, that's what I love about you. We're in crisis mode, and you're worried about whether I've eaten."

"Crisis mode?"

"Merry's view. But, if you like, we can call it a little family drama."

"Does Merry know you came?"

"Are you kidding? She'd knock my block off. That is after she'd knocked *your* block off."

"So I need to tell you that—"

"Mom, here's the thing. You are a loving, kind, generous mother, but—"

"Thank you, dear, what I have to explain is—"

"Listen, Mom. I love you. Merry loves you. At least there are moments when she does. But in this particular situation you—"

"I understand, Evan, which is why—"

"Mom, *please*, listen!" Evan raised his arms up in the air and waved his hands around, as if he was a schoolkid trying to get called on. "Look, I'm used to not being listened to—I grew up in a house of women—you and two sisters—even the dogs didn't listen to me—of course they didn't listen to anyone, but right now I'd be really happy if you just heard me out."

She could save him the trouble of explaining, but she thought it would be better to let him speak. She sat down on the side of the bed and folded her hands in her lap. And then, because she was afraid that might look like a parody of contrite, she placed her hands at her sides.

"OK. Thank you," said Evan, and he scratched the back of his head in that way he had when he was collecting his thoughts. "So here's my little speech. Merry was a wreck when she heard you were flying out here. I know you meant well, but you don't know the whole story about Merry and Josh, so I decided I better come out and try to head you off. Merry's told me stuff, and I'm not going to lay it on the table, but I thought if I gave you enough of a hint, you'd kind of get what's going on, and you'd see why meeting with Josh was a dumbass—" Evan caught himself, then continued, "wasn't a great thing to do. So here I am, trying to do some damage control. That's the short version."

"You are a sweet big brother," said Delia. "But you don't really need to head me off—"

"Somebody does!"

Delia shook her head and patted the side of the bed, next to her. "My turn," she said.

Evan grabbed his coffee and took a sip. "We could sit on chairs," he said, pointing to the little sitting area by the window. "You're paying extra for them."

"I'm already sitting," said Delia.

Evan sat down beside her. "OK. Shoot."

"What I've been trying to tell you is you don't need to head me off, because I've already done that myself. I realized last night that coming out here was a mistake. I don't know what's happened with Merry and Josh, but whatever it is, shouldn't matter. It's Merry's life, and I see now that no matter how much I love Merry and want to help her—I have no business interfering. I haven't called Josh, and I don't intend to. I'm going right back home."

"Wow!" said Evan. "You mean I lost a good night's sleep for nothing? You should have told me."

"I had no idea you were coming."

"That's because you weren't answering my calls."

"I wasn't answering anyone's calls."

"The one who's been squawking the loudest is Kat. She's all worked up that you went off without informing her."

"I'm not concerned about Kat. It's Merry I'm concerned about."

"Yeah, well. Got to agree with you there. Let's say we go downstairs and get some breakfast, then talk about it on a full stomach. You think we can get pancakes in this place or will we have to settle for something trendy?"

"It's a hotel chain," said Delia. "I'm sure pancakes will be somewhere on the menu."

After breakfast, Delia went back up to her room and managed to book a return flight for them for the following morning. She knew that Evan would be calling Merry from the hotel lobby while she was gone. When she came back down, he was standing at the window, looking out on the astonishingly blue swimming pool. No one was in it, and the water was perfectly flat.

"Damn, I wish I'd brought my swimsuit."

"What did you bring?" asked Delia. "I didn't see your bag."

"No bag," said Evan. "I travel light. I don't even have a toothbrush."

"We can probably get you one at the desk."

"Make it a red one," said Evan.

"Was Merry surprised you followed me to California?"

"I don't think anything I do surprises her very much. She asked me to go by her house and pick up two things for her as long as I was here."

"How is she?"

"If you are asking, how is Merry, on her own, the answer is, 'fine.' If you're asking how is Merry about your coming out here. Well, I think that's a work in progress."

"I feel sorry for Bob. He's the one who's been on deck."

"Don't worry about Bob. I think Merry is focusing her wrath on you."

"I hate wrath," said Delia.

"Cheer up, Mom, I'm sure in a few days the sentiment will be downgraded to fury."

In the rented car, on the freeway to Long Beach, Delia shut her eyes for much of the ride. She found it amazing that Merry—or anyone for that matter—could actually drive out here. When she'd last been here for a visit, she'd asked Merry if she took Eloise in the car on the highway, and Merry had given her an exasperated look and said, "No, I make her walk in the breakdown lane."

"Is Merry sure Josh won't be home?"

"She said she's sure. He's never home before six."

Meredith's house looked even more dwarfed by its neighbors than Delia had remembered. It was tan stucco—all hard, straight lines. No softness of old wood, like their farmhouse and barn. The lot was only some fraction of an acre—less space than the donkeys' yard—with a square of brownish grass in front and a short driveway on the side.

Evan pulled the car right up next to the house. "Merry says the key should be hidden in one of those fake rocks, somewhere near the back door."

"Maybe I should stay in the car."

"Why?"

Delia shrugged. "The neighbors might wonder why the two of us are prowling around the back of the house."

"I don't think the neighbors can see into the backyard, and even if they can, don't you think it looks more suspicious if I'm out there on my own? A scruffy guy in running shoes? You'll lend respectability to the project."

Evan came around the car and held the door open on Delia's side. She looked up warily at the neighbor's house. There was no sign of life. She followed Evan around the back of the house. There was only one tree in the small, walled-in backyard. It was heartbreaking to think of Eloise growing up thinking this is what "outdoors" was like.

Evan knelt on the cement walkway along the back of the house and examined rocks that were piled by a bristly plant near the door.

"Can I help?" asked Delia.

"I think I checked them all," said Evan, and he sat up on his heels. "Am I missing any?"

Delia looked on both sides of the back door and up and down the strip of gravel between the house and the path. "I don't see any others," she said.

Evan stood up and wiped his hands on his jeans. He texted Merry, but she was no help. "She said if I can't find the key, I could try to get in through the window to the laundry room. The catch is broken."

"Oh, Evan!"

"Come on, I may need a leg up," said Evan, and he started around the side of the house.

Delia ran behind him. "You can't break into their house, Evan!"

"Sure I can. I'm an old hand at forced entries."

"Please, Evan, this is not a good idea!"

Evan turned around and looked straight at her. "Mom, compared with some other no-good ideas, this one is not so bad. At least it's something Merry *wants* us to do."

"What if someone sees you?" asked Delia, and she looked at the house next door.

"First of all, I'm not sure there's anyone alive on the premises, and if there is, you'll be standing there, smiling pleasantly, looking as if you belonged here. Once I get in, I'll open the back door for you."

"I don't think I should be going in."

"Hey, I may need reinforcements. Merry wants me to get her cowboy boots and Eloise's favorite sweater, yellow with a duck on it."

"But she might not want *me* intruding in her house."

"I don't think she cares about her house," said Evan.

"What about Josh? We can't just take things from the house!"

"You think he's going to notice that a sweater and a pair of boots have gone missing?"

Evan worked at the window and managed to get it to slide open. He hoisted himself up and started squirming through the opening.

"Good thing I didn't have a second order of pancakes," he said.

Everything downstairs in Meredith's house was as neat and clean as if it was ready to be put on the market. When Delia had last visited there had been clothes slung over the backs of chairs, books open face down on counters, crayons strewn across the floor. Josh had obviously picked things up after Merry departed. The only sign that anyone was still living in the house was a coffee mug parked in the sink, with a spoon lying beside it. In the living room the coffee table was bare; the pillows on the sofa were properly aligned. It didn't look like Merry's house anymore, except for the painting that took up most of one wall, an abstract nude with the woman's body barely contained by the canvas, as if she had been squeezed inside the frame.

Upstairs, Delia refused to step in Merry and Josh's bedroom.

"You expect me to dig through her closet and find her boots?" asked Evan.

"I can't go in there," said Delia. "You're on your own. I'll look for Eloise's sweater."

It was obvious that Josh hadn't touched anything in Eloise's room. Leggings dangled from the laundry hamper, dolls were heaped in a toy crib, stuffed animals were piled on the bed. Delia found Eloise's yellow sweater on the floor, where it must have fallen when she packed her suitcase. Delia had sent it to Eloise that fall. And it was her favorite!

"Found them," cried Evan, who was standing in the doorway. He dangled a boot from each hand. "Any luck with the sweater?"

Delia held it up. "Now, can we get out of here, please, before Josh gets home?"

"I was going to suggest sitting in the backyard for a moment and having a margarita," said Evan, but seeing the look on Delia's face, he laughed and said, "Just kidding."

The problem with Evan was that Delia was never sure when he *was* just kidding. In the car on the way back to the hotel, she tilted her seat back and shut her eyes. She held Eloise's sweater in her lap and fingered the edge of the duck appliqué.

Since there were two queen-sized beds in her hotel room, Delia argued that it didn't make sense for Evan to waste money on another room.

"You don't mind if your son hears you snore?"

"I don't snore," said Delia.

When was the last time Delia had slept in the same room as Evan? When he was a little boy he'd sometimes crawl into bed with her in the early morning and then fall back asleep. He liked to cuddle, unlike Kat, and was always nuzzling when he sat next to her on the sofa. He'd been a huggy child—and he still was huggy.

"Evan," Delia asked, when they were both in bed and the lights were out, "was it true, that no one listened to you when you were growing up?"

"Have you been worrying about that too?"

"I hate to think that I didn't give you attention—"

"Oh, you gave me plenty of attention. It's just that once Dad was gone, I was the only male left, and I was surrounded by girl chatter. You and Kat—and later, Merry—were always yakking on about this and that. I didn't get much airtime. Maybe it's just that no one was interested in the things I was interested in."

"I'm sorry, Honey!"

"Hey, Mom. Don't worry about it. It wasn't a big thing. It's not like you stifled me for life. Do I seem like some guy who's reluctant to talk?"

Delia laughed. "No."

The door to the bathroom was open a few inches, and the slit of light was in Delia's eyes. She turned away. Outside the window, through the curtains, the lights of the city throbbed.

Delia wasn't sure she'd be able to ask Evan what she wanted to ask him, but there's something about darkness that makes it easier to talk about things that can't be said in daylight. She was afraid if she didn't ask him now, there'd be no other opportunity. Still she put it off until she was afraid one of them would fall asleep first.

"Evan?" she whispered. "Are you still awake?"

"Yup. What's up?"

"I know Merry has confided in you about what's going on with her and Josh, and I wouldn't ask you to tell me anything she told you—in fact I would hope you wouldn't even if I did ask—but I was wondering if you could just let me know if it's the kind of thing that could be repaired. That is, if you feel it's OK to let me know that."

Delia wished she could see Evan's face.

"I was wondering when you were going to get around to asking me that."

"You were?"

"Mom, I know you! You don't want to meddle in the affairs of your children, but you can't help yourself sometimes. It's because you—"

"Love you so much?"

Evan laughed. "Sure, why not."

"What were you going to say?"

"I was going to say because you're so curious!"

"Isn't everyone curious?"

"Hardly! Most people don't want to know much beyond themselves. But you want to know about everything—and you *care* about everything—me, Merry, Kat, Bob, the dogs, the donkeys, the chickens. You're a one-person Department of Emotional Support. When you're afraid someone might be in trouble—family, friends, neighbors, even strangers!—you've got your emergency kit already packed and in you rush."

"Sounds pretty awful."

"No," said Evan, "not awful. A bit trying for your kids at times, but what's awful is a mother who doesn't care, who'd rather *not* know what's going on. I've had plenty of friends who came from families like that, and they spend the rest of their lives underwriting psychiatrists' vacation homes on Nantucket."

Delia wondered which of his friends Evan might be referring to. Then she asked, "About Merry?"

"OK," said Evan. "Back on topic. Here's my question to you: Does it matter *why* Merry's marriage is shot to hell? Isn't it enough that she feels there's no way she'll go back to Josh? I mean would you feel better if I told you that anything Josh would say or do now isn't going to change things between them? It's not that Merry's just blowing off her marriage; there's some real shit that went on there."

"Oh no, Evan. I can't bear to think that Merry's been really hurt!"

"Of course she's been hurt! You think she'd pick up Eloise and come flying all the way across the country and move in with you and Bob if she weren't? But you've got to let her sort things out her own way. You can't jump in to make things right for her. You just need to support her while she does that for herself."

Delia lay face down and pressed her mouth into the pillow. How had she gotten things so wrong? How had she forgotten what it had been like for her to deal with her own mother, back when she'd decided to leave Phil? She hated herself for her lack of insight, her obliviousness, her stupidity—that's what it was, wasn't it?

"Hey, Mom, are you crying?"

But Delia couldn't answer.

"Mom?" Evan had gotten out of bed and was kneeling beside her bed, his hand on her back. "Mom, are you OK?"

Delia turned to her side and reached around and held his wrist.

She was about to say "I'm OK, Sweetheart," but in the honesty of darkness what she said was, "Don't worry about me, Sweetheart. I'll be OK."

14

Meredith leaned against a maple tree in the side yard of Hitchcock Hill Elementary School, her eyes on the window of the second-grade classroom where she had deposited Eloise, Moosie in hand. Kids were not normally allowed to bring stuffed animals with them to class, but an exception had been made for Eloise for her first day so she could introduce Moosie to her classmates and help her transition to her new school. Eloise, gregarious and fearless in her dealings with adults, was unpredictably shy when it came to interactions with her peers. She'd wet the bed the night before, something she hadn't done for so long that Meredith had gotten rid of the waterproof pad that had once been on Eloise's bed, just in case.

Eloise's teacher, Alicia Bent, was Meredith's age. Ms. Bent—unlike Eloise's private school in California the teachers here went by last names—was married, if you could rely on the rings (a peppercorn-sized diamond) on her left hand—and probably not yet a parent. She was plump and smiley, with a comforting aura and a soft voice that Meredith found irritating, but was probably good for managing seven-year-olds. She seemed unflappable and earnest, two qualities essential for an elementary school teacher, though not qualities Meredith admired. Meredith was relieved that Eloise had been assigned a teacher who seemed likable, yet at the same time felt wary that Eloise might end up liking her too much. Eloise had always cultivated the affection of teachers and babysitters in the past, elevating them to favorites, fawning over them. Meredith wanted Eloise to be happy, but that didn't stop her feeling of rivalry. And now, as she was outside the school, trying to look in, she felt . . . well, banished!—and had trouble tamping down her envy of Ms. Bent, who would have Eloise in her domain for the entire day.

The glare of the morning sun turned the window into a reflective surface, denying Meredith visual access, but she stood there anyway, watching, and listening. She couldn't hear any of the goings-on either. Not that Eloise would be crying; when she was scared or anxious she silently pulled back in, pinched her lips, lowered her eyes. The quiet outside the school was punctured by the roar of a machine—a leaf blower maybe?—from somewhere beyond the trees. A landscaper going about their business. Someone untroubled by thoughts of their only child facing twenty curious kids and having to explain why she was there.

Meredith had never attended this elementary school. When they'd bought the farm and moved to the district, she was already in seventh grade, and forced to navigate the treacherous middle school. Hitchcock Hill was a one-story building with wings that seemed to have been added haphazardly, without benefit of an architect, and the hallways inside were a perplexing maze of corridors. Ms. Bent had reassured Meredith that Eloise would not get lost on the way to the bathroom or the cafetorium—a ridiculous name!—at lunchtime.

"The kids learn their way around here the first day," she'd said. "The grown-ups take weeks—if they get it at all." Not a very reassuring comment on the grown-ups to whom Merry was now entrusting her only child.

There was no point in Meredith lingering here longer, yet she didn't want to leave. Anyone who saw her here might find it odd, even suspicious (these days all sorts of behaviors could be viewed as suspicious): a grown woman, slumped against a tree—and would wonder what she was doing, studying the school this way. And she knew she should leave because it wasn't healthy for her to linger here, clinging to proximity with Eloise, afraid to get too far away in case Eloise might disappear. She wished there was someone to talk to now, someone who might understand this bout of separation anxiety. But she really had no one to turn to. It was too early to call the few friends she had in California—none of them were good enough friends to wake up. Evan was the one person she could call anytime night or day, and even though he didn't get the parent thing, didn't understand that dominating tug, he'd listen to her, but he and her mom had other stuff going on now.

Meredith pulled herself away from the view of the second-grade classroom and hurried to her car before she lost courage and turned back. She had six and a half hours until she could return here to wait in the parent pickup line. Six and a half hours until Eloise would emerge from the building, and Meredith could see her face and try to decipher from that first look how the day had gone, six and a half hours till she could hug her again. Longer, even, than it would take to span the entire country by plane if she were to fly nonstop.

Before she started up the car Meredith checked her cell phone to make sure she hadn't accidently turned the ringer off. She needed to be reachable by the school in case anything happened to Eloise. The thought that it was possible that something *could* happen to Eloise rippled through her. No! She wasn't going to let herself go there! It was enough to worry about Eloise suffering, Eloise missing her, feeling abandoned. But it was probably more likely that once Eloise got immersed in things—introducing Moosie to Rosy, the class pet guinea pig, picking out a book in the Cozy Reading Corner—she would be OK. It was Meredith who was suffering. It was Meredith who was missing Eloise, Meredith who felt abandoned. And it was crazy, wasn't it? It wasn't like Eloise was going to school for the first time. She'd been in preschool and kindergarten, and Meredith had weathered that. There was no reason for this to feel so different, was there? But it did. Meredith drove around to the exit of the parking lot and stopped before pulling out onto the street. Just one look back at the school? Nope, not doing that.

When she got back to the house, Juno and Ralph came running to the car to greet her. Their tails were wagging as if they hadn't seen her for weeks, but they checked beyond her as if to say "No one else with you?" It wasn't just Eloise they were hoping for, but also, most likely, Delia. They'd been stuck home alone with just Bob. Bob, who professed not to like dogs that much, although Meredith guessed that out of view of others he was more indulgent than anyone would know. That was the thing about Bob. He didn't like to be accused of kindness.

Meredith dropped her shoulder bag on the bench in the mudroom and put on her muck boots. She decided she'd go for a ride on Falstaff, then get to work on the barn. A good way to keep her mind off Eloise. She texted Wylie to see if he'd be able to come over sometime later and give her a hand, but he didn't get right back to her. She'd expected to find Bob in the house, but he wasn't there. She spotted him out by the field and walked out to see him. He was working on a latch on the gate.

He looked up when he saw her coming. "Got Eloise settled OK?" He looked somehow older and smaller than the way she usually pictured him.

"Yeah. She'll survive."

Bob stood up straight. "Will you?"

Meredith gave a little laugh. "Maybe." He tilted his head, waiting for more, so she said, "There's a lot going on."

"You know, about your mother—"

Meredith interrupted him. "I'll never forgive her."

"I think you will."

"Don't hold your breath."

Bob set his pliers down on the ground next to the screwdriver and the jar of hooks and eyes. He let the new hook fall into place and gave the gate a tug to test it. Then he turned his full attention to Meredith.

"She loves you, you know."

"Well, if that's what love is, I don't want it."

Bob sighed. "Love is a lot of things—and wanting the people you love to be happy is a main part of it."

"It's not her business whether I'm happy or not."

"No?"

"No!"

Clementine came trotting over to the fence, and Meredith reached over to scratch her under the chin.

"Is Eloise's happiness your business?"

"She's a child. It's entirely different."

"Different. But not entirely. You'll see."

"It's not her life, it's my life. It's my marriage, it's my husband."

Bob bent down to gather up his tools. He put the jar in the pocket of his barn jacket. "I think she knows that," he said.

"You don't need to defend her!"

"I'm just trying to explain things."

"There's nothing to explain!" cried Meredith. "She went out there to talk with Josh. She went out there without asking me, without asking anyone!"

"I gather she didn't talk with him, in the end, though."

"Because my brother got to her in time!"

"There may be more to it than that," suggested Bob.

"You know what? It doesn't matter. What matters now is how this is going to work, my living here with her. How is any of this going to work?"

She turned and walked away. Rude to Bob, who probably didn't deserve it. But she was done talking. She needed to go for a ride. She brought Falstaff back to the barn and saddled him up. She slung herself up on his back and shook out her hair. Fuck her riding helmet! Then she thought about Eloise—she couldn't risk anything happening to her so she wouldn't be here for Eloise—so she got back down and got her helmet. Falstaff, the reins dangling, waited patiently for her to return. She mounted him and walked him across the front lawn, then set off on a trot when they got out to the dirt road. She stayed on the road until she reached the turnoff to an old trail she remembered. She hadn't been on it for years, not since she'd moved away, not since Eloise had been born. And how strange it was to think that she was the same person as the teenager who had last ridden here, coaxing a much-younger Falstaff up this stony farm road, across this small stream, and down through a thicket of laurels where the trail narrowed. She tried not to think about Eloise. Be in the moment, she told herself—but that was such a California thing! Her moment was never clean, on its own. It was always a mixture of what she was experiencing, and the jumbled thoughts in her head. She could lean down to keep clear of an overhanging branch, and her mind would be there, with the bending, with her face pressed against Falstaff's sweaty neck, but then when she sat back up again she'd be both there and in the hallway of Hitchcock Hill Elementary School, the door of Eloise's classroom closing behind her, and only that narrow strip of glass where she could peer through and see the small brown head of the person that was everything she loved most in the world.

Wylie turned up after lunch. He hadn't texted—or maybe he had and she hadn't noticed. Meredith was in the barn, moving a stack of boards that were in the way. She turned around when she heard the slam of the door of his truck. He'd pulled up close to the barn.

"How are you doing?" he asked.

"Could be better. It's Eloise's first day of school."

"First day?" He looked puzzled.

"First day in this new school."

"Ah, got it!" She thought he looked as if he was considering stepping closer to her, giving her a hug, or a pat, but he straightened and said, "Bet it's harder for you than for her."

"That's what I'm hoping," said Meredith.

"How were things up in the tundra with Evan?"

"OK. How were things in New York?"

"I don't know how people live in the city. I feel like I'm holding my breath till I get back on 91 heading north. How'd you ever survive in LA?"

"Long Beach isn't exactly LA, but it's not New England. And I'm here now, aren't I?"

"Yeah." Wylie smiled, and then, as if he just remembered, said, "Brought you something. Come take a look." Meredith followed him around to the back of the truck. He folded down the tailgate and lugged something out of the back.

"What is that?"

"A shop vac. Figured this barn could use it."

"Are you insulting the barn?"

"You could say 'thank you.'"

"Thank you, Wylie."

"You're not good at thank-yous, are you?"

"No. Bet you aren't either."

"Depends on whom I'm thanking. And for what." He handed her a coiled-up extension cord.

"Don't think we need this," she said. "I'm sure we have one."

"You know where it is?"

"Not exactly, but I suppose Bob would know."

"Until then."

Wylie carted the vac into the barn. It took a while before they could locate an outlet to plug it in. Wylie turned the vac on and ran it along a section of the floor. It left a relatively clear strip behind it. Meredith hadn't noticed just how dirty the floor was.

Wylie turned off the vac. "I'm not here to vacuum the whole barn for you," he said. "Just came by to drop this off and say hello. You can get back to work."

"I was about ready to take a break," she said.

There must have been something about the look on her face that made Wylie say, "Feel like taking a walk?"

"Yeah."

Wylie unplugged the vac and set it close to the wall. "Need a hand stacking these boards first?"

"Nah. I'm tired."

"We don't have to walk. We could just sit down somewhere." He looked up at the hayloft.

"Let's go outside. If I sit here, I'll just see stuff that needs to be done."

There were two aging lawn chairs out by the donkeys' pasture. Wylie tested the seat before he sat down.

"Eloise will be fine," he said. "She's a plucky girl. And once you see that she's fine, you'll be OK too."

"Guess so."

"Something else going on?"

"You know about my mom and California?"

"Evan told me he was going out there—he's always going places. He mentioned your mom, but didn't elaborate."

"She went to California to 'help me' by tracking down Josh and trying to shame or persuade or force him to patch things up between us. Evan went out to head her off."

"Whoa!"

"Yup."

"Did he succeed?"

"It appears he did."

"Then crisis averted."

"Not exactly. I still have my mom to deal with."

"Yeah, well. I suppose she meant well."

"Doesn't matter."

Wylie waited a second, then said, "Probably thought she was defending you."

"Whose side are you on, anyway?"

"Didn't know there were sides."

"There are always sides."

"So what's the real problem?"

"I don't know how I can continue to live here with her."

Wylie was quiet for a long time. He fingered a piece of peeling paint on the arm of the chair. Then he asked, somewhat tentatively, "You're not thinking about going back to California, are you?"

"No way," said Meredith. "I've moved back East. My plan was to help out here, take care of the animals, keep this farm going, keep them from selling it. I'm here for good. I got Eloise settled here. I got her enrolled in her new school. I'm not going to uproot her again. But how the fuck can I live with my mother after what she's done?"

Wylie stood up and walked over to the split rail fence. Meredith watched him. He gave the top rail a shake, then turned back to her.

"Can I make a suggestion, Merry, and if you don't like it, that's OK."

Meredith shrugged. "Sure, why not."

"You could come live with me—" He held up his hand as Meredith began to speak. "I mean live in my house, but not *with* me, if you're not ready to do that—and I don't want to pressure you in any way. The lease on The Heap is up at the end of the month. I can let you and Eloise have it."

"It's a huge place!"

"But Eloise would love it. I don't need the money—I rented it out just so someone would be living in it. You'd be able to come over here—it's not that far away—and help out with the animals, have your studio in the barn, but you wouldn't have to live here, with your mother."

Meredith let that all sink in. She wasn't ready to respond, and she sensed that Wylie had something more he wanted to say, but felt hesitant about. His face looked like the face of a child, his eyes squinty, as if he might be about to cry. He pressed his teeth into his lower lip. Then let out his breath in a whoosh. "I was thinking—or maybe it's just that I'm hoping—that someday, once you get things settled with Josh—you might be interested in living with me, sharing the place *with* me, you and Eloise—"

"Wylie!"

"OK, Merry. It's not like you don't already know this, but I've got to say it anyway: I love you."

"You're not allowed to love me!"

"Who says I'm not allowed to?"

"I do!"

"Well, that's too bad," he said. "Because it's just the way it is. Not a whole lot you can do about it. I won't say anything more about it if you don't want me to, but it's not going to go away."

"Jesus, Wylie. You think I don't have enough to worry about already?"

"This isn't something to worry about!"

"Well, that just happens to be my basic operating system."

"The vac is yours for as long as you want it."

"Thank you, Wylie."

"Whoa! Progress! She said 'thank you'!"

"So I did. But don't let it go to your head." She wanted to kiss him, but she was afraid he might think it meant something more than it did. But maybe it did mean something more? She watched him as he got in his truck and backed around, his arm slung around the seat back as he turned in his seat to look where he was going. He looked at her before he headed out, and gave the horn a gentle two-beat tap. Then he drove away.

~

Ms. Bent told everyone that Eloise had moved here from California and had Eloise hold one side of a big map of the United States to show the class how far away that was. California was a long pink shape on the left side of the map. Massachusetts, on the right, was a tiny green rectangle with a curl at the bottom corner. Eloise wondered how everything could fit inside it.

Eloise sat Moosie on her desk so she and Moosie could look at each other. He kept slumping to the side, even though Eloise tried to prop him up.

"I have a moose too," said Charlotte, the girl sitting next to her. "I got him when I went to Maine. They have real moose in Maine. Did you get your moose from Maine?"

"No," said Eloise, "I got him for my birthday."

"Do they have moose in California?"

"I don't think so," said Eloise.

Charlotte looked disappointed, so Eloise said, "They have mountain lions, though."

"Did you see one?"

"No," admitted Eloise. "But my mommy once did."

"Was she scared?" asked Charlotte.

Eloise thought about this. They were on a vacation and her mother had gone out for a walk and her father said it was probably just a big dog, and her mother said she certainly could tell the difference between a mountain lion and a dog, and her father said, "A mountain lion, yeah. You do like to be dramatic, don't you?" and then he had pointed at Eloise and said, "That's where she gets it from."

"Was she?" Charlotte asked again.

"Only a little," said Eloise.

~

Meredith's car was the first one on the pickup line. She wanted to rush out to Eloise when she spotted her walking out of the building, but parents weren't supposed to get out of their cars. A teacher on duty helped Eloise get into the back seat, and Eloise strapped in Moosie next to her. Meredith longed to hug Eloise, but she had to be content with twisting around and sending her kisses in the air. "How was Moosie's first day of school, Sweetheart?" she asked.

"OK."

"Did Moosie make any new friends?"

"No, because he was the only stuffy there."

"What about you?" Meredith asked, but the teacher waved her to move on, so Meredith had to turn back around and drive. When they were out on the road, Eloise said, "I made a new friend, named Charlotte. And there's another girl at our table, Aiden, but I don't like her as much."

"How come?"

"She's bossy."

"Some kids are like that," said Meredith. "Sometimes they outgrow it, and sometimes they don't."

"Like Aunt Kat?"

"Where did you get that from?"

"You said it to Grandma."

"I did? Well, I shouldn't have."

"Even if it's true?"

"Oh, Eloise!" Meredith paused and took a big breath. "Now, tell me all about your day!"

"I will when we get home. Then I can tell Grandma about it too."

"Grandma's not home now," said Meredith.

"Is Grandpa home?"

"Yes."

"Then I'll tell him. And I'll tell Grandma all about it when she gets back."

Meredith was about to say something about Grandma, but stopped. She didn't want to be thinking about her mother now.

When they got out of the car at the house, Juno and Ralph circled around them, tails wagging. Meredith held Eloise against her. "I missed you today," she said. She tried to keep her voice light.

"Juno and Ralph missed me too," Eloise said.

Meredith batted them away. "Go away, beasts!" she said, laughing, but the dogs stuck close beside them as they went into the house.

Eloise found Bob in the living room, reading. She sat down on the footstool in front of him and seated Moosie beside her. "Eloise is going to tell us about her new school," Meredith said.

Bob placed a bookmark on the open page, snapped his book shut, and set it on the table beside him. "I'm all ears," he said.

"That's silly," said Eloise. "If you were all ears, you wouldn't have any eyes, and then you couldn't read."

"I see your point," said Bob.

"So, what was special about your first day?" Meredith asked.

"I made a name sign for my cubby," said Eloise. "We make them ourselves, and you can draw flowers or dogs or whatever you want. And I got to use the smelly markers, only the purple one was used up and didn't smell like grape anymore. And we had worksheets that you filled in letters for words. They have mac and cheese at the cafetorium, so can I get it tomorrow instead of bringing lunch?"

"We'll see," said Meredith. "Do you like your teacher?"

"Her name is Ms. Bent," Eloise informed Bob. "And I like her a lot. She let Moosie sit on my desk for the whole day."

"I trust he behaved himself," said Bob.

Eloise laughed. "Where did Grandma go?" she asked.

"California," said Bob.

Eloise spun around and looked at Meredith. "You didn't tell me *that*."

"Bob!" said Meredith.

"She's going to come back, isn't she?"

Bob saw the look on Meredith's face. "Of course she is," he said.

"When?"

"Tonight, I think."

"How come she went to California?" Eloise asked.

Bob held his hands up and looked at Meredith, but Meredith quickly said, "Let's go out to see Falstaff and the donkeys. They're waiting for you to tell them about your day." She started to walk to the doorway.

"How come she went to California?" Eloise repeated.

But Meredith didn't answer her question. Instead she said, "Since it's a special day—your first day in your new school," she said to Eloise, "let's go give the donkeys apples, as a treat."

Eloise thrust Moosie at Bob. "You can watch him for me," she said.

"An honor," said Bob.

When they got out to the field, Clementine, who had an unerring sense of the approach of an apple, came racing up to them.

"Eloise made new friends at school today," Meredith told Clementine, although Clementine wasn't really listening. She was focused on the apple.

"Just Charlotte and Aiden," said Eloise. "There's a boy who sits at our table, too, but he's not a friend."

"Maybe not yet," said Meredith. "But maybe he will be."

Eloise shook her head. "He has a pen with a top that has a floaty ship inside it. He showed it to me, but he wouldn't let me hold it."

"I don't think you're missing out on much," said Meredith.

"Will Grandma be here when I come home from school tomorrow?"

"I don't know," said Meredith. "I'm not in charge of your grandmother."

Eloise laughed. "I'll tell her about my second day of school," she said.

They gave apples to Tulip and Myrtle and Falstaff, then started walking back to the house.

"Eloise, how would you like to live at Wylie's house for a while?" Meredith asked. "The big house, The Heap. The people who are living there now will be moving out, and the house will be empty."

"Why doesn't Wylie live there?"

"He likes his little carriage house."

"Why would we want to live there?"

"I thought it might be nice for us to have a house all to ourselves. Just the two of us."

"What about Falstaff? And Clementine and Tulip and Myrtle, and Agnes and all the chickens?" asked Eloise.

"They'd stay here. And we would come back to take care of them."

Eloise shook her head. "I want to stay here too," she said. "And Grandma and Grandpa would be lonely if we moved away."

"I don't think so."

"Yes, they would be!" cried Eloise.

"They weren't lonely before we came here," said Meredith.

"They *were*," insisted Eloise, "Grandma told me."

"Oh, for God's sake," said Meredith.

15

Evan drove Delia home from the airport, but refused to spend the night.

"I need to get home," he said. "I've got to be at work early tomorrow."

"I don't like you driving late at night."

Evan laughed. "It's old people like you who shouldn't be driving at night. My night vision is A-OK. And night is a great time to drive. Fewer cops out to catch me speeding."

It was dark by the time they reached the farm. Delia and Bob had never fixed the wiring in the lamppost by the driveway, and the only light was the yellow one by the door, inadequate, perhaps, but comforting, like candlelight. Kat had pushed them to install floodlights for safety's sake around the house, but what was there to keep safe from? Certainly not the darkness. And Delia felt that nocturnal creatures deserved their privacy.

"I'm just going to drop you and keep going," said Evan.

"At least come in and have something to eat."

"Mom, first you say you don't like me driving late, then you try to delay me."

Delia studied his face. "You just don't want to witness Meredith's wrath—even if it's been downgraded to fury—when she sees me."

"Yeah, well, there's that," said Evan. He got Delia's suitcase out of the trunk and popped out the handle.

"I can manage this," Delia said as she took it. "Goodbye, Darling." She reached up and gave him a kiss. "Drive safely." The wheels of the suitcase were defeated by the uneven flagstones of the front walk, but Delia lugged the suitcase up to the door as fast as she could, then turned to wave goodbye to Evan.

The dogs, as always, were reassuringly nonjudgmental, and when she came inside they rushed towards her with the gleeful exuberance that only dogs can muster. Bob, whom she'd texted when she arrived at the airport, did not display gleeful exuberance, and his hug was merely perfunctory. He had not offered to pick her up at the airport, and although she wouldn't have accepted, she was still hurt that he hadn't offered. Not justifiably hurt—since she didn't feel she deserved his kindness in connection to any aspect of this misadventure—but hurt nonetheless. His not offering suggested that he had not yet forgiven her.

"Hungry?" he asked. "We got takeout for dinner. There's some left."

"I grabbed something at the airport," she said. She'd planned to eat the wrap on the ride home, but she didn't feel like eating; she'd just shoved it into her bag. She kicked off her shoes and left her suitcase and her bag in the hallway.

She dreaded seeing Meredith, but she wanted to get it over with. The whole way home on the flight she'd been rehearsing little speeches, explanations, overtures. But it just made her more anxious. How could it be that she was afraid of her own daughter?

"How are things going?" she asked Bob, in a low voice, while they were still alone.

He shrugged. She turned to walk towards the living room, but he caught her arm, held her back.

"Something you should know," he said.

She turned. "What?"

"Merry told me she's thinking about moving out."

"What!"

He held his finger to his lips. And pointed upstairs. "Wylie's offered her his place."

"She's going to move in with Wylie!"

"Not with Wylie. His big house is going to be vacant. He said Meredith and Eloise could have it."

Delia sank back against the wall. She had imagined many things. But she had not imagined this. "Oh, Bob, what am I going to do?"

"Maybe, for once, you're not going to do anything."

She felt as if she had been slapped. Bob saw the look on her face and softened. He tilted his head and held out his arms. She fell against him, face to chest.

"I can't help it," she whispered.

"I know," said Bob, and he sighed. His hands pressed her back.

Bob, of course, would feel differently about Meredith moving out. He'd suffered having her and Eloise living with them—put up with them for Delia's sake—but he hadn't been happy about having his house invaded, having to deal with Eloise every day. He'd be relieved to have them leave.

"Grandma! You're back!"

Bob released Delia quickly, and she turned to see Eloise running towards her. Delia reached out to her and caught her up in her arms.

"I thought you might never come back!" cried Eloise.

Delia kissed her cheek, and then hugged her tight and kissed her again. "Of course I'd come back," she said. "I wouldn't go anywhere and not come back for you."

"It's after your bedtime," said Merry. Delia looked up and saw her standing near the top of the stairs. She was wearing an oversized T-shirt—Evan's castoff probably—and her legs looked pale and skinny, her bony knees, vulnerable.

"Grandma's back!" said Eloise. "I want to tell her about my new school."

"It's late," said Merry. "And you have to get up early tomorrow morning."

"I want to hear all about it," said Delia, "but you can tell me tomorrow."

"I want to tell you now!" said Eloise.

"Bedtime!" said Merry.

"May I come up and read her a goodnight story?" asked Delia.

Merry glared at Delia. "She's already had her story," she said. "Upstairs, now, Eloise!"

"I missed you, Grandma!" said Eloise, and Delia hugged her close, then released her.

"I'm going to count to five," said Merry. And Eloise ran upstairs. Daughter and granddaughter disappeared from view.

Delia went into the kitchen and put the plastic container she'd gotten at the airport into the refrigerator.

"Sure you don't want any of this?" Bob asked, pointing to the Chinese food out on the counter.

"No, thanks," said Delia, and she put that away in the refrigerator, too, and, out of habit, put the dirty dishes that had been left out into the dishwasher.

"Kat called earlier," said Bob. "She's planning to come visit soon."

"Oh no!"

"I think she wants to check up on you. Make sure you're OK."

"What she wants to do is lecture me on the folly of impetuousness."

"Maybe, but she was upset that you went off to California without informing her. And the fact that you didn't answer any of her calls."

"I can't deal with Kat, now. I have enough to deal with, with Merry."

"Well, I'm out of it," said Bob. "They're your daughters. I've been in the hot seat since you took off, and now I'm done."

"Oh, Bob," said Delia. "I'm so sorry I left you with this mess. I just—" Delia didn't know what to say. There really wasn't anything *to* say. "Should we go sit down and have a drink together?"

"I don't really want a drink," said Bob, "but I'll sit with you if you want one."

"Actually, what I'd like better, would be to go for a walk."

"Aren't you tired?"

"I need to walk off California, breathe New England air."

"You do know it's dark out there."

"That's why we have headlamps."

"Are we taking the dogs?"

"Of course. It wouldn't be fair to them to go for a walk and not include them."

"I'm not sure it would be wise to base all our life decisions on what would be fair to the dogs," said Bob.

Delia reached for Bob's hand as they started walking. She felt initial reluctance in his fingers and gave his hand a little shake.

"Hey," she said.

He gave a slow exhale of resignation. "Hey, yourself," he said, and held her hand more firmly.

"I need you, Bob."

"I know that," he said. They walked a bit farther, and then he added what she had hoped he would say. "We need each other."

There was solace in the darkness, and the smell of the dirt road, the surrounding woods and fields. The sky was star studded, and it amazed Delia that only a few hours before, she had been there, up in that sky, as tiny to anyone looking upward as the stars were to her now.

As they started back to the house, Delia asked the question she had been holding back. "Do you think I can repair things with Merry?"

Bob hesitated longer than she would have liked. "I don't know," he said, finally. "She's struggling with a lot of things right now, and you're just one of them."

"Like what?"

"Like her marriage. Like her career as an artist. Like Eloise going off to school."

"Sometimes I feel as if I'm the focus of it all, as if I'm the main thing she's doing battle with."

"Isn't that what mothers are for?"

"What do you mean?"

"You're a safe battleground."

"Safe!"

"She can push against you, and you'll always be there, you'll always love her—isn't that true?"

"Of course it is. But doesn't she realize it's not a battle between us? That I'm on her side."

Bob actually laughed. "I bet you've told her that, too, haven't you?"

"Well, yes."

Bob laughed again.

In bed at night, Delia fought off images of the hotel room in LA, the runway with planes panting, waiting to take off, and images of Merry's house, the backyard with the solitary tree. I'm here, she told herself. I'm home. She pressed close to Bob, making up for their separation, reclaiming that territory. Making love was a way to restore who they were. She wondered if sex was like that for other people—a time-out from all the worries of daily life, a no-man's-land from conversation, from thought.

In the morning, Delia barely had a chance to talk with Eloise before Merry whisked her off to school.

"When I get home I'm going to tell you all about my new school and my new friend, Charlotte," said Eloise. "She can write a whole page in cursive."

"Well, that's impressive," said Delia.

"And let's brush the donkeys."

"OK."

"And will you give me a violin lesson, like you did before?"

"If you'd like."

After Eloise had left, Delia went to her music room and took out her violin. She hadn't played for three days now, and it felt as if she'd been away for much longer. She didn't turn on the chandelier—the morning light was enough. Her G string was all out of tune, as if the peg had slipped in protest of her absence. She took out her book of Bach sonatas and partitas, even though she knew many of them by heart. She'd worked on them almost obsessively that horrible year, when Phil's brokerage firm was in trouble and her father had bailed him out, and Phil, instead of being grateful, had let his misery and self-loathing spill over onto her. It was almost as if Bach had known what it had been like for her then, had given her those sonatas so she'd have something to engage her, a place to go that wasn't words. She played some of them now, in no particular order, but ended with her favorite, the wrenchingly beautiful Largo movement of Sonata No. 3, where she thought of the double-stops and chords as the voices of separate violins, so she wouldn't be alone.

When Meredith returned from driving Eloise to school and went straight to the barn without coming into the house, Delia put her violin away. She knew there was nothing for it but to go out to the barn and face her daughter. Yet when she stepped outside, she didn't feel quite ready, and instead went to the field to be with the donkeys. Their presence was always reassuring: their large, knowing eyes, their quiet sense of purpose. All the difficulties of their relationships were played out in simple terms—Clementine ignored Tulip, Tulip bossed around Myrtle, and Myrtle idolized Clementine. Blame and forgiveness did not play any part in their dealings with each other. Delia thought about brushing them, but she'd do that with Eloise when she got home. It was just stalling now.

Delia walked back to the barn and stood in the open doorway and watched Merry paint. Merry had an enormous canvas propped up against the wall. There were faint black lines outlining shapes, but Delia couldn't tell what the subject was. She thought of the painting in Meredith's living room. The woman, nude, crouching as if she had been trapped within the frame. Merry was sitting on a stool, hunched over, as she worked on a lower corner of the canvas. It looked as if she was painting sky. She must have heard Delia move—or perhaps it was just her sense of being watched.

"Jesus, Mom," she said, as she twisted around, brush in hand, bristles thick with blue paint. "How long have you been standing there?"

"I just got here," said Delia.

"What are you doing here?"

"I came to talk with you."

"Well, I'm not interested in talking with *you*."

"Please, Merry! We have to talk—"

"Actually we don't."

"But we can't go on like this—"

"Says you?" Merry got to her feet and stood facing her. The stool was between them.

"Sweetheart, listen, please, I'm sorry about what happened. I shouldn't have gone. I understand why you're feeling the way you do, but—"

"I don't think you do understand. I don't think you've ever understood me."

"Merry, I just want what's best for you. I went to California because I love you, and I wanted to help you."

"Help me? How about you start by respecting me?"

"I do respect you! That's why I didn't end up going to see Josh at all, I turned around and came back—"

"Because Evan dragged you back!"

"No, it wasn't Evan. I need to explain, I already—"

"I don't want your explanation. You did what you did. That's enough."

"But I didn't—"

"You know what, Mom? I don't want to hear any more about this. I'm working now. At least I *was* working before you barged in. You claim you support me as an artist, but you don't act as if you do." She turned from Delia and sat down again. She gripped her brush, but didn't touch the canvas.

"I do support you as an artist, and as a mother—"

Merry whipped around. "As a mother? What a joke! You undermine me every chance you get!"

"What?" cried Delia. "What are you talking about?"

"Last night, when I'm trying to get Eloise to sleep, you want her to tell you all about her new school, and then, when I say it's bedtime and wait till the next day, you offer to read her a story—"

"But, Merry, I was only trying to—"

"And this morning, you promised her you'll give her a violin lesson when she gets home from school when I explicitly told you I didn't want her to be studying violin."

"But she asked me—"

"And that's your excuse? She asked you? What about what I decided for her? What about what I want?"

"Oh, Merry. I just thought it was something I could offer—something that would be nice for her."

"Like it was nice for me? You pushed me into it when I was a kid. And now you want to push my daughter into it too?"

"But I didn't push you," cried Delia. "I didn't make you practice. I—"

"No. You just made me feel guilty if I didn't."

"You didn't need to practice—not like Kat. She had to work hard to get anywhere with the violin, but it came so easily to you, you were so talented—"

"See? That's what I mean. 'I was so talented'—"

"And you gave it up. And I—"

"You were heartbroken, right? That's what you told me. Disappointed you once again. I was a fuckup as a kid, and I've been a fuckup ever since. And you're still hoping to straighten me out. You were even going to fix my marriage for me."

"No! I saw that I was all wrong about that, and so I—"

"I can't take any more of this!" cried Merry. "I'm getting out of here."

She threw down the paintbrush, scattering blue paint on the barn floor, and ran out. She got into the car and slammed the car door.

Delia pressed her back against the doorway of the barn. Her knees buckled, and she sank to the floor, her spine rubbing along the doorframe. She crouched there on the threshold, eyes closed, and listened to Merry drive away.

16

When they got home from school that afternoon, Meredith took Eloise out for a trail ride. She needed to be outdoors; she needed to be away from the house. And her mother.

"Do you think you can saddle up Clementine all by yourself while I do Falstaff?" she asked Eloise.

"Of course I can!" said Eloise.

Meredith looked over at Eloise while she worked. Eloise was running through the steps in a professional way—taking herself so seriously!—and she was fast. She smoothed the fleece pad on Clementine's back before she put on the saddle. She checked the height of the stirrups. She clipped on the roper reins. Clementine stood patiently through the entire process. Tulip came over to investigate, but Myrtle kept her distance. She clearly had no intention of carrying anyone on her back.

"It's not a race, Honey," said Meredith.

"I know," said Eloise, but she was obviously pleased when Clementine was ready to go before Meredith was done with Falstaff.

"Need a hand up?"

"Nope!" said Eloise. She clicked the buckle of her helmet strap in a decisive way and hoisted herself up on the saddle. "Come on, Mommy!" she said. Clementine was fine for now, but Meredith would have to get her a pony sometime. Or, at least, a bigger donkey.

They cut across the field, side by side. The dogs, who had come along, though uninvited, ran off into the greenness on either side, then followed along more closely when they entered the trail in the woods, an old logging road. Meredith let Eloise lead, and Falstaff, gracious—or perhaps it was the weariness of old age?—allowed Clementine to go ahead of him. He tolerated the donkeys the way he tolerated the dogs. He seemed grateful just to be out on the trail, to have Meredith with him. She reached forward and stroked his neck, which was warm and firm. The sun was full, the sky, nearly cloudless, and it seemed as if winter was so far behind them maybe it hadn't happened at all. Meredith relaxed in the saddle, allowed herself a small taste of joy.

There was a minivan in the driveway when they got back to the barn. A little girl was carrying a violin case out of the house, swinging it back and forth in a satisfied way, her mother behind her. Eloise got down from Clementine and watched, reins in hand.

"Grandma's going to give me a violin lesson too," said Eloise.

"I'm not sure about that," said Meredith.

"Why not?"

Meredith closed her eyes for a second. She hoped an explanation would pop into her head, but it didn't. When she opened her eyes, Eloise was still looking at her, waiting, so instead she asked, "Would you like to go out to dinner tonight?"

"With Grandma and Grandpa?"

"No, with me."

"Just the two of us?"

"Yes."

"Where?" asked Eloise.

"I haven't decided yet," said Meredith.

"Charlotte went to Friendly's. Can we go there?"

Friendly's was not the sort of restaurant Meredith would have chosen, but she said, "OK."

"Eloise and I are going out to dinner, tonight," Meredith informed Delia as they came into the house.

"Oh," said Delia, "I was going to make pasta and—" She stopped herself mid-sentence. She looked at Eloise. "Have a good time," she said.

Meredith hadn't been to Friendly's for a long time, probably not since she was a teenager in flare jeans that dragged on the floor, and it was strange to be going there as an adult now, bringing her own kid. Eloise beside her was proof that all those years had gone by. Amazing that Friendly's was still in business. The menu didn't have much to offer vegetarians, but Eloise got grilled cheese, and Meredith had a garden-vegetable omelet—were there vegetables that didn't grow in gardens? She let Eloise order a sundae from the regular—not the kids'—menu. It was outrageously pink with confetti sprinkles, chunks of nonorganic strawberries, whipped cream, and a maraschino cherry, oozing red dye #40, perched on top that would probably take years off her life. It made Meredith kind of sick to her stomach to look at it, but Eloise stared at it in wonder, unbelieving that such desserts existed, and that her mother would actually let her order one.

"One for you?" asked the waitress brightly.

"I'll pass, thanks," said Meredith. The waitress laid a clean spoon by her place and wrinkled her nose in a knowing way. "In case you want a taste," she said.

Eloise, spoon poised in hand, seemed reluctant to mar the glistening concoction. "You might as well eat it before it melts," said Meredith, though the sundae had a plastic, permanent look. Eloise carefully spooned off a bit and slowly tasted it. At this rate, Meredith thought, they'd never get out of here. She was feeling that prick of anxiety she sometimes got in public places: Friendly's egregious wholesomeness, the horrific dessert she'd actually allowed her daughter to eat, the brightness of it all.

"May I have a bite?" she asked Eloise, hoping to speed up the process, and when Eloise nodded she scooped up a chunk off the side of the sundae that Eloise couldn't see. She was careful not to get too much of the gooey red sauce, but she couldn't avoid a congestion of sprinkles, and they felt like bits of gravel in her mouth.

It took Eloise what seemed like hours to make her way through the sundae. When she finally said she was done, there was still a puddle of strawberry-tainted ice cream abandoned at the bottom of the glass dish, and gooey smears along the sides. It looked like the remains of an accident.

As they left Friendly's and started towards their car, Meredith spotted her old classmate Nora coming across the parking lot towards the entrance with two little girls in hand, and a man—probably husband—carrying the toddler who had been destroying the items in the shopping cart at the supermarket. She would have circled around a van to avoid running into her, but it was too late. Nora had seen her and called out, "Meredith!" and waved. Meredith stood where she was and braced for the approach.

"Oh, Meredith!" Nora cried. "How nice to see you again!" She turned to the man beside her. "Donny, Meredith was in my class in high school, and she's just moved back to town from—where was it? Someplace out West?"

"LA," said Meredith.

"Well, that's a change," said Donny.

"You bet," said Meredith. Her voice sounded like someone else's.

"This is my husband, Donny," said Nora. "Maybe you knew each other. Donny was a year ahead. Lacrosse?"

Lacrosse. Was that a noun or an adjective? Meredith shook her head but instantly had an awful thought that maybe she had not only known Donny but had let him feel her up at some party when she was dead drunk. Or was that someone else who looked like him?

"Don't think so," said Donny.

"How are things going?" asked Nora.

"Oh fine," said Meredith. She was tempted to say "just dandy," which would have been as alien to her as the "you bet," but she resisted. "Eloise and I thought it would be fun to come to Friendly's."

"How nice, just the two of you?" asked Nora, and she looked to the empty air on either side of Meredith for confirmation.

Meredith smiled harder. "Just the two of us!" She gripped Eloise's hand. "Well, we've got to be off now," she said. "Have a good dinner!"

"See you!" said Nora.

"See you!" said Meredith, just as brightly, and she walked towards their car, holding Eloise's hand.

"That girl is in my class," said Eloise.

"Which one?" Meredith looked back.

"The taller one," said Eloise, as if Meredith should have known.

"She is? How come you didn't say hello?"

Eloise shrugged. "We're not friends."

"What's her name?"

Eloise shrugged.

"Why aren't you friends?"

"You can't be friends with everybody," said Eloise.

Meredith thought about this for a moment, then she said, "I suppose technically you could, but there wouldn't be much point in it, would there? But why aren't you friends with that girl? What's wrong with her?"

"Nothing, I guess. But Charlotte doesn't like her."

"Why not?"

"She just doesn't," said Eloise, and Meredith was content with that. There were a lot of people she just didn't like, without being able to explain why.

When they got back to the house, Eloise ran into the kitchen, then the living room to find Delia. "I got a sundae," she announced, "with confetti sprinkles and a cherry on top!"

Delia looked over at Meredith with some surprise, but said only, "That certainly sounds like fun."

Meredith blinked. Had she and her mother both used the word "fun" in the past half hour?

In the morning Meredith went straight to the barn after dropping Eloise off at school. She stood back from her painting, studying it from different angles. She'd thought she knew what she was doing, but now she wasn't so sure. The blue paint had hardened on her brush. She stamped it on the table, so the bristles crinkled. She considered tossing it—it was one of her old brushes anyway—but carried it over to the barn sink, filled a jar with water, and stirred the brush around till the water turned blue. That was the advantage of acrylics: water, not turpentine, which gave her not only a headache but a rash on her hands. She held up the jar and looked through it. She thought she'd like to capture that blue, that liquidness. She looked back at her painting. But she wasn't ready to paint. The residue of the fight with her mother was still there in the air of the barn. She set the jar down in the sink and went outside to the field. Falstaff came trotting right over to her, and she nuzzled against his soft nose. She went back to the barn and got the pail with the brushes and tools. She brushed Falstaff, combed his tail, and cleaned out his hooves with the pick. She looked over at the donkeys.

"OK, ladies," she said. "Your turn."

Clementine was resigned to having her hooves cleaned, but the look on her face said it was unlikely she would forgive Meredith anytime soon. Tulip was OK with her front hooves, but kicked the back, and Meredith had to wrestle with her to hold on to her leg. It was a miracle, she thought, that she hadn't gotten her nose bashed.

Myrtle, who had watched with alarm while Tulip put up the losing battle, ran around the field and sprinted out of catching distance anytime Meredith got close. When Meredith lost patience with the chase, she went back to the barn for an apple, and managed to coax Myrtle close enough so she could grab her halter, something she should have done at the start. Somehow, when she was chasing a donkey, she lost sight of that. It was like that with a lot of things, wasn't it? You got so involved in the chase you didn't step back and strategize a better way. She had just managed to secure Myrtle's rope onto the ring on the side of the shed when she heard a truck drive up. She turned and saw Evan coming out towards her, hands behind his back.

"Didn't expect you!" she said.

"That's a fine greeting!"

Meredith laughed. She ran up to Evan, flung her arms around him, and gave him a loud kiss. "Better?"

"Yeah, well, except now I'll smell like donkey all day."

"How come you're here?"

"Brought you these." Evan's hands came around, holding out her boots.

"Oh, great!"

"I forgot to give them to Mom when I dropped her off. Found them in my truck last night."

Meredith set the boots outside the gate. "You drove all the way out here to deliver my boots?"

"Well, not exactly."

"Didn't think so. What's up?"

"Shouldn't you untie that miserable animal first?" asked Evan, and he pointed to Myrtle, who was trying to pull herself free from her tether.

"Took me half an hour to get her there. Want to help me do her hooves?"

"No. But I'll watch."

"Maybe you could entertain her while I work on the back ones?"

"I'll do my best," said Evan. "Has she heard the joke about the dogs online? It's a cartoon I just saw. It's about dogs, but could be about donkeys."

"What are you talking about?"

Evan crouched by Myrtle's head. She eyed him suspiciously. "Two donkeys are sitting—or rather, standing—in front of a desk. They're looking at a computer screen. One says to the other, 'Online, no one can tell if you're a donkey.'"

"That's good," said Meredith. "Not sure Myrtle gets it."

"Then I guess I'll have to sing, instead."

"Spare us!" cried Meredith. "You know what? Her hooves don't look that bad. I should file them, sometime, but no hurry." She released Myrtle and hung the rope back on the hook in the shed.

"How's the painting going?" Evan asked.

"Some days better than others."

"Can I have a look?"

Meredith shrugged. "I don't usually like to show work in progress. But I'll make an exception for you."

"I'm touched," he said.

Meredith picked up her boots as they walked up the hillside to the main level of the barn. She set them on a chair by the door, straightening them so they were lined up perfectly side by side. She stood there and watched Evan while he looked at the canvas.

"Wow! It's big!" he said.

"Thanks. I'll take that as a compliment."

"I won't ask what it is."

"Good move. It's not the best thing to ask any artist."

"I can see why you needed a barn to work in."

She waited a minute, then asked, "OK, now tell me what brought you out here."

"I thought I'd bring your boots and just have a moment to see how you were doing."

"And?"

"I heard from Wylie that you might be moving out there."

"You talked to Wylie?"

"We talk now and then."

"And?"

"So you and Wylie are, ah—" Evan paused while he searched for the word and settled on "together."

"No! Did he tell you that?"

"Not exactly."

"Well, I thought I made it clear. I'm not planning on moving *in* with him—he offered me The Heap—a place for Eloise and me."

"That's a lot of house for just the two of you."

"Yeah, well."

"You know, Merry, I hope you're not leading Wylie on."

"What do you mean 'leading him on'?"

"If you live in his house, he might expect that eventually he can end up moving in with you—"

"So?"

"So, it's not fair to Wylie if you have no intention of it."

"So, now you're suddenly worried about Wylie getting hurt? That's a new one!"

"Not just Wylie. I'm worried about you."

"What's there to worry about?"

"I thought you might want to have kind of a break to think about things before you got yourself tied up in another relationship."

"I wouldn't call it tied up!"

"What would you call it?"

"Wylie and I are friends. He lives nearby. I don't have a lot of friends here, Evan, in case you haven't noticed."

"Enough said," said Evan, and he held up his hands. He walked to the barn door and looked out at the fields. Meredith came up beside him.

"So you drove all the way out here to warn me about getting too involved with Wylie?"

"Well, not just that. There's the issue about you moving away from the farm."

"Why are you calling it an issue?"

"Well, you'd led everyone to believe you were planning to be here for the long haul."

"I thought I was, but it's just not healthy for me to be living here anymore. I need to get some distance from Mom."

"You know Kat will be ballistic. She'll say you're bailing on Mom after having upended her plans to sell the farm. Typical Merry."

"She'd already accused me of that a while ago."

"And you told her you were sticking it out, but now you're not. So she was right?"

"Evan! I can't believe you'd see it that way."

"I'm just telling you how Kat will see it."

"So I should care?"

"Well—I imagine Mom and Bob will see it that way, too."

Meredith paused for a moment. "I thought you were my ally. I thought you'd understand."

"Hey!" Evan put his hand on her shoulder and gave it a gentle shake. "I am your ally. Aren't I the guy who made a trip to California for you when I thought you needed my help?"

"I *did* need your help."

"Turns out, not really. It was a wasted trip."

"I wouldn't call it wasted. You kept Mom from butting into things with Josh."

"Actually I didn't."

"What do you mean?" Meredith was alarmed. "She didn't see Josh, did she?"

"No, Merry, she didn't. When I got out there I found out she'd already decided not to see him."

Meredith scowled. "Huh?"

"Mom didn't get in touch with Josh, but not because of me." He tilted his head and looked at Merry. "Didn't she tell you that?"

"Tell me what?"

"That before I got there she'd realized it would be a mistake to interfere in your life. She was already planning to come straight back."

Meredith looked at him. They stood there in the barn, looking at each other. Behind Evan's head, her painting loomed big, and blue, and answerless.

"What? She didn't tell you?" he asked.

"No."

"I can't imagine why not."

"Well, we didn't actually talk."

"You didn't?"

"I mean we *talked*, but—well, I was pretty angry at her."

"Jesus, Merry!"

A muscle on the side of Meredith's forehead started pulsing. She pressed her fingers against it.

"Sounds like the two of you need to talk. I mean, you really don't have a lot of reason to be angry with her."

"She went out there, though! She was planning on talking to Josh."

"Whoa! Stop shouting at me, Merry. Mom went out there, thought better of it, and came back. No harm done."

"She did go out there!" said Merry.

"If you want to go on being angry at Mom even if there's no good reason for it, that's your business, but I don't want any part of it." He walked away from her and down the hillside to his truck. He'd never walked away from her like that before. If he'd looked back he would have seen her standing there, making herself not cry. But he didn't look back.

When Meredith picked up Eloise from school that afternoon, Eloise asked if she could start taking the school bus home.

Meredith turned full around in her seat. "I thought you liked having me pick you up."

"I do, but I want to go with the other kids too." Eloise pointed to the main entrance to the school, where the buses—big and bright yellow—were waiting, doors folded open. Meredith could see why Eloise would find them appealing, and she remembered, too, her own longing as a child to be with the other kids, to fit in.

"Well, maybe sometime," she said.

"When?" Eloise asked.

"I'll look into it," said Meredith. "I don't even know what the route is like. You might be on the bus for a long time."

"That's OK. Charlotte said if I took the bus, I can sit with her. We can play puppies."

"She might not even be on your bus route."

"She *is*," insisted Eloise, and Meredith decided not to ask her how she could possibly know that. She wasn't ready for Eloise to take the bus. She needed to deliver Eloise safely to school, watch her walk into the building, and she wanted to be with her the moment school was over, to hear all about her day. She'd become, she realized, not just one of those horrible overprotective mothers, but a *needy* mother. When she glanced in the rearview mirror, Eloise was staring out the window, her face set in grim resignation, and Meredith tried to think how she might make it up to Eloise for everything she was denying her. When they got back to the house, she asked, "Would you like to have a playdate with Charlotte sometime?"

"Yes!" cried Eloise, her face transformed by surprise and joy. "And I can see her new climbing gym."

"Let's have her come to our house. Maybe on a Saturday?"

"This Saturday?" asked Eloise.

Meredith hadn't been thinking of a playdate that soon, but she said, "Well, I suppose so. I have the class list somewhere. I'll text her mom."

That evening Meredith contacted Charlotte's mother, who said that Charlotte had soccer on Saturday mornings, but she could come over afterwards, and she was fine about Charlotte having lunch with them. She seemed perfectly fine with entrusting her daughter to someone she'd never met.

Saturday morning Eloise baked chocolate chip cookies with Delia, and they made little sandwiches and cut them out with the bunny cookie cutter.

"Quite a spread!" said Meredith. "I just hope Charlotte ends up coming."

"What do you mean?" cried Eloise.

"Well, sometimes, things happen and people have to cancel."

"She'll come!" said Delia cheerfully.

"Thanks, Mom," said Meredith.

"No reason to be pessimistic," said Delia, in that same irritating cheerful voice.

"Eloise needs to learn that things don't always go according to plan."

"I think Eloise already knows about that," said Delia.

Meredith was about to say something, but managed not to. In truth, her mother was right about this.

Eloise went outside to wait for Charlotte fifteen minutes before she was supposed to come.

"She's not going to be here for a while," Meredith pointed out.

"I don't care," said Eloise.

Meredith understood. She looked out the window as Eloise sat there, and wanted to put her arms around her, protect her from the anguish of waiting. But she held herself back, even when Charlotte didn't turn up at the expected time. When Meredith was a kid and she was waiting for Evan, she used to close her eyes and count to ten, then twenty, then a hundred, as if there was something magical in the numbers that would make Evan appear. Counting, that objective activity, kept her from crying out, "Come! Please come!" Evan was often late, but he always turned up. But that wasn't true about other people. She remembered a girl she wanted to be friends with in middle school who said she'd meet her at the playground and never came, and when Meredith said something about it in school the next day, she didn't offer an excuse, just shrugged her shoulders and said, "So?"

Josh, unlike most of the guys Meredith had dated before him, was reliable. That was one of the things she'd liked about him—he showed up when he said he would. Meredith was often late to things. "You don't take time seriously," he once said to her, laughing. He didn't seem to mind waiting for her—at least he didn't at the beginning. Then, later, he did. He was constantly impatient with Eloise, who—like most kids, Meredith thought—moved at her own unpredictable pace.

After ten minutes had passed, Meredith wondered if Eloise would come inside and check on the time, but Eloise didn't move, as if she was afraid if she abandoned her post for a second, Charlotte might come and, seeing her absent, leave. Meredith checked her cell phone in case Charlotte's mother had texted to say they were running late. But nothing. Surely, if there were a change of plans, she'd get in touch? Meredith began to dislike this mother, who seemed so unconcerned, and after another ten minutes passed, she disliked even this child, Charlotte, who had such power over Eloise's happiness.

When she was just about to call Charlotte's mother, she saw a grey car coming up the driveway and stepped outside to join Eloise on the porch. Charlotte got out of the car, lugging a big canvas bag with her. The man who was driving—presumably Charlotte's father—yelled out the window, "I'll be back at three!" and waved before he pulled around in the driveway.

"Hi, Charlotte," Meredith said. "Isn't your dad coming inside?"

Charlotte didn't seem to think there was any reason why her father *should* be coming inside and said in a matter-of-fact way, "Liam's with him."

"Who's Liam?" asked Eloise.

"My little brother."

"I didn't know you had a brother," said Eloise.

"Well, I do," said Charlotte. "Do you?"

"No."

"Sister?"

"No."

"Well, maybe you will sometime," said Charlotte, and she looked at Meredith.

Meredith opened the door. "Come inside, girls," she said.

"What's in the bag?" asked Eloise.

"Barbie dolls," said Charlotte. She set it on the kitchen floor to show Eloise. "So we can play."

"I don't have any Barbie dolls," said Eloise.

"You don't?"

"I have other dolls, but not Barbie dolls."

"That's OK," said Charlotte. "I brought six so we have enough for both of us. And I brought their clothes."

"You can go upstairs and play," said Meredith, "and I'll call you when it's lunchtime." She watched Eloise take one handle of the canvas bag and help Charlotte lug it up the stairs.

When she came upstairs to call the girls to lunch, she stood just outside the door to Eloise's room, watching them before she said anything.

They were both involved in what looked like a doll's beauty parlor session. The Barbie dolls were lined up, and doll hairbrushes and clips were strewn around. Eloise was showing Charlotte the doll Bob had gotten her at the auction.

"Are you allowed to play with her?" Charlotte asked.

"Yes. But I can't drop her, or her head would crack in two."

"What's her name?"

"Sofia. I named her for my friend at school in California."

"Are you going to go back to California?" asked Charlotte.

"No," said Eloise.

And just as Charlotte was asking "How come?" Meredith stepped into the room. "Lunchtime!" she said.

Delia had laid a tablecloth on the kitchen table and set the table with the china bird plates.

"You're letting them use those?" Meredith asked.

"What am I saving them for?" said Delia.

Charlotte peeled back the bread from her sandwich, and looked inside.

"What are these?"

"Some arc peanut butter and jelly," said Eloise. "And some are hummus sandwiches."

"Do you have any ham sandwiches?"

"We're vegetarians. We don't eat ham," said Eloise.

"Why not?"

Meredith wondered what Eloise's explanation would be.

"Because pigs are cute," said Eloise. "And they have to kill them to get the ham."

"That's only the grown-up pigs," said Charlotte. "They don't kill the baby pigs."

"We have cookies," Eloise said, and she slid the plate of cookies towards Charlotte.

Meredith decided if they didn't eat the sandwiches, it was OK with her.

After lunch Eloise brought Charlotte to meet the animals. Meredith could tell that Charlotte was afraid of Falstaff, and although she said the donkeys were cute, when Eloise told her not to stand behind them because they kicked, Charlotte asked if they could play inside, instead.

"We can play in the hayloft in the barn," said Eloise. "We can pretend we're puppies and make beds for ourselves."

"Just don't pull the bales apart," said Meredith. She watched them climb up into the hayloft and went to her painting area and sat on the stool and studied her canvas. She could hear Eloise and Charlotte barking and yipping and giggling. It had been a long time since Eloise had played with a friend outside of school, and her happiness had an almost hysterical quality to it. When Meredith heard a squeal from Charlotte, she got up and hurried over towards the hayloft.

"You girls OK up there?" she called out.

"We're OK!" said Eloise.

"What happened?"

"Charlotte saw a spider, but it's just a daddy longlegs, not the poisonous kind."

"Can we go back and play with dolls now?" asked Charlotte.

"Sure," said Eloise. Meredith stood at the bottom of the ladder while Charlotte climbed down. Eloise—obviously showing off for her new friend—swung down on the rope that hung from the rafter.

~

Eloise would have liked to play longer in the hayloft, but they went inside because Charlotte was her guest, so she got to say what they'd do. When they walked past Bob on the stairs, Eloise told him, "This is my friend Charlotte, and we're having a playdate."

"Well, that's nice," said Bob.

Upstairs in Eloise's bedroom, Charlotte asked, "Is that your daddy?"

Eloise laughed. How could Charlotte think he was her daddy? He was old. Not as old as Sofia the doll, but old. He had a beard! "No, that's my grandpa."

"Where is your daddy?" asked Charlotte.

"In California."

"Is he going to come here too?"

Eloise had wondered about this, but she hadn't asked her mother. They hardly ever talked about her father. When he'd called recently her mother had her talk to him, but she didn't know what to say, and she was relieved when he told her to put her mother back on. And then her mother had shooed her out of the room and shut the door.

"I don't know," she said. She sat Sofia on the floor next to her, but it was hard to get her to sit up straight, so she propped Sofia against her side.

"Are your parents getting divorced?" asked Charlotte.

That was something else Eloise didn't know.

"If your parents get divorced, then they have a custard battle to see who gets you."

"They do?" asked Eloise. She'd never heard of a custard battle. If this happened, her mother would get her, wouldn't she? It had never occurred to Eloise that maybe she wouldn't get to be with her mother. The mere thought of it made her suddenly feel like she couldn't breathe, and when she tried to swallow she couldn't swallow either. Maybe something had gone wrong inside her. But that would be OK because if something went wrong inside her, then she would have to stay with her mother, right? She took a big, gaspy breath, and Sophie slumped to the side. Eloise caught her just before her head crashed to the floor.

~

That night Meredith felt obliged to check out the school bus route and was relieved to see there was an objective reason for her driving Eloise to and from school.

"You'd have to get up too early to catch the bus, and it would get you home too late in the afternoon," she told Eloise in the morning.

"I don't care!" said Eloise. "I still want to take the bus!"

"Not this year. School will be over for the summer soon."

"Then can I take the bus next year?"

"We'll see," said Meredith. "Depends where we'll be living."

"You said we weren't going back to California. Didn't you?" Eloise asked.

"Yes."

"Are you and Daddy going to get divorced?"

"Where did that come from?"

"Charlotte asked me."

Of course, Meredith thought. She wasn't prepared to have this discussion with Eloise yet, but she had to say something. "Maybe," she said.

"If you do, you'll get to keep me, wouldn't you?"

"Of course," said Meredith. She could be sure about that.

"Then why wouldn't we be here?"

"Oh, Eloise!" cried Meredith. "I'm still figuring things out, OK?"

"What things?"

"Just—" Meredith didn't know where to begin. "Just a lot of things!"

"I'm going to stay right here with Grandma and Grandpa and the animals," Eloise said. "No matter what!"

"Oh, Sweetheart!" said Meredith. She reached towards Eloise and tried to draw her close, but Eloise kept her arms at her sides, and just stood there.

When Meredith was younger, before she became a mother, all her decisions had seemed relatively easy. She just did what she wanted. Or what she thought she wanted. But it wasn't like that anymore; she was different now. Josh didn't get it. He wanted her back the way she'd been when they were first together, what Josh called "B.E.," Before Eloise. And that was never going to happen.

When Meredith picked up Eloise from school the next day, Eloise was carrying her art project, a collage, which was too big to fit in her backpack.

"We cut out different shapes—rectangles and squares and parallelograms"—she enunciated the word precisely—"and stuck them on the paper," she explained. "I'm going to show Grandma and Grandpa when we get home."

"I'm sure they'll like it," said Meredith, which was an understatement. When she was a kid, her mother had always praised her artwork and displayed it on the refrigerator, but she'd gone overboard with Eloise. She treated every scrap Eloise brought home from school as if it were museum-worthy—even a stupid coloring sheet—and taped it up all around the dining room on the wainscoting.

Meredith followed Eloise into the kitchen when they got back.

"Very artistic!" said Delia, when Eloise handed the collage to her, and she laid it on the table.

"It goes this way!" said Eloise, and she turned it so it was right side up.

"Look what Eloise made!" said Delia as Bob came into the kitchen. Meredith was surprised to see he'd shaved off his beard. His mouth looked naked and raw.

"Well, Bob, so you do have a chin!" she said.

"What you got there, Eloise?" Bob asked, and he walked over to the table.

Eloise looked up at him. Then she looked over at Meredith. Her mouth was half open.

"Looks like Grandpa decided it was time to shave his beard," said Meredith, and she smiled.

Eloise looked back at Bob. Then she burst into tears.

"It's OK, Honey," said Meredith. "It's still Grandpa."

But Eloise ran out of the kitchen, crying out "No! No! No!"

17

Delia stood in the center aisle of the Unitarian Church, waiting for the piano tuner. She could have squeezed enough folding chairs into her music room for the spring recital, but she wanted her pupils to have a chance to stand up on a stage (actually it was more of a platform) and experience their music filling this spacious room. Even quarter-sized violins sounded full bodied here. The church rented out its space to the local community, but the minister, a former Suzuki parent, waived the rental fee. Instead, Delia made a donation to the church's food pantry and paid to have the lovely old Steinway tuned.

Light poured in through the high windows, windows unblemished by stained glass, and the unadorned two-hundred-year-old church had a serene dignity to it. It felt like a privilege to have this place all to herself. Delia took in the silence and the light—the silence more profound, perhaps, because of the light. The air smelled fresh rather than ecclesiastical. She'd never attended a church service, but she'd been here for concerts and memorial services, and even with a full audience, it felt uncrowded. In spite of being a house of a particular religious denomination, it maintained a dignified neutrality. It didn't instruct you on what to think or what to believe. It was just a sanctuary that said: Rest here in this quiet, figure things out at your own speed, find peace from whatever is troubling you.

"I thought you were thinking about retiring!"

Delia turned to see Jules Crowell coming up the aisle, piano-tuning gear in hand. He was a short man with a round belly and a large head adorned with soft now-grey curls. Delia could picture him as a cherubic baby.

"Not yet," she said. And she laughed. "I don't see *you* retiring!"

"I'm getting there! My back keeps urging me to quit," he said.

"Please don't! Not while I still need you."

"I'm starting to cut back, but don't worry, I'll keep a few old pianos—like yours."

Jules propped open the lid of the piano and laid out his tools, like a surgeon laying out his instruments, thought Delia. The piano waited patiently. "You're doing your recital early this year, aren't you?"

"It's so hard to find a time everyone can come," said Delia. "My students all have a dizzying number of activities, and it gets impossible towards the end of the school year."

"Tell me about it! All those ambitious, determined parents pushing their kids to be star soccer players or virtuoso soloists. Poor kids!"

Delia didn't imagine he was referring to her, but she couldn't avoid thinking of Merry. Had she been an ambitious, determined parent, hurt when Merry turned away from her? Was that at the bottom of everything?

"Doing the recital early makes it more a work in progress—removes the pressure to be perfect. I've never really been big on 'perfect'—not when it comes to music."

"That's a relief. Takes the pressure off my tuning!"

Delia laughed. "That's a different story," she said. She settled onto a pew and slipped out of her jacket. At least they had cushions on the seats now. Two centuries earlier, when this had been a Congregational church, the parishioners had hard seats as well as the hard backs to keep them from dozing off.

"You don't need to hang around," said Jules. "I can let myself out when I'm done."

"I like listening to you work."

"It's rather monotonous."

"Soothing monotony. And you always play some schmaltzy Chopin when you're done."

"I'll do my best!"

Delia was happy to have an excuse to be away from the house for a while longer, a moment of calm before the all-too-predictable prerecital anxiety set in. She worried about each of her pupils' performances—not how they played, but how they felt about playing. She wanted so much for them! She wanted them to feel how magical it was to make this unlikely wooden object swell with music. She wanted them to sense—even if they couldn't quite understand it—the almost-visceral connection with composers who'd written the music, some of them who lived even longer ago than the building of this church.

And she liked listening to Jules work. There was something reassuring about the simplicity of pitch, the intervals all exact and predictable. It was an oasis of objectivity. When she'd asked Merry if she'd bring Eloise to the concert that afternoon, Merry's reply had been "Why would I want to do that?" If only you could tune people's interactions so there was nothing discordant between them!

When Jules had finished tuning the piano, he put away his tools, then sat on the piano bench and played a Chopin waltz for her. He started playing with comic flair, imitating ridiculously emotive concert pianists, but not far into the piece, almost as if in spite of himself, he let that go and just played. Delia rested her head against the back of the pew and closed her eyes. She tried to think of ladies waltzing, the swish of silk skirts, but she wasn't successful. An image of Merry intruded, Merry standing in the kitchen, the cuffs of her baggy flannel shirt rolled up to expose her thin forearms. "Why would I want to do that?" Merry had said—not angrily, but more as a genuine question, which was more hurtful because Delia could think of several obvious reasons Merry *should* come.

After she'd closed up the church, Delia walked out into the gravel parking lot with Jules. When the lot was full—at the annual holiday fair—cars parked on the grass as well. Now theirs were the only two cars, and they looked out of place, as if they'd been abandoned here. Delia got into her car and turned on her ignition, but she sat for a moment after Jules took off and looked out at the field behind the church. Some farmer had plowed under the old cornstalks, and the land lay bare and welcoming for whatever was coming next: brown awaiting green. It was a perfect companion for the plain, white church. The church, like her, was in a state of quiet suspension now, but things would be different for both of them that afternoon. Delia shifted into drive and went home to face the fray.

Kat arrived right after lunch. She came to the spring concert every year to help out and offer support. Delia didn't need Kat's help, but had to appreciate Kat's good intentions. Kat had made lemon squares and brownies, and she arranged them on a tray along with the cookies Delia had bought at the Italian bakery. Delia had succeeded in keeping Kat from driving down to check on her after she returned from California, and mollified her now by promising that if she ever decided to get on a plane and take off for someplace far away, she'd let Kat know about it.

"And, Mom," insisted Kat, "you do need to answer phone calls."

"I can't promise that," said Delia. "I don't always have my cell phone with me."

"Then check your messages!"

"I'm not sure how to do that."

"I'll teach you!" cried Kat.

"I don't think she wants to be taught," said Bob, who was sitting in his usual spot, coffee in hand, the newspaper spread out on the table before him.

Kat sighed. "I was afraid that was the case."

Eloise came into the kitchen and spied the desserts. "Can I have one?"

"They're for after the concert," said Kat.

"I don't think Eloise will be there," said Delia. "Merry's not coming."

"How come?" asked Kat, and then she looked at Delia's face. "She's still fuming about California? Evan told me about that and—"

Delia gestured with her chin towards Eloise, and Kat stopped midway through her sentence.

"Why can't I go to the concert?" asked Eloise.

"You'll have to ask your mother," said Delia, and Eloise ran out of the kitchen calling "Mommy!"

"I can take her with me if Merry doesn't want to go," said Kat.

"It's complicated," said Delia.

"It doesn't *have* to be."

Delia gave her a look. And Kat said, "Well, I guess with Merry it usually is."

"Usually is what?" asked Merry as she came into the kitchen.

"Forget I said anything!" said Kat.

"Nothing like having your mother and your sister gang up against you!"

"No one gangs up *against* you, dear," said Delia. "We gang up *for* you!"

"Right!" said Merry.

"I was just suggesting I could take Eloise to the concert—if you're not going, that is," said Kat.

"I'm not going. I've done more than enough time at Suzuki recitals," said Merry. "I think I can be spared this one."

"But why can't *I* go?" persisted Eloise.

Merry looked at Delia and Kat as if they were responsible for this insurrection. She sighed. "All right, then, I won't deprive Eloise of the dubious pleasure of bad Boccherini."

"What's that?" asked Eloise, but no one answered.

"Mom's going early to get things set up," said Kat, "but I'll go with Eloise a bit later."

"Doesn't Mom need someone with her to keep her calm before the big show?" asked Merry.

"That's what she has me for," said Bob.

"I have you for carting the refreshments," said Delia.

A phone rang somewhere in the front hall.

"I think that's yours, Delia," said Bob, and Delia ran off to rescue her cell from her pocketbook, which was on the hall table. It was Lindsey Klebanoff-Stark, calling to say she wasn't able to play in the recital. Her mother wasn't home, and she couldn't get ahold of her dad, so she had no way to get there. Delia was surprised that Lindsey's parents had willingly missed this opportunity to oversee their daughter's performance and suspected Lindsey had failed to tell them the date. But she didn't say so. What she said, instead, was that she'd arrange for someone to give Lindsey a ride, after she got the OK from Lindsey's mother.

When Delia returned to the kitchen and explained Lindsey's dilemma, Kat took a program from the stack on the kitchen table. "I see she's your grand finale," she said, "so it will be a problem if she doesn't show up."

"I don't care about a finale for the concert," said Delia. "It's Lindsey I care about. She's really into her piece—Bach's unaccompanied Partita No. 3, the Gavotte en Rondeau—and she deserves to play it. I'm sure she was skipping the concert because it would be stressful to have both her combative parents there in the audience."

"I'll get her," said Merry.

"I thought you weren't coming to the concert," said Kat.

"I offered to drive her to the concert," said Merry. "I didn't say I would attend it. I'll drop her off. I assume someone else can bring her home."

"I will," said Kat. "Can Eloise go home with you?" she asked Delia.

"Of course!"

Delia's old friend Simone Hoffman had volunteered to be the accompanist for the recital. Sometimes Delia accompanied her students herself, but it was nice to be able to concentrate on helping the violinists. Simone, a professional pianist, had filled in during the years her own daughter did

Suzuki, and still liked filling in, now and then. "It keeps me young!" said Simone. "It's fun."

Simone was not young, and looked even older than she was. Her scanty frizzle of hair was almost white, and her eyebrows were so pale they were nearly invisible. Delia would never have described her recitals as "fun," but she appreciated Simone's good nature, and her innate uncompetitiveness. Simone's daughter, Lucy, was Kat's age. They'd started violin at the same time, but Lucy was quickly two Suzuki books ahead of Kat before she was even seven. She'd gone on to be a professional violinist—no surprise!—and had earned a seat in the Cleveland Orchestra, which would have given Simone bragging rights, but Simone was not that sort. Instead, she laughingly described the quartet Lucy was part of as one that "focused on work by well-respected contemporary composers that no one really wants to listen to."

Delia had come early, as she usually did, but there really wasn't much to do until the students arrived. The music was on the piano, the programs were stacked on a chair by the door, and Bob was reading in the church activity room, on guard next to the table of after-concert goodies.

"How are you holding up?" Simone asked Delia, and put her soft arm around Delia's waist.

"I'll be fine, once we get through this!"

Simone laughed. "Don't worry about the kids. If they goof up, it's no big deal."

"As long as *they* feel that way!"

"They'll be fine."

"And their parents?"

"That's another story, of course!" said Simone, and she laughed her long, unmelodious laugh. She sat down in the front row of seats and patted the place next to her, so Delia sat down too. "I heard Merry's back in town. I can't wait to see her later!"

"You won't," said Delia. "She's not coming."

"She isn't? Why not?"

Delia sighed. "Long story."

"Short version?"

"She said she's done enough Suzuki recitals in her time."

"I get that," admitted Simone. "But she still plays, doesn't she?"

Delia shook her head.

"Oh merde," said Simone. "I'm sorry, Darling." And she sounded genuinely sorry.

"I thought you knew that she quit when she was in high school."

"I knew *that*," said Simone. "But she was a teenager then. Teenagers do all sorts of things to punish their parents for all the loving things their parents do for them. But I assumed she went back to the violin. She was so good!"

Delia wasn't going to say anything, and then she realized she *needed* to. And Simone was one of the few people she could talk to. "She doesn't play at all. And she doesn't want Eloise, my granddaughter, to play either."

"Oh, that hurts!" said Simone, and she hugged Delia and planted a kiss on the side of her face.

"Lots of old, unresolved issues."

"Then, you know what? It's time to resolve them! It's criminal for someone like Merry to squander her talent."

Delia couldn't help laughing. "I'll tell her you said so!"

"You do that," said Simone, and she pointed to the doorway and stood up. "Your first victim."

Nathan came running into the church. He had his violin case in one hand and in the other hand, a plastic pterodactyl that he was swooping through the air.

"I guess I'm on duty," said Delia.

"I'm here!" shrieked Nathan when he saw Delia. His mother, perpetually weary and apologetic, trotted behind him. "I told you to leave that thing in the car!" she said.

Nathan dropped his violin case and circled around, growling. The pterodactyl in flight looked more like a fighter-bomber than a prehistoric creature.

"Give that to me now!" said Nathan's mother, and she attempted to grab the toy from Nathan, which made him growl louder.

Delia crouched in front of Nathan and held her finger to her lips. "Shh," she said. "Pterodactyls didn't make any sounds. They were silent."

Nathan stopped spinning mid-growl. "They were?"

"Oh yes. They didn't want to be noticed and gobbled up by the other dinosaurs."

Both Simone and Nathan's mother looked at Delia quizzically. But Delia gently took the pterodactyl from Nathan's hand and stood up. "I imagine your pterodactyl has come to watch you play, so let's put him somewhere where he'll have a good view." She placed him on a windowsill. "Now let's get you tuned up."

"What can *I* do?" asked Eloise when she arrived with Kat.

Delia looked around and then pointed to the doorway. "You can be in charge of handing out programs when people arrive. They're on that chair." Eloise ran off, and Delia was sad that Eloise was being fobbed off with this minor task while the other kids were getting to perform onstage.

"Where's Bob?" asked Kat.

"Hiding out with the refreshments until the last minute."

"Shall I save a seat for him?"

"No. He prefers the back. And you should sit up close so Eloise can see."

As Delia's students arrived, they went up to the piano to have her tune their violins. Then they sat, instruments on laps, in the front row. Delia had arranged the order so that the wiggly kids would go first. When they were done playing, their violins could be returned to their cases, safe from danger. Delia kept watching for Lindsey. She was afraid she might change her mind and decide not to come at all, but just as Delia was about to start the concert without her, she saw Lindsey creep up the aisle and grab a seat.

The first child on the program, Julietta, wore a princess dress and a tiara. Delia had given in to her mother's pleading and taken her on as a new pupil, in a moment of weakness. Delia squatted beside her, smiling encouragement, as Julietta played a scratchy version of "Twinkle." The applause was punctured by Nathan's shouting "I'm next, I'm next," as he ran up to the stage, nearly trampling Julietta. Nathan whipped his violin up on his shoulder and began playing "The Happy Farmer" before Simone had touched the piano, so Delia had him stop, take a deep breath, look over at the windowsill to make sure his pterodactyl was watching (it was), and begin again.

He was followed by Sasha, playing Paganini's "Theme from Witches' Dance." "But I'm already up to Lully Gavotte!" Sasha had protested when Delia had assigned her "Witches' Dance," but someone more advanced was already doing the Lully, and one Lully was enough.

Delia had kept the concert to under an hour. Although two students were working on the Vivaldi A minor, she hadn't included it on the program. It was too long, even for the worshipping grandparents in the audience, and she found it tedious. When Kat had been a student, she'd practiced that Vivaldi dutifully for what had seemed like months, but Merry, at just Eloise's age, had sailed through it effortlessly, surprising Delia with a vibrato she'd acquired without any instruction at all.

Lindsey, last on the program, shuffled reluctantly to the front. She was wearing camo cargo pants and flip-flops. She took a place onstage where she was half hidden by the piano, and Delia motioned her to move forward. She slunk towards the audience, lifted her violin to her shoulder, and shook her hair back before she settled her chin in place. Her hair, which had been blue at the previous week's lesson, was now an alarming shade of purple. The waistband of her pants had slipped down on one side, exposing a band of surprisingly tender-looking pale skin. But once she started playing, any sartorial distractions disappeared: musician disappeared into the music. Bach's Gavotte en Rondeau was all there was in the room—just that profoundly beautiful melody—and Lindsey, eyes shut, let the music lay claim to her. She became the music and forgot about the audience. It was, Delia thought, as if Bach had written the piece for her.

At the end Lindsey remained frozen while the last, long note slowly vanished in space. She stood still in the silence, then looked up surprised, almost as if she'd just awakened, and lifted her bow from the strings. She gave a quick nod to the audience and darted off the stage. Delia looked out at the applauding audience and spotted Merry, sitting far in the back. She might have been there all along.

After the concert Delia found Lindsey by the refreshment table, a brownie in her hand. Lindsey smiled and shrugged. "Guess it wasn't that bad," she said.

"No," said Delia. "It was luminous and elegant."

Lindsey screwed up her face.

"It was," said Delia, and she touched Lindsey's shoulder.

"Your daughter's giving me a ride home," Lindsey said. Delia wasn't sure if she meant Kat or Merry. But when Lindsey said, "She's cool!" she knew which daughter it was.

Eloise, who had felt left out during the recital, asserted her connection now by snuggling against Delia. She had a brownie in one hand and in the other a cookie, which she was licking the sprinkles off.

"*One* dessert!" said Merry as she came up behind her.

"I'm saving this one for later!" said Eloise, holding up the brownie.

"Oh, all right," said Merry. She turned to Lindsey. "Loved your Gavotte, and it's a harder piece than it seems."

"You played it?"

"A thousand years ago," said Merry.

"Did you do Suzuki with your mom?"

"For a while."

"I want to do Suzuki too!" said Eloise. "I want to play that piece with the da dida dida da!"

"Which piece, Honey?" asked Delia.

"I think she means 'Witches' Dance,'" said Merry, and she hummed the tune.

"Yes, that one!" cried Eloise.

After Eloise had gone to bed at night, Delia went upstairs and tapped cautiously on the door to Merry's bedroom.

"It's open!" called Merry.

Delia stepped into the room, careful not to look around. She didn't want to be perceived as noticing Merry's predictable mess, and being accused—just by the look on her face—of passing judgment on it.

Merry was sitting in the middle of the double bed, her knees up, her laptop balanced against her thighs. Her feet were bare.

"I wanted to thank you for picking up Lindsey today," said Delia. She wasn't going to say anything about her trip to California. She and Merry seemed to have arrived at peace about that indirectly, which is the way it usually was with forgiveness.

"No big deal," said Merry. "By the way, she thinks you're wonderful—the only person in the world who understands her."

"Oh, that's nice, but I hope it's not true. I'd like her to feel that her parents understand her too."

"Fat chance of that! They're so wrapped up in their epic divorce nothing else matters to them."

"I think Lindsey matters to them!"

"Don't count on it."

"I like Lindsey. This is a hard time for her, and I want to help her, if I can."

"You already do! I think you've kept her from going off the rails. You know, Mom, you're pretty good at that." Merry laughed. "At least with *other* people's kids."

"It's always easier with other people's kids. Maybe because you love your own kids so much."

"Maybe because you have so much invested in them, and they don't always measure up."

"Can I sit down?" asked Delia. There was so much she wanted to say, but she wasn't sure how to begin.

Merry set her laptop to the side and leaned forward to push aside a pile of clothes so Delia had room at the foot of the bed.

Delia turned to look at Merry. "Is that how you imagine I felt about you? That you didn't measure up?"

"Imagine? That's how it was! You had this goal for me! You wanted me to be something I didn't want to be: a concert violinist. And I failed you. You reeked of disappointment all the time."

"I didn't want you to be a concert violinist!"

"No?"

"No! Why would I want that for you?"

"Because you hadn't done it yourself. And you wanted me to be your surrogate."

"Not at all!"

"Why didn't you do it yourself? That's what I want to know!"

"Because I wasn't good enough."

"You weren't?"

Delia had to think about this. "I'm not sure," she said after a moment. "My father didn't think I was good enough, so in the end, that's what counted."

"He said you weren't good enough?"

"Not exactly. But I felt it."

"What about your mother? Did she hope you'd be a concert violinist?"

Delia sighed. "My mother was an opinionated woman, but when it came to music, she deferred to my father."

"Was she disappointed when you gave it up?"

"I think she was relieved. Her true goal for me was to be a wife and mother."

"What about you? Weren't you disappointed?"

Delia ran her hand along the edge of the blanket. It was an old fleece blanket, pink roses on white, that had been Merry's when she was a girl. She must have dug it out from the closet.

"Maybe," she said. "For a time. But I'm not sorry I didn't pursue it. Even if you're one of the very few who are lucky enough to be successful—it's not an easy life."

"But you are sorry that *I* didn't."

"I didn't really care about you having the violin as a career, Merry. I just wanted you to play. You were so gifted!"

"Gifted! I hate that word! It was this thing about me that set me apart, tried to control my life. I was told I had all this 'potential.' My 'potential' was like a voice, crying, 'Live up to me! Live up to me!' Maybe I didn't want to have potential. Maybe I just wanted to be like everybody else."

"Did you really want to be like everybody else?"

Merry stretched out her legs. "What kid doesn't?"

Delia looked down at Merry's foot, beside her. It was small and looked as vulnerable as a child's. She reached out and laid her hand on the top of it, and was relieved when Merry didn't pull away.

"What saddens me is that you gave up playing. I can imagine all the music that might be coming from you, and it's not coming! It was your way to express yourself, a way to let your feelings out—" Delia paused for a moment, then added, "Even your anger towards me."

"I paint."

"I know—but you should have music too. And it used to give you pleasure." Delia hesitated. "It did give you pleasure, didn't it?"

"I don't know about that."

"Ever?"

"It was hard to have pleasure in it when I felt that you were always there, wanting—*expecting*—something from it."

"I'm sorry, Darling," said Delia. "The last thing in the world I wanted to do was to ruin it for you." She wrapped her hand around Merry's foot. The skin was taut over the bones. She rubbed her thumb up and down along the curve of the arch.

18

Meredith got a call from Josh at midnight. After she finished talking with him, she shoved her cell phone under the quilt, to smother the residue of his voice, smother Josh himself. With his typical arrogance he'd called that late, as if his Pacific Time, not Eastern Standard Time, was the real time, and he didn't apologize, even when she said he'd woken her up. There was a lot in their lives he hadn't apologized for. Since she'd left California they'd spoken with each other only once—he didn't want to talk with her any more than she wanted to talk with him. They communicated—when necessary—via email, which was toneless, but brutal enough.

She'd flipped on the light when he'd called, and she reached up now and turned it back off, but in the dark, Josh was even more present than he had been in the light. Not an image of Josh when she'd first known him—Josh speeding down the highway with one hand on her knee—but the Josh he'd become, Josh in that bilious green shirt—where had he gotten it?—standing in the kitchen doorway, yelling at her, her hand gripping Eloise's. "If that's what you want to do, then go ahead and do it. I don't give a fucking damn." And Eloise's hand so small and moist in her own.

She turned the light back on. She'd go downstairs and get herself some chocolate ice cream. No, maybe a drink would be better. Hey, why not both? She walked quietly past the door to Eloise's bedroom, then went back and opened the door to check on Eloise. The curtains closed off the night, and there was just enough light from the night-light to enable her to creep towards the bed without stubbing her toe—or worse. Eloise lay on her side, Moosie squashed beneath her shoulder. One of her legs had escaped from the quilt and lay on top of it. Meredith freed the quilt and pulled it over the bare leg. She leaned down and kissed Eloise. She didn't have to worry about Eloise waking; when Eloise slept, she slept. "I love you so much," she whispered. What she did not say aloud was "I love you so much it hurts."

Downstairs, moonlight illuminated the kitchen, and the shadow of the window—the grid of mullions between the panes—lay on the floor, dark against light. Meredith stepped into it, her own shadow interrupting the design. She stopped for a minute, so the bars lay across her; then she moved away to the other side of the kitchen. She dug a spoon out of the silverware drawer and was reaching for a bowl when she heard a noise behind her and turned to see her mother. They were equally surprised to see each other. The dogs rushed up to Meredith, tails wagging.

"Since when are you up after midnight?" Meredith asked.

"Ralph needed to go out. Or rather Ralph *wanted* to go out."

"You take him out this late?"

"I usually let him whine for a while and try to go back to sleep, but when he nudges me and yips, he probably needs to go out. And then Juno decides she needs to go out too. How come you're up, Merry?"

"I wanted some chocolate ice cream. Correction. I *needed* some chocolate ice cream."

"Come outside for a moment, first," said Delia. "There's a full moon."

So that's why the kitchen had seemed so bright. Meredith set the bowl on the counter and followed her mother out the back door into the dense moonlight. The dogs pushed past them. The yard was lit up as if it were a stage in the still moments before the actors entered the scene. Juno stayed close beside them, but Ralph ran out onto the grass; then, bedazzled, he froze in the silverness and stared back at them with glimmering eyes.

It would get warm later when the sun was up, but now it was still cold. Meredith would have gone back inside to grab something warm to wear, but she didn't want to break the spell. The night had that mystical, unworldly quality that made her imagine she might even expect to see a unicorn canter across the field. Delia noticed her shivering, took off her sweater, and placed it on Meredith's shoulders. "I'm warm enough," she said. "Your body's still in California mode." Meredith drew the sweater around her.

The moon was as big and as round as a moon in a child's drawing.

"The mother in the moon," said Meredith. She laughed. "You certainly indoctrinated me!"

"Why call it the man in the moon?" asked Delia. "It's definitely a woman's face. And it has a calm, beatific look."

"The Madonna in the moon?"

"Too religious," said Delia.

"True. The moon is definitely pagan." They stood, side by side, almost touching. It smelled like spring, and Meredith felt that quivery sense of promise, of being on the edge of some great transformation. That was the problem with LA: no real spring. *One* of the problems. Juno nudged her arm, and Meredith scratched her behind the ears.

"Why the need for chocolate ice cream?" asked Delia.

There was no point in not telling her. "Josh called to inform me he accepted a job offer from a new start-up, and he's moving to Hong Kong."

"What!"

"He wants to sell the house. If I want to keep it—which I don't—I'd need to buy out his share."

"When is this happening?"

"End of the month. He says if there's anything I want in the house—who is he kidding? It's like everything I own—I need to come get it. The real estate person he's lined up—without even asking me—probably some girl he's fucking—is 'staging' the house and will dispose of anything that doesn't 'work.' So I'm going to have to go out there and grab whatever I want to rescue."

"Oh, Honey, I didn't realize Josh was such a—"

"Such a shit, is that what you were going to say? It's OK, Mom, you're allowed to say a word like that!"

"But what about Eloise? How can he move so far away from her?"

"Yeah, well, the guy isn't the most involved father in the world. In case you hadn't noticed."

"I'd been wondering about how you'd work out custody—I mean if you were on different coasts—but now, Hong Kong! I mean—"

"It's not a problem. A lot of things *are* problems, but custody is not one of them. Josh doesn't want Eloise."

"Doesn't want Eloise?"

Delia looked so stung that Meredith had to stifle an urge to comfort her. "It's OK, Mom. It makes some things a whole lot easier."

"What's wrong with that man?"

"A lot. As I tried to tell you."

"You're cold," said Delia. "Let's go inside."

"You're cold." A statement, not a question, as if she knew—*had a right to know*—what Meredith was feeling. Ordinarily Meredith would have called her mother on it—even though she *was* cold—but she didn't. It didn't matter enough now. And somehow a statement like that—her mother's assumption—didn't infuriate her the way it once did. She'd sort of gotten past that now.

Bob, in a bathrobe and red flannel pajama pants—probably a gift from some Christmas past—came into the kitchen. "What are you ladies up to?" he asked.

"I'm sorry I woke you," said Delia.

"Wasn't you, it was the damn dogs."

"Moon gazing," said Meredith.

"Huh?"

Meredith pointed outside. Bob gazed out at the yard. "Good thing we don't have a rooster."

"Josh is moving to Hong Kong and wants to sell their house," said Delia.

"In the middle of the night?"

"And Merry needs to go out there and collect all her things before he throws them out."

Bob took a moment and looked at Meredith, as if expecting her to add something. His untied bathrobe was open, exposing the fuzzy grey hair on his bare chest. An old man's chest.

"Is your mother's estimate of the situation at all accurate, or is she unduly dramatic?"

"Josh is being a shit," said Merry. "But that's nothing new."

Bob took this in, then said, "What I suggest you need is a good lawyer."

"Kat will be here for dinner on Sunday," said Delia.

"If I remember correctly," said Bob, "Kat's a member of the bar in Massachusetts, but not in California."

"But she may have contacts in California," said Delia. "And in any case, she can offer Merry some basic advice."

"I'm not sure Kat would want to get involved in this," said Meredith.

"She's your sister! She'll want to help you out."

"I'll leave you two to work this out," said Bob quickly, "and if you'll excuse me, I'll repair to my humble bed and see if this creature"—Bob leaned down and pointed at Ralph—"will permit me to go back to sleep."

Ralph, who Meredith suspected was actually Bob's favorite, did a little dance of excitement, his toenails clicking on the tile floor, then followed Bob upstairs.

"Do you still want that ice cream?" asked Delia, as she headed to the refrigerator.

"I think I'd rather have a glass of wine," said Merry. "Is there some white in there?"

Delia found a bottle of pinot grigio, and Meredith got two glasses from the cabinet and held them up. "Join me?"

"Why not."

They sat at the kitchen table, and Meredith was happy that her mother was content not to talk, happy for them to just drink the cool wine and let the glow of moonlight settle on them. Moonbathers. When had they last sat this way, just drinking together? Maybe never. When she'd finished her glass, Meredith got up and retrieved the bottle from the counter. There was only a little left, and she poured it equally into their two glasses.

"How long do you think you'd need to be in California?" asked Delia.

"A few days at least. I'll have to go through everything, arrange for shipping."

"Would you bring Eloise with you?"

"I wish I didn't have to. I don't want to take her out of school, if I can help it. And it's not going to be pleasant," said Meredith. "Not if Josh is there. But I don't know there's anything else to do."

"You could leave her with Bob and me. If you can trust us."

"I'll think about it."

"We could plan some special things for her. Maybe Evan would come—she loves Evan—and we could get out the camping stuff, pitch a tent in the yard and—"

"I said I'd think about it." Meredith tried to keep her voice level. The thought of leaving Eloise behind—anywhere—frightened her. But the thought of Eloise in their old house, watching Meredith packing up all their things, the thought of Eloise there with Josh—Josh, irritated, finding her in the way, as Meredith expected he would, Josh saying things she didn't want Eloise to hear—was maybe even worse.

"I'm sorry, Merry, I'm just trying to help."

Meredith sighed. "I know."

Delia got up and carried the empty glasses to the counter. She turned to Meredith.

"You didn't deserve this, Sweetheart. I wanted you to have a husband who loved you properly."

"Yeah, well, things don't always work out the way we want them to, do they?" Meredith considered for a minute, and then said, "Is that how it was for you, with my dad?"

"More or less," said Delia.

"And what about Bob? Does he love you *properly*?" Meredith emphasized the word and gave a little laugh.

"He loves me in the ways that count," said Delia.

Meredith thought suddenly of Wylie. He had nothing to do with this. Nothing to do with any of this. But she couldn't stop herself from picturing him standing by the split rail fence, telling her he loved her, and when she'd told him he wasn't allowed to, he'd said "It's just the way it is. Not a whole lot you can do about it." That's what he'd said.

Meredith got up from the table. "Goodnight, Mom, I'm going up to bed."

"Goodnight, dear. Sweet dreams," said Delia, just the way she said it to Eloise. Just the way she used to say it to Meredith, when Meredith was a little girl.

Meredith walked out of the kitchen into the darkness of the hallway, leaving the moonlight behind.

A few days later, Meredith was working in her studio, trying to finish a project before dinner, and looked up when she heard someone knock on the side of the barn. Kat was standing in the doorway. Kat, wearing black leggings under a short flowered dress—not her usual style—her hair fluffed, as if she'd just washed it and let it dry in the wind.

"Hoped to catch you for a minute before dinner," she said, "but looks like you're in the middle of something."

Meredith laid down her canvas pliers and staple gun. "I'm just stretching canvases, not painting."

"Aren't you working on that?" asked Kat, pointing to the big canvas against the wall.

"Yeah, I am. But I'm taking a break to do some small paintings the gallery in town might be able to sell. Not much of a market for ones that size."

Kat stepped farther inside the barn and tilted her head to study the painting. "I like all the swirly blues," she said. "Water or sky?"

"Yes," said Meredith.

Kat laughed.

"I thought you'd be inside on dinner duty with Mom," said Meredith.

"She's got Eloise helping her. And I wanted a moment to talk with you."

Meredith was afraid it was something like this. She didn't have the emotional energy to grapple with Kat about anything, but she was stuck now. She pushed the frame she'd been working on towards the back of the table and nudged the pliers and staple gun so they were parallel. "What's up?"

"I just wanted to say—" Kat hesitated and fingered the neckline of her dress. It was rare for Meredith to see her awkward. "Well, Mom told me about Josh and the Hong Kong business, and I just wanted to let you know I was sorry."

Meredith was about to say "That's nice of you," and was checking to make sure she wouldn't sound sarcastic, but Kat continued, "The truth is I never really liked Josh—not that I know him very well—and so I'm not entirely surprised he'd do something like this. I *was* surprised, though, when you married him. I mean he didn't seem like your type at all."

"What did you think was my type?" asked Meredith.

"Someone not quite so—what's the word for it? Slick? Someone more in tune with the arts, perhaps."

"Is that a euphemism for a bearded hippy?"

"Well, maybe. But not necessarily bearded."

Meredith laughed. "Did Mom send you out here?"

"No!"

"But I bet she put you up to offering me legal advice."

"That, she did." And now Kat laughed. "And I'd be happy to. I do have a friend in LA who'll know some good divorce lawyers—should you decide you want one—but actually I came out here to offer you something else."

Meredith was caught off guard by this. She couldn't imagine what Kat might be offering, and it made her feel uneasy and wary. Kat seemed uncomfortable, too, almost apologetic, so unlike her usual assertive self.

"Yeah?"

"I thought that if you were going out to California to gather your stuff and settle things—maybe I could come along and help you. Be your advocate."

Meredith had no idea what to say. In fact, she had no idea what to think. Kat didn't seem to notice her amazement and was talking now, faster than before, as if she wanted to get out what she had to say before she reconsidered saying it. "I imagine you don't want to spend much time there," she continued, "so I thought maybe I could help you sort and pack things and make arrangements for shipping. And if you did want to meet with a local attorney, I could set that up and go with you."

"Why are you offering to do all that?"

"Because Josh is being so rotten to you."

"And you feel sorry for me?"

"I wouldn't dare!" said Kat. "I know you well enough, Merry, to know you'd hate anyone feeling sorry for you! It's more that—well I realize I haven't been particularly supportive since you came out here—we've been in kind of a snarl over the stuff with Mom, and I'd like to make, uh—"

"Reparations?"

"Something like that."

They were both quiet for a moment. Meredith looked at her big canvas. She wished she could just plunge into all those swirly blues. She wished that Josh and the house in LA and all the stuff there in closets and drawers and bookcases would just disappear. She wished she couldn't even remember it. "What about your job?"

“I’ve got weeks of vacation time owed me.”

“It would hardly be a vacation!”

“Actually I rather like projects like this. Cleaning out houses. Organizing moves. Dealing with soon-to-be ex-husbands.” Which, Meredith realized, was probably true. And Kat—naturally bossy, highly organized, and not easily intimidated—was probably good at it too.

“The thing is, I’m not sure I’m up to any of it at all,” said Meredith. “Especially the Josh part. It could get ugly. Which makes me not want to bring Eloise along. But I’m not sure I’ll be able to go off and leave her behind.”

“That’s another reason I’m volunteering. If you do go, you might like to have someone along to hold your hand. Evan’s already made a trip to California on your behalf. Mom and Bob would need to be here to take care of Eloise. So that leaves me.” Kat smiled and pushed back her hair. “Look, whatever you decide is OK—it’s just that if I’m going with you, I’ll need a few days’ notice so I can clear the rubble off my desk.”

Kat left the barn and was already walking towards the house when Meredith realized she hadn’t said thank you. She got up and ran to the doorway and called out, “Kat!”

Kat turned around.

“Hey!” The word “thanks” was forming in Meredith’s mouth—she could almost taste it—but she didn’t quite say it and waved, instead. Kat gave a little wave in return and turned and walked on to the house.

When they made it out to California three weeks later, Kat, as Meredith had expected, was a whirlwind of efficiency. She took over all practical matters, freeing Meredith to focus on the emotional labor of closing out her California life. Even before they landed in LA, Kat had arranged for packers and movers and set up an appointment with a divorce attorney. At the house she photographed each room and the contents of every closet. She got plastic bins, cardboard boxes, and acres of bubble wrap. Meredith surrendered herself to Kat’s clarity and energy and abdicated most decisions to her. Not because she didn't care, but because facing this house—the house she and Josh had bought together, the house she'd brought Eloise home to when she'd been born, the house where Eloise had spent her entire life—had depleted her.

It had once been her home, but after she'd walked out with Eloise, the word "home" no longer applied. It had been demoted to a house where she had once lived. But that wasn't quite true, and it wasn't fair to her past either. When she and Kat got there and she turned the key in the lock and pushed open the door, she was immediately conflicted: This *had* been her home. When she'd escaped back East she'd put all her feelings about it on hold; they overwhelmed her now. This was the house she and Josh had been so excited about buying, after living in that garden apartment with the moldy shower and chipped concrete steps. Their first night there they'd polished off a bottle of champagne saved from their wedding, and made love on the floor of the unfurnished living room. And when she'd done the cha-cha—yes, the cha-cha!—bare-assed around the room, Josh had said, "My sexy bride!" and pulled her back down, and they made love again.

It had been her house. This was the sofa she'd chosen, the walls she'd painted, the art she'd hung. Josh, absorbed more and more in his job, was not so much joining her in making choices as acting as critic of the choices she'd already made. That was one of the things that had changed.

"What color is that, anyway?" he'd asked when he'd first seen the dining room walls she'd painted.

"Pumpkin."

"Where's the turkey?"

Did he find that funny? Did he think *she'd* find that funny?

Kat had informed Josh that she and Meredith were planning to stay in the house, and he had to clear out for the time they were there. "Josh complied," she told Meredith, "because he wants to sell the house and get his share of the money soon as possible. He's afraid we'll stall on selling—that's our leverage." She quickly corrected the "our" to "your," but Meredith didn't care either way. There was only so much she could care about.

"I do need to warn you, though," Kat continued, "Josh may still turn up and poke his head in."

"I don't want to lay eyes on him."

"I know," said Kat.

They worked through the downstairs of the house to Kat's drumbeat. Meredith, desperate to get through it all and fly home to Eloise, chose things without much thought, and laid them on the kitchen table. When they lifted the art off the walls there were faint outlines left behind, as if the walls were remembering what had once covered them.

Upstairs, Eloise's room was the easy one. Meredith decided to take every last thing—bed, lamp, rug—strip the room down to its bones. Screw the real estate lady—Josh's lover or friend or maybe nobody, but screw her anyway. Meredith didn't want to leave a speck of Eloise behind here.

"I think you can forget those," Kat said, when Meredith started gathering the hangers off the rack in the closet, but when Meredith shook her head, Kat quickly said, "OK, I'll just label this for the shipper as 'All contents, entire room.'"

Meredith's bedroom was emotionally treacherous, and since Kat was sleeping on the futon in the back bedroom, Meredith had chosen to sleep in Eloise's room, rather than in her old own bed. Kat, noticing her wavering at the bedroom doorway, said, "Let's wait on this. Why don't I do the linen closet while you do the bathroom?"

The bathroom vanity had a white marble counter with double sinks—totally unnecessary, since Meredith and Josh had never brushed their teeth at the same time. In the mirror above, Meredith confronted her pale, naked face. Her face and her reflection. Two faces. Sinks for the two hers.

The makeup drawer was a jumble. Black eyeliner—which she once used too much of—mascara, eye shadow, and false eyelashes—had she ever worn them?—that looked creepy, as if they had been ripped from someone's face. She'd stopped wearing any makeup the past year or so. No point. She dumped all the makeup into the wastebasket. She filled a plastic box with the contents of the lower drawer: combs, brushes, Eloise's hair bows, and her barrettes with flowers and animals, paired as if for Noah's Ark. She picked out a barrette with a pink daisy—an Eloise favorite—and stowed it in her pocket. She was jolted by the scent of sandalwood, and she noticed the cluster of Josh's shaving stuff, lurking at the side of his sink. He used an old-fashioned razor rather than an electric one—an affectation she'd once found charming. She picked up the shaving soap in its wooden bowl and dropped it into the toilet. Then she added Josh's razor and his badger shaving brush—a Christmas gift from her, years before. They looked absurdly helpless lying there in a pool of water. She shut the lid and flushed. She didn't care if they went down or not.

"I'm done with the linen closet. Ready to tackle the bedroom?" asked Kat. She was holding a suitcase in each hand.

"No," said Meredith. "But I never will be."

Although the downstairs rooms had all been tidied and cleaned, the bedroom looked as if Meredith's things hadn't been touched since she'd left. Perhaps Josh wasn't sleeping here. The novel she'd been reading was open, face down on her nightstand, her jar of skin cream, lid beside it, sat on her dresser top, the silk scarf she'd bought at a craft fair hung from the knob of an imperfectly shut drawer. It was uncanny, as if her things had been caught midlife and were waiting in place for her to resume using them. It was as if the bedroom had expected her to return and pick up where she had left off.

Nothing in this room was neutral; everything held the scent of something from the past. The bed was a confusion of desire, of hurt, of hate.

"You OK?" Kat asked.

Meredith sank onto the side of the bed. She'd never thought she'd tell Kat this—Kat, of all people!—but it all just rushed out of her, the words unplanned, unmanageable. She kept her eyes on her lap.

"I had a miscarriage," she said. "I was pregnant, and I lost the baby. When I came home from the hospital, I didn't want to get out of bed. I just lay here. I lay here for days."

Kat sat down on the bed beside her.

"Josh said I was making too much of it. He didn't think it was a big deal. He told me he never wanted to have a second child anyway. In fact, he never wanted to have kids at all. I wouldn't ever have gotten out of bed, except for Eloise. I had to get up to take care of her. I couldn't just leave her with Josh."

"How come Mom didn't come out to help you?"

"She didn't know about it."

"You didn't tell her?"

"No. I didn't want anyone to know."

"You could have told her. Mom's good at keeping secrets." Kat paused for a moment, and Meredith wondered if she was going to say anything more. Then Kat went on. "When I got pregnant in high school, Mom never told anyone. She just helped me deal with it and move on with my life."

Meredith looked up at Kat now. "You got pregnant?"

"Yeah, me. I was sixteen. Not popular, not pretty. So when this guy on the football team—a game I pretended to like, since you were *supposed* to like football—took an interest in me, I was flattered. You can fill in the rest."

"Where was I then?"

"You were just a kid. You had no idea what was going on. No one did. Except Mom."

"Did you tell Roger about it?"

"Yes. Of course. We tried to have a baby together—but it didn't happen."

"I didn't know you'd wanted to have kids. I thought you didn't really like them."

"I may not be *good* with kids," said Kat, "but I like them. I've envied you having Eloise." She caught the look on Meredith's face and said, "You're surprised?"

"I didn't think—" Meredith began, but Kat jumped to her feet, as if she'd heard something, and went to the bedroom door.

She turned back to Meredith. "That might be Josh."

"Jesus!"

"You can stay up here," said Kat. "I'll go talk to him."

Meredith got up and walked to the doorway and watched Kat head down the stairs. She leaned back on the doorframe. She pressed her hands against her chest to quiet her heart. It pounded under her palms. She tried not to listen to what was going on downstairs, but how could she not listen? The voices, not quite audible at first, grew louder.

"She can't take all of these!" Josh said. "The walls look like hell."

"They're *her* paintings." Kat's voice was cold and even.

"You're the lawyer, aren't you? California is a joint-property state."

Meredith flew down the stairs. Josh was standing there in the living room, his hand on the frame of her large painting of a woman that had been hanging over the sofa. "Don't touch that!" she screamed.

Josh blinked and held his hands in the air, as if she were pointing a gun at him. "Hey, Meredith," he said, "no need to get hysterical! Just want the house to look good, so we can get the best price for it." His voice was conciliatory and false.

She was about to say "I'm not hysterical," but Kat said quickly, "Josh, any art that you and Meredith purchased jointly can remain with the house for now. But anything she painted, goes with her."

"You're going to leave that wall bare?" Josh pointed. He was petulant now.

"What are you doing here?" asked Meredith.

"Just checking you're not taking things you have no right to."

"I don't think this is a profitable use of your time, Josh," said Kat. "We aren't going to remove anything that's clearly your exclusive personal property. Trust me."

"Right!" said Josh, but he turned to leave. He walked towards the back door but stopped to look over the items out on the kitchen table, including some mugs that Meredith had made years before in a ceramics studio. He lifted the one she'd glazed cobalt blue. It was the mug he often chose for coffee in the morning. He gripped the handle with his fingers and stroked the ripples of clay with his thumb, then he set it down again and looked at the other things on the table. He picked up the blender. “Hey, *this* is mine!” he said, and he started carrying it out of the kitchen.

“Oh no, it’s not!” cried Meredith. “I won that last year at the Art Council’s silent auction.”

“Fuck you!” said Josh, and he slammed out the door. He started walking towards the driveway, blender in his arms, the cord dangling behind him. Meredith ran after him and snatched the end of the cord, but Josh tugged it away from her. Meredith reached for it again, but was grabbed from behind. Kat’s arms came around her waist, held her firmly.

“It’s just a blender,” said Kat. “Let it go.”

Meredith watched Josh—the back of him, a sweat line down the center of his grey T-shirt—as he dashed around the side of the house to the driveway. They hadn’t even said hello to each other. And they hadn’t said goodbye. She felt her sister’s arms hugging her, and leaned back against Kat’s chest. She must have been crying, because Kat was rocking her gently, side to side.

“It’s OK, Baby,” Kat said. “Let him go.”

19

Eloise knew that her mother wasn't going to be there when she got home from school, but it was different when she got back and her mother was really not there. She hadn't missed her mother at school because her mother wasn't *supposed* to be at school. But she was supposed to be here. Now, all the missing that had been stored up inside Eloise came out in a rush. Eloise went to the front hall and looked up the stairs, just in case. But she could tell no one was upstairs by how heavy the quiet was. The afternoon sun glinted on the brass rails that held the carpet in place, and they looked as if they would sting if she touched them. What if her mother didn't come back? What if she never came back?

~

Delia bought Eloise a cupcake with pink icing at the bakery, but Eloise didn't eat it.

"I thought you liked strawberry," said Delia, and when Eloise didn't say anything she sat down beside her and lifted her onto her lap. She pushed her string of beads over her shoulder so Eloise could snuggle against her chest. "Oh, my sweetheart," she said. "Your mommy will be coming back soon."

"How soon?"

"Soon as can be. She and Aunt Kat are packing everything up as fast as they can. And in the meantime we're going to be doing lots of special things, and Uncle Evan is going to come tomorrow."

"And stay over?"

"Maybe. And now I need your help with the donkeys because the vet is coming."

Eloise sat straight up. "The vet! What's the matter with them?"

"Don't worry, nothing's the matter with them, Honey. It's time for their checkups and spring shots. They're scared of the vet, so I bought treats for them when I was at the bakery."

"Cupcakes?"

"No, that was just for you. I bought them baguettes—French bread."

"Which is quite as ridiculous as buying them cupcakes," said Bob, as he came into the kitchen.

"There is nothing ridiculous at all about it!" said Delia. "The donkeys love baguettes. Right, Eloise?" She slid Eloise off her lap and walked over to set Eloise's plate on the shelf above the counter. "We'll put your cupcake up here so the dogs won't get it, and you can have it later if you want."

"Did you neglect to buy cupcakes for Ralph and Juno?" asked Bob.

"Dogs don't eat cupcakes," said Eloise.

"These dogs? They'll eat anything!"

When Delia and Eloise went out to the field, the donkeys trotted up to them happily.

"That's because they don't know about the vet," said Eloise.

The donkeys were wary of Dr. Morgan, but she talked to them softly, and eventually they let her get close. They didn't realize she was a vet until it was too late. Dr. Morgan pronounced them healthy but said they were getting fat. She looked at the baguettes Delia was giving them and smiled and shook her head.

"Just today," said Delia, defensively. "A special treat because you're here."

"Clementine could use more exercise," said Dr. Morgan. "I have a feeling she mostly stands around and eats."

"I ride her!" said Eloise.

"That's good," said Dr. Morgan.

"I want to be a vet when I grow up," said Eloise, and she was delighted when Dr. Morgan gave her a roll of stretchy blue bandage, a plastic syringe, and rubber gloves that were so long they came up to Eloise's shoulders, which Delia felt squeamish about when she learned they were useful for pulling out baby calves that got stuck during birth.

"So did they appreciate the baguettes?" asked Bob after the vet's truck had left.

"They always do," said Delia.

"Dr. Morgan doesn't think they should eat baguettes," said Eloise. "She said they're getting fat and need more exercise."

"I wonder what she'd say about me," said Bob.

At night Delia read Eloise three picture books, then two more. Eloise clung to her when she turned out the light. The night-light cast a small circle of light against the wall. "Don't go!" she pleaded.

It was just what Merry used to say to her when she was a little girl, and just as she had then, Delia said, "I'll stay till you fall asleep." It was as if the years had telescoped together, and the child who had clung to her then had been substituted with this other child, and Delia, although technically three decades older, was the same woman, this night, the same night.

"No, keep staying after too," cried Eloise, and Delia, awash in love, whispered, "All right, for a bit, and then I'll be in my bedroom, right next door, if you need me." She closed her eyes and breathed in the smell of this small creature beside her. Eventually she felt the fingers that had gripped her arm slowly loosen. And she thought she wanted nothing more in the world than this: the trust of this sleeping child, and her delicate beauty, this child whom Merry had—in spite of everything—entrusted to her. She didn't intend to fall asleep, but she must have, and she awoke thinking she was in her own bed, but realized she was wearing the clothes she'd been wearing that evening, and her head was slumped at an odd angle, a pile of picture books wedged on the bed beside her.

Evan came for lunch as he'd promised, but he got there late, so knowing Bob's appetite, Delia had them start eating without him.

"Wylie's coming over later," he said. "He's got a surprise for Merry."

"What sort of surprise?" asked Delia.

"Don't worry, Mom," said Evan. "You'll like it." He got up and gave her a loud kiss on the side of her face.

"As long as it's not a beagle," said Bob. "I draw the line at beagles."

"Can I see the surprise?" asked Eloise.

"Of course!" said Evan. "You're not only going to see it, you're going to help us set it up."

When Wylie came he backed his truck right up to the barn doors, then he came inside. "Glad you're here, Eloise," he said. "We're going to need your assistance."

Delia took Eloise's hand and followed Evan and Wylie outside. They slid a large flat box from the back of Wylie's truck, then struggled to carry it into the barn and lay it on the floor. Inside were yellow metal ladders and bars, a wood plank, and a set of wheels.

"What is it?" Eloise asked.

"A scaffold," said Evan.

"It's a platform so your mom can reach up high when she paints," Wylie explained. Delia sat down on Merry's stool, and watched while he showed Eloise how to push the bolts through the holes as they assembled it. When it was together, Evan lifted her up so she could stand on the platform. She stroked an imaginary paintbrush back and forth in the air. "Look, Grandma," she called to Delia, "I'm Mommy. I'm painting up high!"

"I wanted to get it all set up while your mom's away," explained Wylie, "so she can be surprised when she gets back."

"Some girls like fancy jewelry," said Evan, "but Wylie knows your mom's the kind of girl who'd prefer a scaffold as a gift." Delia wondered if this was true. Josh had given Merry a diamond engagement ring, but after Eloise was born she said it got in the way and stopped wearing it, and when Delia had asked if she'd put it in the vault, Merry shook her head and said, "It's around, somewhere."

"But it's not her birthday, is it, Grandma?" Eloise asked.

"No," said Delia. "Her birthday's not till the fall—September twenty-seventh."

"It's a 'just because' gift," said Wylie.

"Because what?" asked Eloise.

Wylie shrugged.

"Because you like her?"

"Yeah, that kind of because."

Wylie had brought a roll of white paper and a set of colored markers for them to make wrapping paper. He unrolled the paper across the barn floor, and he and Eloise lay on their bellies to draw, their heads close together, sunlight from the barn window touching their hair. "What kind of animals should I draw?" he asked.

"Donkeys," said Eloise. "And horses. And chickens."

"Then why don't you draw some grass and carrots for them."

"And I'll draw them baguettes!" said Eloise.

Delia watched Wylie's hand move across the paper, leaving a trail of whimsical animals behind. Some of them were wearing jackets and outlandish hats. They were as inventive and detailed as the illustrations in a picture book. Delia had forgotten that he'd gone to RISD.

"Are you an artist, too, like Mommy?" Eloise asked.

"My buddy Wylie is a man of many talents," said Evan. "But don't ask him to sing."

"Why not?"

"I don't want him to embarrass himself."

But Wylie started singing anyway. He sang "Old MacDonald," and the animals on the farm were donkeys and horses and chickens. Evan joined in. He didn't sing very well, either. "Enough, Evan," said Delia laughing. She got up off the stool and helped them wind the paper around the scaffold, and Eloise taped it on.

"Guess we didn't quite cover the bottom," Wylie said.

"Don't worry, Wylie," said Evan. "Merry will never guess what it is."

"Don't you need to make a card so she'll know who it's from?" asked Eloise.

"She'll know," said Evan.

In the morning Delia helped Eloise pack the saddlebag for Juno. She put dog treats in the pouch on one side and a water bottle on the other side with a rubber dog dish. Eloise showed her how it flattened and then popped up again.

"Uncle Evan, can Ralph come even if he doesn't have a saddlebag?"

"Up to you," said Evan.

"He should come," said Eloise, "because he's the kind of dog who doesn't like to be left behind."

"Where are you going hiking?" Delia asked Evan.

"The old logging road up the hill behind the barn," said Evan. He grinned at her. "I can put a GPS on Juno, Mom, so that you can track her, without admitting you want to keep track of us."

"That's all right, dear," said Delia. "I may not trust the dogs, but I do trust you."

"I rode up there with Mommy," Eloise said. "I rode Clementine, and she rode Falstaff. When I get bigger she's going to get me a horse. Or maybe *Grandma's* going to get me a horse." Eloise looked over at Delia and smiled.

"That sounds more like it," said Evan.

"Is this something you were planning on telling me, Lili?" asked Bob.

"Of course not," said Delia. "It's better you be surprised."

Evan and Eloise returned for lunch, hungry in spite of the granola bars they'd brought, and not at all tired, though the dogs did a great show of panting.

"See, Mom," said Evan. "We made it back in one piece. So you can stop worrying."

"Your mother wasn't the least bit worried," said Bob. "She knew you had Ralph and Juno to look after you."

"Ralph smelled the dog treats in Juno's backpack and tried to get them out," said Eloise.

"Did he succeed?" asked Bob.

"Uncle Evan grabbed them and stuffed them all in his backpack."

"Poor Ralph," said Bob. "He hates to be thwarted."

Evan hung around with Eloise for the afternoon, but Delia couldn't persuade him to stay for dinner.

"I'll come back soon, though," he said, "if your grandma will let me."

"She has to let you," said Eloise. "She's your mother!"

"Hear that, Mom?" asked Evan.

"I heard," said Delia.

"Do you think Mommy's going to like the scaffold?" Eloise asked him as she and Delia walked him out to his truck.

"I think she will," said Evan.

"I *hope* she will!" said Eloise. "Wylie would be sad if she didn't."

"You bet," said Evan.

"Wylie really likes Mommy, doesn't he?"

"I'm afraid so," said Evan.

Eloise stopped walking and turned to Evan. "Why are you afraid so?"

"Well, I'm not sure how your mom feels about him."

"Oh, she likes him a lot," said Eloise, and she started walking again. "I know, because when he was coming over last week she ran upstairs and changed into the new sweater she'd bought."

This was news to Delia, but it didn't alarm her. She pictured Wylie and Eloise the day before, lying on the barn floor, quietly drawing. She wasn't sure how she felt about him anymore.

"I'm happy to hear that she likes him," said Evan.

When Delia was getting ready to start making dinner, Eloise said she was going out to brush the donkeys.

"I hope they'll be grateful," said Bob. "Though I'm not sure how you can assess gratitude in donkeys."

"Remember not to stand behind the donkeys when you brush their tails," said Delia.

"I *know* that," said Eloise.

~

Eloise walked out to the big field. Clementine was standing near the gate, nibbling at a bit of hay that had blown against the fence. Eloise put on Clementine's halter and led her towards the stable. She didn't need to tie Clementine up because Clementine always stuck near the barn, since that's where the hay was stored. Eloise brushed Clementine and was careful to stand beside her when she did her tail. Her belly, with winter-long white fur, was big and round, and her bony legs looked too thin to hold her up.

"You *are* fat!" said Eloise. "But I love you, anyway." And she kissed Clementine's soft muzzle. "Dr. Morgan says you need more exercise, so I'm going to take you for a ride." Clementine blinked her enormous brown eyes, but did not object. Eloise saddled her up, and before she got up on Clementine's back she remembered to put on her helmet. She wished there was someone there to see what she had done all by herself. She picked up the reins, gave Clementine a soft kick, and said, "Walk on!" Clementine didn't budge, so Eloise kicked again, just a little bit harder. When Clementine still didn't move, she called out, "Let's walk," the way Mommy did, and reached back and gave Clementine a slap on her rear. Clementine, surprised, started trotting. She slowed to a walk when they got to the hilly part of the old logging road. When Clementine stopped to sample long grass, Eloise yanked her away. "This is exercise," Eloise told her, "not dinner!"

Eloise knew the trail well, since she'd come this way with Uncle Evan only that morning, and she'd ridden Clementine this way before, with Mommy. She remembered the rocky part, where Clementine had to walk carefully, and the little stream Clementine had refused to cross, so they took a path that went around it. She'd never been this far from the house on her own before, but she wasn't really alone because Clementine was with her.

When they came to a spot where the trail split in two, Eloise guided Clementine to the right, but as they went farther along, the trail grew narrower and overgrown with weeds. There was a place where branches hung low over the trail and Eloise had to duck. She didn't remember having to do this before. She pulled back on the reins and got down from the saddle. She looked around for something familiar, but the trees looked different here, and she didn't see the stone wall that bordered the old road.

"Do you think this is the right way?" she asked Clementine, but Clementine didn't answer. She'd spotted some fresh dandelions farther back, and she spun around, yanking the reins from Eloise's hand, and took off to claim them.

"Stay, Clementine!" Eloise cried. But Clementine snatched up a clump of greens, and before Eloise could grab the reins she trotted off, weeds dangling from her mouth. Eloise lunged to catch her tail, but Clementine galloped away, and she didn't look back to see Eloise running after her.

"Clementine! Wait for me!" cried Eloise, but Clementine was soon far out of reach, her fat brown body on thin little legs getting smaller in the distance.

~

When Delia opened the oven to check on the casserole, Ralph, who kept an ear out for promising sounds, came dashing into the kitchen in hopes there might be a morsel of food he could snatch up from the floor before Delia intervened. It wasn't hunger; it was the delight of the chase. He clearly found Juno's indifference to food incomprehensible. Delia sometimes wondered if these two creatures could be the same species. Witnessing the disappointment in his eyes, Delia gave him a dog treat to make up for it. She could hear Bob's voice: "My God, Lili, are you rewarding that beast for being a nuisance?" But Bob was safely ensconced in his workshop, doing whatever he did there. And she smiled because she knew—and Bob knew she knew—that he'd sneak Ralph undeserved tidbits when he thought *she* wasn't looking.

Delia wondered if Eloise was still busy with the donkeys, and she stepped outside to get a view of the field. She didn't see Eloise there and guessed she'd gotten tired of donkey grooming and was probably playing in the barn or—and she hoped this wasn't the case—she was in the workshop, pestering Bob. The view of the field was, as always, restorative: the dark shapes of equine against the paler background of the well-trod field, the stretch of grass embraced by trees. Winter had bleached out the color, but the young grass renewed it now. The world was returning to green. Crocuses had come up along the stone wall, frail little harbingers of spring, white and purple. The slender tendrils of daffodils were just emerging. Delia had planted tulips along the wall, too, even though the deer and chipmunks relished them. The tulips would come up, or they wouldn't, and you were happy when they did. Delia picked two crocuses and left the rest for Eloise. They were delicate as baby birds, and she carried them in her open palm, then set them in a tiny vase on the kitchen table. She'd go call Eloise and Bob in for dinner shortly, but she retreated to the music room for the few moments she had to herself.

After the violin recital Merry had given her license to "inflict" (Merry's word) Suzuki violin lessons on Eloise. "I know you, Mom," she'd said. "You're never going to give up on this."

"I don't want to do anything you don't want me to do," Delia had protested, and Merry had laughed and said, "What? Are you kidding?"

Delia got out the case with the quarter-sized violin and examined the bow. It could use rehairing, but it probably made sense to wait. Eloise might not want to continue with lessons after she tried them. Kids were like that. Once the excitement of producing sound was over and they were expected to practice, many of them would abandon the violin if there wasn't an ambitious parent prodding them along. Delia was not going to take that on. She just wished Eloise would fall in love with the violin. If she enjoyed playing, it didn't matter if she had any talent or not. And Delia had no idea if she did. Josh, she knew, was peculiarly unmusical.

Delia put the bow back and closed the violin case. She hadn't wanted to think about Josh, but he'd pushed his way into her mind, unbidden. Delia hoped he wasn't going to turn up at the house while Merry was there in LA. Thank goodness Kat was there, supporting Merry and keeping her from getting diverted. Kat was so good at that! It was a miracle that Kat and Merry were out there together—her two daughters who had always been at odds, as if they had no genes in common. It was as surprising to her that Kat should have volunteered to accompany Merry to California, as it was that Merry had accepted her offer.

Delia sank down on the sofa and stroked the nap of the worn velvet armrest. Josh had invaded the serenity of her music room, and she was stuck with him. It was interesting that she'd been afraid of Wylie and yet she hadn't been afraid of Josh. She'd been so glad Merry had ended up with someone who seemed solid—a relief after all Merry's turbulent years, her knack of connecting with men who were unconventional and unstable—she'd ignored how ill suited he was to Merry. And she hadn't anticipated—and she guessed Merry hadn't either—that he had no interest in being a father. He didn't love Eloise the way she deserved to be loved. And that was as unimaginable as it was unforgivable.

Evan had disliked Josh and mistrusted him from the very start, but he'd always trusted Wylie. She'd never thought of Evan as a good judge of character—she'd never credited him with that kind of insight—but he'd seen fundamental things about Josh and Wylie that she'd missed. She'd been wrong about both Josh and Wylie. She'd been wrong about Evan too. Delia pushed herself to her feet. She'd been obtuse about so many things! She'd always felt she knew what was best for her children. She'd confused that with loving them.

Delia went outside to look for Eloise. She checked the stalls and tack room in the lower level of the barn, then she went upstairs in the barn and called up to the hayloft. Eloise didn't answer. She went out to the workshop, where Bob was engrossed in a project.

"Have you seen Eloise?" Delia asked.

Bob looked up at her. "Didn't she say she was going to brush the donkeys?"

"She's not out there."

"Probably went back to the house."

"I didn't hear her come in."

"I don't believe she feels it's required to check in with you."

"What are you up to?"

"Tinkering," said Bob. "A time-honored tradition." He pointed to the birdhouse on his worktable, then held up a dowel. "The perch fell off; I'm replacing it."

"I thought you were going to try to fix the mower."

"You thought correctly, but I didn't have much success. I'm taking a break with this." Bob tapped the birdhouse. "Wood is more compliant than metal. There's always the possibility the mower will fix itself on its own."

Delia laughed. "Why don't we just get someone to repair it?"

"I am at peace with my relative incompetence, but I do not surrender easily."

"I'm going back to the house to find Eloise. Dinner will be ready in fifteen minutes or so."

Ralph followed Delia back to the house. "Stop looking hopeful," she told him. "You're not getting anything before dinner." While she'd been in the music room, she wouldn't have noticed if Eloise came into the house through the back door, but as she walked through the downstairs rooms, Ralph at her heels, Delia saw no sign of Eloise. She called up the staircase, and when Eloise didn't answer, she climbed upstairs. Eloise wasn't in her bedroom, and she wasn't in Merry's bedroom either—where Delia had expected she might find her, curled up with a book in her mommy's bed. Delia called out "Eloise?" anyway. There was no answer. Delia checked the other bedrooms, but there was no sign of Eloise. She stood for a moment in the hall and tried to imagine where Eloise might be. Ralph whined and nudged her shins, but it was only because he wanted pats. Neither he nor Juno were of any use in situations like this. Downstairs she worked through room after room more carefully—kitchen, pantry, dining room, living room, music room, Bob's study—calling Eloise's name. But there was no trace of Eloise. She fought against the anxiety that had started growing inside her, but she started to run as she headed out to the workshop.

"I can't find her!" she cried, as she burst in on Bob.

Bob got up and placed his hands on her shoulders. "Catch your breath, Lili, there's no need to panic. She's somewhere. She hasn't evaporated."

"I'm not panicking," insisted Delia. "But I've looked through the house, and she doesn't answer when I call."

Bob laughed. "Since when do kids answer when you call them? Go back and look again. And you might check the attic—she likes to rummage up there. I'll look around out here. It's possible she's with the chickens, trying to teach them rudimentary math."

"You're trying to reassure me, aren't you?"

"Have I succeeded?"

"Not entirely," said Delia, but she did feel reassured as she walked back to the house. Eloise had to be around somewhere; there wasn't anywhere else for her to go. Yet when Delia started searching through the house again, calling out "Eloise" and meeting nothing but silence, her anxiety started to edge in again. She couldn't believe Eloise would deliberately not answer if she called. If Eloise were hiding she'd give herself away with giggles, wouldn't she? Delia walked through the house again. She looked down the basement stairs, but the basement was dark and moldy, and it seemed unlikely Eloise would venture down there on her own. She went upstairs again and checked the closets in her bedroom and the extra room at the back of the hall. Then she climbed the stairs up to the attic. The staircase was narrow, and where it turned at right angles halfway up, the steps were slender triangles. The light hadn't been turned on, but there was still sufficient daylight through the windows, and Delia caught her face—the worried face of an old woman—in the mirror propped against the wall.

"Eloise?" she called. "Are you up here, Honey?" Nothing. There was a lot of stuff in the attic Eloise found enticing: a brass birdcage that once imprisoned some poor canary, a trunk full of shapeless lace dresses and a fur stole that was a real dead fox, biting its own tail. There were lots of corners to hide in, if you didn't mind the dust and were not afraid of spiders—which Eloise was not. Delia poked around the old furniture: chests of drawers with missing pulls, chairs with broken appendages, and a horsehair sofa that had served as a nursery for many generations of mice.

"Please, Eloise," said Delia. "Let me know if you're here." Still, nothing. Delia leaned against the wall and came to terms with the silence. The feeling of relief she'd felt after talking to Bob had eroded. Her tongue felt too thick in her mouth, and she couldn't swallow. She went back downstairs and retraced her steps, hunting for clues to Eloise room by room. She checked the pantry and the mudroom again; then she went back to the kitchen. The casserole was beyond salvaging. Even Ralph wouldn't be tempted. Delia sat down at the kitchen table and tried to calm herself. She had to think productively. If Bob had found Eloise he'd have come back to the house to let her know. Was it possible that Eloise was still here in the house? What had Delia missed? Her eye was caught by something brown on the floor. She bent down to look: It was Moosie. He must have slipped off a chair where Eloise had left him. His legs were akimbo, and his stuffed antlers were flopped to the side. It was his position, the way he lay there helpless and distorted, that struck Delia. Fear invaded her body, her neck, her shoulders, her hands and left her weak, as if she'd been in free fall.

What if Eloise wasn't answering because she was lying somewhere, injured, unconscious? Where was she?

Delia went through the house once again, still calling Eloise's name, but now looking for Eloise's small body. Upstairs she searched the depths of the closets and looked under the beds. She pictured Eloise curled up, in pain, Eloise with a broken arm or leg. Or worse, Eloise with a head injury, a concussion. "Eloise, darling," she pleaded. "I'm trying to find you. If you can, let me know where you are!" She listened for a whimper, for a movement, for a breath. The house was resolutely quiet.

Meredith had gone off to California full of misgivings, but in the end, in an incredible act of faith, had entrusted her mother with Eloise. She'd turned to Delia for help, for the first time in so many years. She'd relied on Delia to keep Eloise safe, and Delia had failed not just Eloise, but failed her daughter. She wasn't worthy of Meredith's trust. She wasn't worthy of anything.

Delia climbed back up to the attic to search more carefully. The light coming through the small windows was frailer now. There were treacherous pieces lurking everywhere: a dismembered brass coatrack propped precariously against a table, an ancient sled with rusty runners, a picture frame with nails sticking out, eager to rip young flesh. Delia lifted tarpaulins, opened antique trunks that could trap a child inside, got down on her hands and knees and searched behind boxes. There was no trace of Eloise, anywhere. Delia collapsed back on her haunches and tried to make herself breathe slowly, fought against her fear. She couldn't panic; she had to think. Where would Eloise go?

There was only one place in the house Delia hadn't looked: the basement. Maybe Eloise *had* gone down there. Eloise was an imaginative child, and she might have invented a game that involved a dungeon or a dragon's lair. The basement stairs were just rough boards laid on stringers—no risers, or railings, and Eloise could have tumbled down. Delia pulled herself to her feet and started running downstairs, nearly tripping over Ralph. He stared up at her, but she kept running. She flung open the door to the basement: Eloise was not lying at the bottom. Delia descended the stairs cautiously. She stood in the bleak semidarkness and surveyed the basement, then called Eloise's name while she searched behind the coal bin, the old furnace, the oil tank, the abandoned wringer washer. The light from the basement window was meager, but when she pulled the cord for the light, the single bulb had nothing more to reveal. "Eloise!" Delia wailed. Her own voice echoed against the rough stone walls. There was no other sound here. Even the mice were silent.

There was still one place left Delia hadn't looked, and that was outside. She knew Bob had checked the chicken coop and the fields, so she ran towards the road. At the end of the driveway she leaned against the mailbox to catch her breath. Could a car have come along when she wasn't looking, and could someone have snatched Eloise and driven off? The ugly possibilities—outlandish as they were—made her shaky and weak. She forced herself to appeal to logic. There was no reason a stray car would come along this road, and, more important, there was no reason Eloise would come out to the road; there was nothing to lure her this way. The surface of the dirt road was smooth, undisturbed. The road was innocent, beyond reproach.

Delia looked back at the house and then the barn. She realized she hadn't really considered the hayloft. She'd called up there, when she'd first searched for Eloise, but she hadn't climbed the ladder, hunted through the hay. Eloise may have been hiding up there, not answering, and after Delia had left, she could have fallen out of the hayloft as she reached for the rope she used to swing down—that dangerous rope that was dangling there!

Delia stumbled as she ran to the barn. She stood for a moment in the barn door: Eloise was not lying on the floor below the hayloft. But maybe something had happened to her when she was playing up in the hay. Delia gathered her strength and started climbing up to the hayloft. "Eloise," she called out, "are you up here?"

"I'm over here, Grandma." Eloise's voice was coming from the other side of the barn. Delia gripped the ladder and turned around, slowly, afraid if she moved too quickly Eloise's voice might disappear.

"Where are you, Sweetheart?" she asked.

"Here!" insisted Eloise, and Delia steadied herself and climbed down the ladder. She found Eloise sitting on the barn floor, in Merry's studio area, coloring on a stretch of white paper. Her riding helmet was beside her.

"Mommy's present needed more wrapping paper to cover it," she said. "So I'm making some."

Delia sank down on the floor beside Eloise. She wanted to catch her up in her arms, but she didn't want to overwhelm Eloise with her own relief. She laid her hand on Eloise's back, felt the certain warmth of her body beneath her cotton shirt. Took in the smell of her.

"I've been looking for you, Sweetheart," she said. She tried to match Eloise's matter-of-fact tone. "Have you been here a long time?"

"Nope, I came up here to get a drink when I got back because I had to run after Clementine, and I was so thirsty, and then I saw that you could see the whole bottom of the scaffold. And that would ruin Wylie's surprise."

"Back from where?"

"The trail. I took Clementine for a ride because she needs exercise, but when I got off her to check the way, she ran off to eat grass and I called her to stop and wait for me, but she didn't. She kept running ahead of me and stopping to eat grass, and every time I got close she ran off again. She ran back here to the barn all on her own, and I had to walk."

"Where's Clementine now?"

"Down by the stable. She wants her dinner. But she'll have to wait. I'll go take the saddle off her, soon as I finish taping this paper on."

Delia got to her feet and held out her hand for Eloise. "Come, Sweetie," she said. "Let's take care of Clementine and feed Falstaff and all the donkeys now. I'll help you tape this on afterward, OK?"

Eloise sighed. "OK," she said.

"Did you talk to Grandpa when you got back?"

"No. I didn't see him."

"I need to let Grandpa know you've been found. He's been looking for you too."

Clementine was standing resignedly by the barn with her saddle on and the reins dangling over her neck, but Bob wasn't anywhere around. Delia checked Bob's workshop and the chicken coop. She went to the field with Eloise to lead Falstaff, Myrtle, and Tulip back to dinner and was surprised when Falstaff wasn't there. Falstaff wasn't in his stall, either, when they got the donkeys back to the stable. Delia couldn't imagine where he could be, but when she looked in the tack room and saw Falstaff's bridle was gone, she suddenly pictured what might have occurred. Bob had seen Clementine galloping back towards the barn from the trail, an empty saddle on her back, reins loose, stirrups dangling, and he'd seen that Eloise's helmet was not on its hook. By chance, Eloise had gone straight to the upper barn when she got back, and Bob, who'd been in the stable below getting Falstaff saddled up, had missed seeing her return. Bob, who hadn't ridden a horse in years, who'd sworn he'd never ride one again—not on your life!—had gone off on Falstaff to look for Eloise.

"Give the donkeys their hay and carrots, Eloise," said Delia. "I'm going to look for Grandpa."

The sun had already set, and the fields had a fragile, rosy glow that would disappear soon. How long had it been since Bob had been on a horse? Decades? Falstaff was gentle and old, but Bob was old too. Delia walked outside the barn and strained her eyes to search across the fields to where the trail began. Finally, she spotted Bob riding towards the barn and waved to him. "Bob!" she called, and she kept waving. He rode up to her. "We've got to call for help," he said, breathlessly. "It's getting dark out there." He flung himself out of the saddle.

"It's OK, Bob. She's back."

Bob stumbled towards Delia. "What did you say?"

"I found her," said Delia. "She's all right."

"All right?" It took him a second to grasp it. "Where is she?"

"Here I am, Grandpa," said Eloise, and she ran towards him. Bob collapsed to his knees and covered her with his arms. He pressed his face against hers.

"You don't need to cry, Grandpa," said Eloise. "I'm not lost anymore."

Delia knelt beside them and put her arms around them both. She could feel Bob's crying, the great heaving sobs of someone pulled from the deep.

"Oh you dear, sweet man," she said. "You dear, sweet man."

20

When Meredith got back from California, all she wanted to do was hug Eloise and sleep. She'd left Kat to close up the house. "Go on home," Kat had said, using the word "home" for the farm, as Meredith realized she now did, as well. "I can finish up everything here."

"Are you sure you don't still need me?" Meredith had asked.

"I can manage just fine," Kat had said. "It's Eloise who needs you." Meredith knew that it was clear to both of them that it was she who needed Eloise now.

Meredith was so tired when she arrived, the dogs nearly knocked her over as she stepped into the house, and she had to summon all her strength when Eloise flew into her arms.

Eloise, wriggling with excitement, wanted Meredith to come out to the barn with her that night, but Meredith just longed for bed. "I'll say hello to the donkeys and Falstaff in the morning," she said.

"It's not because of *them*," said Eloise. "It's because there's a surprise for you there."

"If it's a surprise, you shouldn't be telling me, should you?"

"I told you there is a surprise," said Eloise. "I didn't tell you what the surprise *is*."

"I guess that's all right then," said Meredith. "And the surprise will wait, won't it?"

"It will wait," said Delia. Which made Meredith wonder what her mother had acquired in her absence.

The night was filled with the tiny buzzings of insects and the rustling of young, wind-stirred leaves. From the swampy place beyond the field a full orchestra of spring peepers tinkled—softly and persistently. Eloise nuzzled against her and eventually fell asleep. Meredith's arm ached with the weight of Eloise's head, but she didn't move it. The air coming in through the partly opened window was laden with the smells of spring, and Meredith took big, grateful breaths. She felt she was on the edge of weeping. But then she, too, fell asleep.

In the morning, Eloise led Meredith out to the barn, dancing at her side. Meredith was initially baffled by the large object, swaddled in white paper, standing in front of her painting. A fat white cloud against the blue.

"Guess! Guess!" Eloise sang out. And when Meredith guessed "A tractor? An armchair? An elephant?" Eloise laughed wildly and yelled "No!" It looked as if the paper was covered with colored drawings. Perhaps that was the gift, not what was under it?

"Is this for me?" Meredith asked.

"Yes!" screamed Eloise, bouncing with excitement.

"If it's from Grandma and Grandpa, shouldn't they be out here to watch me unwrap it?"

"It's not from them," cried Eloise. "It's from"—she caught herself—"somebody else. There's no card, but Uncle Evan said it didn't need one, that you'd know who it's from."

Meredith wondered if it was from Wylie, and when she stepped close enough to see the drawings decorating the paper, she knew for sure. There were horses, donkeys, and chickens, sporting a wild assortment of hats: straw hats with streamers, beanies with propellers, bowlers with feathers. Floating around them were flowers, carrots, hearts, and an occasional baguette.

"Wylie?" she asked.

Eloise nodded. "He drew the animals, and I drew everything else. That's Agnes," she said, pointing to a chicken carrying a parasol. She pointed at one of the donkeys, who was wearing a sun hat festooned with daisies. "That's Clementine. But before she was bad."

"She was bad?" asked Meredith.

"I took her for a ride, but then she ran off without me and wouldn't let me catch her. Then Grandpa rode Falstaff to look for me, but he didn't have to because I was already found."

"Bob rode Falstaff?"

"I didn't think he could ride a horse anymore," said Eloise, "but he did." She tugged at Meredith's arm. "Aren't you going to unwrap it?"

"Yes, but let's do it together, so the paper won't tear." Meredith peeled off the tape and rolled the paper up carefully—almost tenderly—as she circled the object. The animals curled in on themselves. She laid the rolled-up paper on her worktable; then she stood back and looked at the scaffold. The black wheels at the bottom of the four metal legs made her think of the donkeys' small hooves and their skinny legs, supporting their sturdy bodies.

"It's so you can paint real high up and not fall off a ladder," said Eloise. "I helped Uncle Evan and Wylie put in the bolts. But I didn't tell you because it was a surprise. Even when we talked on the phone!"

"You are a super secret keeper," said Meredith.

"Do you like it?"

"Of course I do!" said Meredith, and she hugged Eloise against her side.

"That's good, because Wylie would be disappointed if you didn't."

"Maybe tonight, after you go to sleep, I should drop by his house and let him know. Would that be a good idea?"

"Yes," said Eloise. "And let him know I didn't tell you who the surprise was from, that you guessed all by yourself."

"I'll do that," said Meredith. "Shall we sit up there now?"

"Yes!"

Meredith lifted Eloise onto the scaffold and climbed up next to her. Eloise, done with talking at last, lay her head against Meredith's shoulder. Meredith ran her hand along the smooth plywood platform, then up along one rail. The metal was cool in her palm. The old barn around them was somber and still, graciously accepting of this modern, bright-yellow intrusion. In its long history, the barn had sheltered a variety of objects, as well as animals. This was just one more thing.

Meredith saw her mother appear in the doorway, Ralph and Juno beside her. Delia looked around the barn before she spotted Meredith and Eloise up on the scaffold. She didn't say anything; she just smiled at them and nodded, as if she had hoped—even expected—to see them there.

"Going to do Falstaff and the donkeys?" Meredith asked.

"On my way," said Delia.

"We'll come with you," said Meredith. She slid down from the scaffold, held her arms out to Eloise, and swung her down.

"Mommy liked the scaffold," said Eloise, as she ran to catch Delia's outstretched hand.

"I thought she would," said Delia.

Meredith took Eloise's other hand, and the three of them walked together down to the stable, where Falstaff and the donkeys were waiting for them, the dogs following in their wake.

Epilogue

This is the first time in many years that Meredith's been alone here at night. She goes out to the barn to feed Falstaff and the donkeys, then returns to the house, where she feeds Ralph and Juno. She heats up some leftovers she scrounges from the refrigerator and pours herself a glass of wine. She eats in the living room, in the wing chair by the window, looking out on the darkening field. The house is so quiet she can hear the trickle of water through the pipes, the wind pulling at the shingles on the roof, the dogs breathing as they settle themselves by the sofa.

Meredith's been back from California for a few weeks now. Long enough so Eloise is OK going out tonight with her grandparents to dinner and a community-theater production of *Annie*. Long enough so Meredith has shaken herself free of California, of the house there, of Josh, of the woman she'd once been. Long enough so she's had time alone with Wylie, and doesn't need to spend this evening with him.

"I'd like us to live together," he told her. "Whenever you're ready."

"And if I'm never ready?"

"That's OK too. As long as you let me hang out with you now and then."

Whenever. She pictures herself and Eloise living together with Wylie someday, but there's no hurry. She's settled in here for now, like the dogs curled up on the carpet, snoozing, trusting in the peace of the moment.

Meredith brings her plate into the kitchen. The dishwasher is full of clean dishes, and she doesn't feel like unloading it. She sets the plate in the sink. The house welcomes the growing darkness. Meredith walks from room to room. So much is unchanged from when she lived here as a girl: the blue-glazed pitcher she'd made in a ceramics class, still on display in the corner cupboard; the way the hall rug curls up on the bottom edge; even the misshapen wreath she'd created with grapevines, still hanging on the back door. She walks to the front of the house. The sliding wooden door to the music room had been left half open. She wouldn't have opened it had it been shut firmly, but the way it's open now seems like an invitation. She pauses in the hallway, hand on the doorframe, then is drawn into the room. She touches the light switch, and the chandelier, its ten glass candleholders still in need of dusting, sends out its gentle light.

The closet on the side of the fireplace is filled with violins. The quarter-sized violin, the one her mother saved for Eloise, is on a middle shelf. Meredith sees her old violin case on the top shelf and pulls it down. It's heavier than she remembers it, sturdy enough to survive her years in school. She lays it on the table, runs the zipper around the sides, and lifts the latch. She keeps her palm on the lid for a moment, then opens it. And now it's too late. Her violin is there, facing her, as she is facing it. There's old rosin on the wood below the strings, but it's impossible to tell if anyone has played it since she last touched it, but someone—her mother?—must have, because the strings aren't wildly out of tune when she plucks them. She lifts the violin out of its case. The maroon velvet lining, which held her violin safe all these years, has been flattened where it lay, the violin's imprint left behind. It's been so many years since she held her violin—held any violin! It's as familiar to her as her own hand—its smell, its shape, its weight—as if it is bone and flesh, not mere wood.

The hair of the bow sags forlornly. She tightens the bow and rosins it. The rosin, in an oval wooden case, was a present in her Christmas stocking when she was how old? Fourteen? Fifteen? When she turns the violin over to attach the shoulder rest, the varnish on the back of the violin reflects the light, and the stripes of the tiger maple shimmer. She runs her fingers along the exquisitely smooth surface; then, quickly, before she can stop herself, she lifts the violin to her shoulder. Her body remembers how to receive it, her arm curves into position, her wrist swivels, her fingers fall across the strings. It is achingly familiar, this position. She grasps the bow, and it feels at home in her hand, balanced, almost alive. She plays the A on the piano and leans down to tune her violin to it. Then she tunes the other strings. The D-string peg pops out, and she has to work it in again, but after a while the violin is sufficiently in tune. She lays the side of her face against the chin rest and succumbs.

Her playing is instinctive, not remembered, her body recapturing what it once did so often, so well. She plays a few scales, a few double-stops, shakes out her hand, runs some arpeggios up and down. She knows what she wants to play, but she is afraid to play it. She's not afraid of stumbling—it won't matter, no one's here to witness that—she is only afraid of how it will hurt. But she's come this far. She'll play because she has to.

She hears the concerto in her mind, the orchestra thrumming around her. She needs them, this orchestra to ease her in, so she won't be alone. She stands, with the bow at her side, waiting; then she lifts it, and places it on the string. And then it's the moment when all the instruments in the orchestra hold their breath and let the soloist take off loose on her own, like a horse, breaking away from the herd and racing across the field, mane and tail aloft, body lighter than air. She hears the opening notes in her mind before she's begun moving the bow; then the music in her head becomes the music on the strings. She is both the girl that she was and the woman she is now.

When she's finished, she lowers her violin and her bow and stands there, eyes shut, breathing hard. She's in no hurry to put her violin away. The evidence of what she's done will be there, if her mother ever checks.

But she doesn't mind if her mother knows. This has nothing to do with her mother. Nothing to do with anything from the past. She lays down her bow and sinks into the sofa. She cradles the violin in her arms.

Outside the window, a small moon, coaxed by the music, makes its way into the dark sky.

Acknowledgments

Behind every book there's a whole crew of people who help bring it to life.

Special thanks to two miracle workers: my agent, Jennifer Weltz (and the Hive at Jean V. Naggar Literary Agency), and my editor, Nancy Holmes (and the behind-the-scenes folks at Little A).

I'm grateful to my supportive family and friends; to violin teachers Martha Knieriem, Barbara Wright, Linda Laderach, and Suzuki maestro Diana Peelle; to fellow writers Karen Osborn, Betsy Hartmann, Roger King, Robert Redick, August Thomas, Rosanne Thomas, John Clayton, and Sharon Dunn; and to HCHS classmates Anne Kaufman, Judy Klotz, Nancy Lynch, Beatrice Rogers, and Virginia Tang.

I'm indebted to my wise and wonderful manuscript readers—Elaine vonBruns, Carol Baim, and Joseph Baim—and to my extraordinary Writing Group—Jeannine Atkins, Barbara Golden, Ruth Sanderson, Holly Thompson, and Jane Yolen.

Boundless thanks to Artemis Roehrig and, as always, to Matthew Roehrig, who makes all my books possible.

About the Author

Photo © Matthew Roehrig

Corinne Demas is the award-winning author of thirty-eight books, including six novels (among them *The Road Towards Home* and *The Writing Circle*), two short story collections, a memoir (*Eleven Stories High: Growing Up in Stuyvesant Town*), a poetry chapbook (*The Donkeys Postpone Gratification*), a play, and numerous books for children (*Saying Goodbye to Lulu*, *The Littlest Matryoshka*, and *The Perfect Tree*). Her short stories have appeared in more than fifty publications. She is the editor of *Great American Short Stories: From Hawthorne to Hemingway*.

Corinne is a professor emerita of English at Mount Holyoke College and a fiction editor of *The Massachusetts Review*. She divides her time between Western Massachusetts and Cape Cod.

Visit Corinne's website at www.CorinneDemas.com.